HOW TO SLAY ON HOLIDAY

SARAH BONNER

Boldwood

First published in Great Britain in 2025 by Boldwood Books Ltd.

Cover Design by Head Design Ltd

Cover Illustration: Bella Howard and Shutterstock

A CIP catalogue record for this book is available from the British Library.

Paperback ISBN 978-1-83633-542-9

Large Print ISBN 978-1-83633-543-6

Hardback ISBN 978-1-83633-541-2

Ebook ISBN 978-1-83633-544-3

Kindle ISBN 978-1-83633-545-0

Audio CD ISBN 978-1-83633-536-8

MP3 CD ISBN 978-1-83633-537-5

Digital audio download ISBN 978-1-83633-540-5

This book is printed on certified sustainable paper. Boldwood Books is dedicated to putting sustainability at the heart of our business. For more information please visit https://www.boldwoodbooks.com/about-us/sustainability/

Boldwood Books Ltd, 23 Bowerdean Street, London, SW6 3TN

www.boldwoodbooks.com

To everyone who's looked at their spouse and wondered if perhaps they could get away with it... this one's for you

DAY ONE

CHLOE

1

The airport at six in the morning is a law unto itself. Chaos reigns supreme as thousands of sleep-deprived people – simultaneously knackered and wired like toddlers on Christmas Eve – shuffle through the cavernous space. At Security they're faced by what many appear to think is a wall of incomprehensible rules and regulations, even though it couldn't be much more simple; liquid miniatures in a clear bag, laptops and iPads out, jackets off, shoes on unless they're super chunky.

'Come on,' I whisper under my breath as the man in front of me stands stock-still staring at the plastic bin in front of him as if it might jump up and bite him. His hand hovers at his belt and my frustration rises. I just want to get through Security and get to the lounge where a cold glass of Prosecco awaits. Travelling is stressful enough at the best of times, and this week is very much *not* the best of times. Given what's going to happen when we return home.

The man turns to look at me, the panic of indecision etched into his face. How is it even possible for a man to be both ruthlessly competent and an utter imbecile? And what is it about airports that encourages the switch?

'Take it off,' I tell him, even though the last thing I want to do is take any ownership of him. Yes, ladies and gentlemen, the idiot is my husband, Scott.

'But...' he says, his eyes darting to his mum in the queue behind me. Like you can trust her for a second opinion. I travel almost monthly for work – corporate finance does rather love an international meeting that could have been email – and have the routine down pat. His mum hasn't flown since before Covid.

'Just take it off.' This time the words come out as a hiss; I can't be arsed to pretend I'm calm any more.

But then I remember the whole purpose of this trip is to convince the world my marriage is happy and healthy and that I am madly in love with Scott. My grieving widow act has to be convincing enough that the finger of suspicion never swings in my direction.

I've been planning this for a long time, turning over the options in my mind, searching for every angle, every potential pitfall. In the end, I decided that the best plan for getting away with murdering my husband was just to convince everyone I couldn't have possibly had anything to do with it.

That's why we're at the airport at this ungodly hour in the morning. What better way to convince our extended families than by a group villa holiday on the Greek island paradise of Mykonos. I just wish I'd remembered what a fucking nightmare they all are. And I include both sides of our families in that assessment. At least the Wilsons – my parents and my brother – are travelling separately so I only need to worry about the Coopers for now.

We finally get through Security, even though my sister-in-law's boyfriend kicked up a fuss when he got selected for a hand search. If only the fool hadn't left his vape in his pocket and triggered the alarm. Not that he'll accept any responsibility, of course.

There are six of us travelling together this morning. Me and the future dead husband, Scott. His parents – more on them later. And his younger sister, complete with her aforementioned other half.

'It's hollibobs o'clock!' Jack bellows at the top of his lungs as we make a beeline towards the Clubrooms Lounge. For a split-second I imagine tripping him up so he goes flying face first into the shiny fake marble floor of the duty-free shop. He links his arm through mine. 'Come on, Chlo,' he shouts in my ear. 'This is going to be amazing.'

I hate it when people call me 'Chlo'. But I tamp down my irritation. Brave face and all that. 'To the lounge,' I exclaim, injecting so much faux joie de vivre into my tone I almost convince myself.

'To the lounge,' Jack echoes, dropping my arm so he can point towards the façade of the Clubrooms which just came into view. 'Whoop whoop!'

Jesus Christ. Someone please kill me now.

The one – and potentially only – saving grace of this morning is my family's refusal to fly out to the villa with us.

'Chloe,' my mother had told me when arrangements were discussed, 'we can't possibly all travel together.' If we'd been having the conversation in person, she would've offered me a patronising little pat on the arm. 'Imagine what would happen if there was an accident?'

Ah yes. The Erin Wilson tendency towards her own special

brand of quiet melodrama. My mother has lived every one of her fifty-two years on this planet in the shadow of catastrophe, always thinking of the worst possible case scenario and making sure we're all aware of it. But she is never hysterical – that's what I mean by quiet melodrama – it's more that she simply accepts the possibility and then makes plans around it. Hence, we can't all travel together. Because, if we did, we'd all die. And that would be bad. Obviously.

My family believe in planning for the worst and preparing for all eventualities. My husband's family, however, believe they are the chosen ones and that luck follows them always. Well, pretty soon their luck's going to run out.

It's half past six in the morning, but, because we're through Security and into the main departure area of the airport, we now exist out of time itself. Which means the sun is over the yardarm somewhere in the world and therefore a liquid breakfast is entirely reasonable. It's one of those airport rules I've never been able to fathom, but I always ensure I uphold. To be honest, at this particular moment I don't take much convincing to day drink, and everything feels more manageable with a glass of vino to soften the edges a little.

Clubrooms is the fanciest lounge at Gatwick – and the most expensive, but the Coopers have deep pockets and like to flash the cash as much as is physically possible – and we walk into a sea of dark wood and plush velvet. I booked us a huge table in the corner and we make a camp, the men sprawling themselves across the seats. The Coopers – and, trust me, I'm not including myself in this – believe the menfolk are the paragons of hard work and should be allowed to rest on holiday. Which – given the place is packed and the staff already run ragged – leaves Tori and me to play waitress and gather up the drinks orders.

The men decide to have pints, which feels somewhat of a waste given we've paid a small fortune for unlimited drinks and they could've just gone to Wetherspoon's. Anyway, we women are going to drink a vat of Prosecco to compensate. Even if it makes us look like the ultimate clichés.

The barman asks for Tori's ID to check she's over eighteen. She giggles as she hands it over. He tries the same bullshit with me but I'm having none of it. I'm twenty-nine for Christ's sake; this doesn't impress me, it just makes me realise he definitely thinks I'm older than I am and he's trying to be cute. Eughh. Men.

'You alright, Chloe?' Tori asks me as we wait for the drinks to be poured.

'Of course,' I reply, trying to inject some joviality into my voice.

'You seem kind of...' She pauses as if she's thinking of the word. 'I dunno. Pissed off?'

'Just, you know, travel and stuff,' I reply, a flick of the wrist to dismiss it as trivial but irritating.

She arches an eyebrow. 'Trouble in paradise?' She glances at my husband.

'No.' I'm quick to quash that idea. *Scott and I are madly in love. Scott and I are madly in love.* If I keep repeating it to myself, perhaps I'll eventually believe it.

'You forget I grew up with him and know what a fucking cretin he is when he's travelling.' She's doing that thing where she leans in as if she's sharing secrets. Tori is a chameleon, she changes her entire personality depending on who she's with, and for some reason she's always acted as if we're best friends, like sisters who whisper secrets in the dark. It's exhausting to be around, I always have to check I'm not being pulled into her orbit, make sure I'm not inadvertently allowing her to wheedle into my subconscious and make me loose lipped. I can only imagine she would run to my husband with any titbit I told her. And that would be a total disaster.

However, she isn't lying about Scott being a cretin when he's travelling. The airport is a great leveller, a place where people's true personalities really come to the forefront. Some people are planners; they like to know exactly which gate they're departing from and when they need to start making a move. They look at where the toilets are, where one of the fourteen WHSmiths is so they can buy a book for the flight, where they might pick up an emergency bottle of shampoo. Other people are *not* planners and they allow someone else to take control of all the airport related admin. My husband is – you won't be surprised to discover – the latter. He's done absolutely nothing to prepare for this holiday and simply assumed that, as his wife, I'll take responsibility; that I'll make sure he has enough pants and socks for the week, that his favourite hat is laid out with his hand luggage, that his iPad and headphones are charged for the flight, that I'm in control of his passport and his ticket. For a moment I imagine the look on his face if I were to 'accidentally' lose his documentation.

While I was still debating my grand plan, I did consider just booking another flight and leaving them at the airport. Telling the family I was nipping to the loo but instead jumping on a flight to somewhere entirely different. Simply running away. But that would leave a trail, one which would lead them right to me. No, it wasn't the answer.

The answer is altogether more intricate.

Next week I'm going to kill my husband.

I will wait until we return from Mykonos. This trip isn't about sullying a stunning holiday destination, it's about convincing everyone that my marriage is happy. That *I* am happy. And then, once the dust has settled and the life insurance policy has paid out, then – and only then – will I go to the airport and get on a flight, and no one will ever even bother looking for me.

Two Italian Summers

2

Three glasses of Prosecco later and my rictus smile is starting to make my cheeks ache. Tori is sitting so close to me she's practically in my lap, hanging on to every word I say, like a dog with its master. Sorry, that was mean. And possibly a little unfair. I think she's just trying to be nice, to be the little sister she assumes I always wanted. But I never wanted a sister, or if I did when I was tiny, that notion died when I was a teenager and saw how it was for my best friend. She was the eldest daughter whose baby sister was treated like the second coming, the chance for her parents to correct all the things they got wrong with Rosie.

'Show me the pictures again,' Tori asks, leaning over me a little to top my glass up again. I'd better be a tiny bit careful with my alcohol consumption, getting pissed before we even get to Mykonos is probably a bad idea, however appealing it might seem at this moment.

I pull out my phone and navigate to the Villa Bougainvillea website. Tori scooches even closer to me so she can see the screen. I can feel the warmth of her Prosecco-soaked breath on my cheek.

'So pretty,' Tori whispers. She's right, the villa is gorgeous. Nestled into the rock face but with a winding path down to a tiny strip of private beach, an infinity pool looking out over the ocean, a huge patio area dotted with chunky wooden sun loungers complete with cushions that look softer than clouds. And, of course, the gorgeous bright pink bougainvillea that gave the villa its name, in perfect contrast to the white stone walls. 'You did such an amazing job finding this place.'

I haven't told the Coopers that the villa kind of fell into my lap; they don't need to know all the details. So, instead, I shrug nonchalantly. 'I'm just good at planning stuff,' I say.

'You really are,' Tori replies. If only she had any idea what I'm really planning.

Our flight is called and the next stage of the airport dance begins. My mother-in-law, Libby, has not yet actually bought any of the things she needed to buy in the main shopping area, choosing instead to head straight for the Prosecco in the lounge. This means we still need to visit Boots and WHSmith and Accessorize because – of course – she needs yet another bikini or coverup or whatever else it is the women of her age decide to take on a villa holiday.

You may think I'd hate my mother-in-law – because, let's be honest, the rest of the family dynamic is a total cliché – but, actually, out of all the Coopers she's the one I like most. Which admittedly might not be saying much, but I don't actually think I hate her. I do pity her though. She's intelligent and witty and rather fun when she's in a good mood, especially if there's a poker game afoot. Just imagine the life she's had married to Peter Cooper for thirty years. If only she'd had the strength to break free from him, maybe the whole rest of this sorry story could have been different. Or perhaps I shouldn't lay the blame at the innocent victim's feet.

Eventually we make it to the gate, which of course has to be the furthest possible one from the lounge, a slog over a giant bridge as I desperately try to stop myself from killing my husband and his entire immediate family right in front of all the other passengers.

We board the plane and I attempt to ignore the bitching and moaning from Tori that she isn't in a window seat. 'But I need the photos for Instagram,' she wails. I dig out my headphones and congratulate myself for getting decent noise cancelling ones.

There's turbulence about half way through the flight and once again I'm grateful for the Wilson rule of not travelling together. I can only imagine the 'I told you so' look my mother would have given me at thirty thousand feet as the bottom dropped out of my stomach.

But, in the end, we land safely into Mykonos and the whole Cooper clan – lubricated by another two drinks onboard – breaks into a round of raucous applause. I wish for the ground to swallow me up.

It doesn't.

'Have you got my passport, babe?' Scott asks as we begin the walk to border control.

I hate it when he calls me 'babe' but I bite down the rebuttal on the tip of my tongue. The alibi is more important. 'Of course, sweetie,' I reply, voice sugary sweet.

'You two are just adorable,' Tori says from behind me. There's a hint of something – sarcasm, maybe – in her tone.

Scott shoots her daggers and she giggles and blows him a kiss. This is the role the siblings play in public: Tori is the baby sister who loves to tease her big brother and he permits her ridicule. But it's all an act, behind closed doors he's just as much of a bully to her as he is to me.

'Couple goals,' she says as she speeds up to get in front of us in the queue. The sarcasm bubbles to the surface. Gone is the sisterly camaraderie towards me she showed in the lounge. She's in 'taking the piss out of Scott' mode now, once again her whole personality changing to the whims of the people around her.

'Please just be civil to each other,' Libby tells them with the weariness of a mother who has refereed almost three decades of fights between the siblings.

The passport check is laboriously slow. The queue full of the kinds of wankers who voted for Brexit and then did a surprised Pikachu face when it resulted in the shambles it promised all along. I'm stuck, sandwiched between Tori in front, my mother-in-law behind, and a couple called Maureen and Clive to my left who were promised sunlit uplands and blame 'remoaners' for deliberately destroying their Brexit dream. Idiots.

Things start looking up when we finally get into the baggage reclaim hall. I can see my own case already resting on the belt, twirling a slow dance as the carousel spins. I treated myself to a new luggage set courtesy of my husband's credit card for this holiday. After all, that's what happy couples do, isn't it? Buy nice gifts for each other? And Scott is definitely the kind of man who would think his wife would like a new luggage set rather than some transient frippery. Flowers die and leave no trace of their existence to prove affection; an anodised aluminium Rimowa suitcase with fancy leather handles and ball-bearing mounted wheels, however, will act as a lasting memento. 'He was so thoughtful and bought me a fifteen-hundred-pound suitcase and now he's dead… boo hoo' will all add to the story I'll spin.

I even tied some sage green ribbon around the handle of my case. It's the same colour as the scheme for our wedding. A tiny detail my mother-in-law notices instantly, even though the wedding was three years ago. 'Such a beautiful day,' she whispers in my ear as she runs her fingers over the satin. 'You two are such an adorable couple.' I make a mental note to spend a bit more time with Libby this week, she'll be an ally in this farce and will likely be instrumental in making sure the others in the family remain convinced.

Of course, my good luck with my case is not matched by my husband's. 'Our cases were together,' he hisses as he motions towards mine.

I want to tell him that just because they're checked in together doesn't guarantee they come out together the other end. It isn't like we've never travelled before. Last year, our cases ended up on different carousels as the flight was so full they'd had to overspill. We had the conversation then about guarantees. Sometimes being married to this fool is fucking exhausting. Actually, scrap the word 'sometimes'.

So instead I say, 'I'm sure it'll be out any second,' imbuing my words with as much positivity as I can muster.

'It'd better be,' he replies. Yet another thing he will make my fault. I cross my fingers behind my back, sending up a silent prayer that his case hasn't actually been lost.

But, after another five minutes, it still hasn't arrived and I pull up the app and check the location of the AirTag in his case. 'And you couldn't have just fucking done that in the beginning?' he hisses in my ear as he looks over my shoulder at my phone screen.

He was the one who said he didn't want the AirTag. Who

told me it was a government conspiracy to track people. I slipped it into the side pocket of the case without him looking. 'It's over there,' I point across the baggage hall in the direction the app is showing.

'Fuck's sake,' he mutters and strides off in the direction of my finger. I can see his case in a pile being loaded onto a trolley by a rather harried man in a white polo shirt and chino shorts. He is obviously a tour guide collecting his clients' luggage. 'Oi, mate!' My husband shouts at him, his voice booming across the space.

The tour guide looks stricken as Scott barrels towards him. My husband may be a fool and an idiot and a total prick. But he's also six foot three, weighs one hundred and twenty kilos, and obviously spends a lot of time in the gym. Think Travis Kelce in terms of build, but without the soft teddy bear demeanour.

There's a conversation between the men that I can't hear. I'm going to assume from their body language and gesticulations, plus the way the people around them shrink away, that Scott is threatening the tour guide with serious bodily harm unless he hands over the case immediately. I'm just about to head over there to break up the inevitable fight – which would otherwise end with my husband in a Greek police cell for the night, because it isn't like we haven't been here before – when the tour guide decides it's best to just do what the angry man mountain in front of him is asking and hands over the case.

Crisis averted. But at least now you have a better idea of the mental state of the man I married.

3

We're met in the Arrivals Hall by the villa concierge.

'Grace,' she says to introduce herself as she shakes hands with each of us in turn. She has a surprisingly firm grip and I wait for Mr Cooper to make some kind of vaguely misogynistic comment, but he exercises an unusual level of self-control.

Introductions complete she guides us towards the exit like the Pied Piper leading a pack of unruly and a little unkempt – day drinking and five hours on an aeroplane will have that effect – children to their fate. The hot sun beats down on us the second we leave the air-conditioned luxury of the airport. Wow, it is seriously hot here.

'Another sunny day in paradise,' Grace says in the sing-song voice of the mortally enthusiastic. 'There's only a one percent chance of seeing some clouds this time of year,' she adds. It feels like the kind of erroneous claim touted by travel brochures, but I'm more than happy if it proves to be true. Bad weather could ruin this whole trip, especially if the combined Cooper and Wilson families end up stuck inside together for too long. I cannot be held responsible for my actions if that particular nightmare comes to pass.

I can hear my father-in-law grumble under his breath as Grace motions towards our transport. 'I didn't come on holiday to travel in a pissing van.'

Now, in his defence it *is* a Mercedes Sprinter. But it's also black and sleek and has Mykonos VIP stencilled on the side in silver. I don't think this is the kind of van the labourers of Croydon are hauling bricks in. A man in a black suit and chauffeur's hat opens the door and we pile inside. The interior is all pale grey leather airline seats with tables, like a luxury train carriage or private jet. My father-in-law lets out a short harumph. Not even he can find fault with this setup. And there are mini bottles of champagne – actual little Moets, not even Prosecco – for everyone. It's probably a good idea for none of us to sober up too much.

It's less than half an hour's drive from the airport to Villa Bougainvillea. My first impression is of the high white stone wall surrounding the place, giving it something of a compound vibe. Tori wrinkles her nose slightly and leans in to whisper something to her on/off boyfriend, Jack, who she's otherwise ignored for most of the trip. Scott shares a look with his dad; I can't see them both but I'm assuming they're appraising the relative security of the place. Like I would have booked somewhere that wasn't secure. This is hardly my first rodeo: I've been a Cooper a long time now, and a Wilson my entire life.

There's a set of wooden double doors in the middle of the wall, like some kind of medieval castle. They sweep open to reveal the villa hiding behind them. It looks like it's been hewn straight from the rock, the brilliant blue of the sea in the distance. Around the front door is one of the huge bougainvillea that give the villa its name, flowering in a gorgeous fuchsia, even more vibrant than the pictures on the website.

'Wow,' Tori whispers, before falling silent again, momentarily rendered speechless.

The place is huge, and you can just tell that luxury drips from every part of the villa. As well it should, I've convinced the Coopers this place cost over fifty thousand euros for the week. Yes, you read that right. Fifty thousand euros. Total madness. They paid without even a question, not that I would've admitted it actually cost half.

A wall of cold air hits us as we cross the threshold, the aircon must be turned up to the max. Everything inside is white, punctuated by touches of a soft dove grey. The effect is something akin to an upmarket hotel, obviously expensive but slightly lacking in personality. It's perfect.

I've already decided who's having which room and sent floorplans to everyone in advance. We all trundle off to unpack a little and refresh for the rest of the afternoon. Scott is in front of me, kicking his suitcase in frustration as the wheels catch on the spaces between the tiles. Mine glides smoothly and I smile to myself. Perhaps I should have bought him a matching Rimowa, but then I wouldn't have been able to enjoy these petty little moments.

Thankfully I don't need to keep up appearances of being happily married when I'm alone with Scott. It isn't like he'll be able to talk after he's dead and trash my alibi. And he's definitely not going to confide in anyone this week about our marriage being in tatters; that is certainly not his style. He would consider it a weakness and men like my husband do not show weakness, not even to their mothers – and certainly not to their fathers – so he'll put on a brave face when we're with the others. He's like the perfect partner in crime, even if he has no idea he'll become the victim of it.

'I suppose you want the side by the patio?' he asks as the door closes behind us and we drop our masks. Obviously, he has no idea I want him dead, but he is starting to think we need to work on our relationship. He's been asking for months what's wrong with me, and every time I've given him the same simple answer. 'There's nothing wrong with *me*.' At first, he assumed that meant everything was actually fine, but maybe one day he'll realise the way I emphasise the word 'me' means it's actually him who there's something wrong with. Not that my husband has ever been particularly astute. And I guess he doesn't have that long left to realise his mistake.

Anyway, I always take the side of the bed closest to the window or the patio. He burns hot like a furnace and so I need to offset that with a cool breeze. 'Please,' I reply. I'm not really saying please, but it takes too much energy to hate him for every single moment of the day, and a little common courtesy is just the path of least resistance at this point.

He grunts and then wheels his case to his side of the bed, heaving it up onto the bedspread.

I bite my tongue over the way he's spreading germs onto the sheets from the wheels. 'One four zero one,' I tell him. I packed for him and that is the code I chose for the lock on his case. I watch for a reaction. There's none. Not even a flicker of recognition. 'Fourteen, oh-one,' I repeat, putting a deliberate space between the fourteen and the oh-one. Still nothing. Bastard. How does he not remember that date? How is it not written across his brain in indelible ink like it is on mine?

Scott doesn't unpack, just rummages through until he finds

a pair of swim shorts. He pulls off his t-shirt and slips out of his cargo shorts. He's been commando on the flight and I gag a little at the thought. I used to think it was sexy that he didn't wear underwear. That illusion has been well and truly shattered.

'Any chance...?' he starts, standing buck naked in front of me.

'Period,' I reply, the perfect excuse.

'Again?' His lip curls with disdain, although whether it's for me specifically or simply for the mention of a normal biological function I'm not sure.

Damn. Perhaps my perfect excuse is one I've used a little too often recently. 'Holiday stress. Messed with my cycle.' The lie is smooth on my tongue.

'Fuck's sake,' he says as he pulls on the swim shorts.

* * *

I didn't always hate my husband. There was a time when I was besotted with him, like he was the greatest man to ever grace this universe.

I was just seventeen the first time I met Scott Cooper.

Chelsham Park School, nestled in the Surrey countryside, was meant to be the perfect place to raise young ladies away from the prying eyes of modern life. I mean, my father genuinely thought if I was imprisoned within its ivied walls I would never get into any trouble. And by trouble, he meant boys.

Now, what happens when you tell a teenage girl she can't have something? It'll come as no surprise that we used to sneak out of school. We were only a few miles from the nearest town and less than two from a small pub that turned a blind eye to the fact most of us hadn't turned eighteen yet. I'd ridden my horse – yes, horse, don't ask – to the pub. How's that for a cliché? Scott was in the beer garden, holding court over a group of other guys about his age. He was twenty-one and I thought he was so sophisticated. So mature. So dreamy. *Scott is so dreamy* I literally remember writing in my diary of teenage angst, big looping letters and a heart instead of a dot above the 'I'. If I could go back in time, I would slap that stupid girl round the face and tell her to get a fucking grip, to finish her A-levels, go to university and leave that greasy little shit to his shitty little life.

'What's your name, gorgeous?' he'd shouted across the beer garden at the group of gangly girls who'd just arrived, all of us in the regulation uniform of horsey teenagers: leggings, crop t-shirts, posh wellies, hair braided to avoid the negative effects of wearing a helmet. My friends and I had exchanged glances, unsure which of us he was talking to.

'Blondie, in the white,' he'd clarified and my cheeks had blazed when I realised *I* was the one he was talking to.

'Chloe Wilson,' I'd called back to him before kicking myself for using my full name. I sounded like an idiot.

'So then, Chloe Wilson, how about you let me buy you and your friends a drink?'

That was it for me. I was a goner. I fell so far and so fast in love with him it made my head spin.

Of course, though, the course of young love didn't run smooth. At Christmas, Dad organised a family skiing trip to Val d'Isère. Scott begged me to find a way to stay in England for the holidays, telling me he couldn't bear to be without me for so long.

'You can come and stay with us,' he said, kissing my neck,

his fingers stroking my hip. 'Think of all that time we could spend together. Just the two of us.'

He'd been asking me to have sex with him for over a month by this point but I kept fobbing him off with a litany of excuses. It wasn't that I didn't want to sleep with him, it's just that one of the girls had smuggled in a dog-eared copy of *He's Just Not That Into You*, which was very clear in its message of making him wait so he doesn't lose interest.

'Come on babe, just stay with me for Christmas. Please.' He'd all but begged but it was hardly as if I could say yes, even if I'd wanted to. My father would one hundred percent have never allowed it.

And so off I went to Val d'Isère and there I met Sébastien. Sébastien was a semi-pro snowboarder with dark floppy hair, a thick accent and the kind of body mere mortal men like Scott could never compete with.

I broke up with Scott the day I came home, guilt over my holiday fling eating me alive. But Scott didn't listen and he continued to turn up everywhere I went, even sneaking into the school grounds a number of times. Some of my friends thought it was romantic and begged me to give him another chance.

I remained stalwart, until... well, until Rosie. After that everything went to absolute shit and I found comfort in the only place I knew. Scott and I have been together ever since. If only I knew then what I know now. It might not have saved Rosie, but it would have saved me.

'I'll see you out by the pool,' Scott tells me and I snap my attention back to the present.

'Yep,' I call after his retreating back. I carefully remove the necklace and bracelet I've been wearing. It's cheap costume jewellery and likely to turn my skin green if I wear it for too long; certainly not something I want anywhere near a swimming pool. A few months ago, I told Scott I was in love with the set in the window of a fancy jeweller's and convinced him to cough up the cash to buy it, but it was all a lie, just another way to siphon off a few more pennies to help shore up my escape fund.

Now, I'll admit, 'escape fund' is kind of a euphemism.

But hitmen are very expensive.

4

What? You didn't think I was going to kill him myself, did you?

The service I've found is very discreet. Very expensive. Very brilliant in its simplicity. I have no idea how he will die. Or exactly when. All I know is that it'll be sometime between 15 and 22 July – basically one day, or night, next week. That's the true beauty of the plan, my reaction will seem genuine because it will *be* genuine.

Except there is one downside.

I cannot stop it. The plan's in train and nothing can stand in its way. So, I need to be convincing this holiday. If I let the mask fall – even for a second – and someone starts to become suspicious, then there's a chance I'll become a suspect in my husband's untimely demise. And if I do make a mistake this week? Well, it isn't like I can just not kill him.

This is happening. All I can do is make sure no one even dreams it could've been me behind it.

* * *

I head outside and claim a sun lounger in the corner of the terrace, the perfect place to watch the others. Last week I traipsed to Westfield and tried on a million – which doesn't feel like hyperbole, it took *forever* – pairs of sunglasses, looking for the perfect pair. I need to be able to keep an eye on them all, but without them knowing I'm hiding behind the oversized lenses and observing their every moves.

Tori, however, did not do the same kind of research. I can tell she's staring at me from behind her black and gold Miu Mius, those big blue eyes constantly trained on me. She is effortlessly gorgeous, all blonde blow-dry, porcelain skin, cheekbones that could cut glass and a figure any Victoria's Secret Angel would kill for. It's probably not a shock that she's a model, a career Mr Cooper was more than happy to push her towards. You might wonder why a father would want his daughter to be a model, given the well-known downsides of eroded self-esteem and drug abuse. But Mr Cooper isn't like normal fathers and he's more than happy to sell his daughter's soul for access to the very lucrative market of her peers. Lots of addicts in the modelling world. Lots of travel too, and plenty of younger girls at the start of their careers who might be persuaded to carry a little something extra. Yes, my father-in-law has zero qualms about exploiting Tori's impressionable young friends.

Just as I'm becoming paranoid about her staring she gets up and walks over to me. 'I just love that colour on you,' she says, motioning to my bikini. It's a deep teal and I fell in love with it on the Prism website.

'Oh, thanks,' I stutter in reply. I hate people complimenting me. 'It was on sale,' I add and instantly want to punch myself in the face. I always do this, it's like some kind of tic. I can never just say thank you and bask in the glory that someone appreciates my taste, I always have to ruin it.

'I have a dress that's similar. I'll lend it to you when we go to Elysium.' And then without missing a beat she turns and walks back to her own lounger.

'Great. Thanks,' I call to her retreating back. Eughh. The last thing I want to do while we're here is go to the Elysium Club. It's *the* place to go on the island and will be full of people just like Tori. All tall and thin and rich and posting everything to Instagram.

'Did Tori say something about Elysium?' Scott arrives by the side of my lounger, dripping water from the pool onto my towel and blocking my sun.

'Yeah,' I reply, trying to sound totally non-committal. Part of me wants him to say he doesn't want me to go out and then I'll have an excuse to stay at the villa. But, then again, it's hardly the sign of a happy marriage if your husband refuses to give you your freedom to go for a few cocktails with your sister-in-law. Damn it. I'll have to leave it to chance and hope Tori decides not to follow through with the trip. Or, even worse, that she decides we all have to go and then I'm stuck with Scott too.

* * *

Grace, the concierge, heads over to my spot on the lounger at twenty to five. We've exchanged so many emails over the last weeks I feel like we've known each other for ever; she's promised to make this my dream holiday.

'I'm just going to pick up your parents from the airport,' she tells me. 'We'll be back in around forty-five minutes.'

Right then, I have three-quarters of an hour to prepare myself. Now don't get me wrong, I love my family. But they can be a bit... *much*. In a completely different way to the Coopers, though. Where the Coopers are loud and raucous and live their lives like they want everyone to watch and gawp, my parents are quiet, almost subdued, and especially in public. The Coopers hide the truth of themselves in plain sight. The Wilsons, however, believe if they appear dull and unpretentious no one will look at them too hard. The Wilson name though... well, that causes people to take notice. Certain people. It carries a weight, a heaviness layered on year by year as the Wilsons established themselves and then ruled their burgeoning empire. And my father will never let me forget it.

'Oh darling, don't you look healthy,' are the first words from my mother's lips when she arrives. I can only assume 'healthy' is a euphemism for the extra few kilos I've gained in the past couple of months. The truth being that my husband likes me thin, but I like biscuits, and I'm no longer prepared to starve myself for him. It's been a revelation. I did wonder if it might look suspicious, undermine my whole 'perfect marriage' charade, but the reality is most people won't notice. And I can always tell the few people who would actually say anything – namely Tori, Mum and my mother-in-law – that Scott and I are thinking about babies and a little extra weight might help. I do feel a little bad dangling the carrot of grandparenthood in front of my mother and in-laws, but then I'm about to kill my husband and tear the family apart so one more tiny lie won't hurt.

My father folds me into a hug and kisses the top of my head like I'm still tiny. His affection is like the rest of him, quiet and reserved. But still full of warmth, his arms a place of safety. 'Ignore your mother,' he whispers in my ear, 'you're perfect.'

'What time is your brother arriving?' Mum asks.

'Another hour or so,' I tell her. 'Just before dinner.'

She rolls her eyes. 'He always has to make an entrance,' she replies dryly.

'You know what he's like.' I match her tone. We've always bonded over Rob, who is so far removed from the rest of the Wilsons in terms of behaviour, it's like he was born a Cooper and swapped in the hospital. My grandmother always said he was a changeling.

We're interrupted by a roar from the pool area and both my parents turn to me with raised eyebrows.

'I guess the water polo has started,' I tell them. The Coopers aren't just loud, they are also phenomenally competitive. I'm surprised none of them have killed each other yet over a game of Monopoly.

'We'll just go and unpack,' Dad says, pulling up the handles of the two large cases next to him. 'Then we'll come join the fun.'

'I'm not playing water polo,' my mother sounds horrified.

'They'll have finished by then,' I assure her. Another roar, even louder than the first, ricochets around the courtyard. 'Hopefully,' I add under my breath. 'Right then, I'll show you the room.'

I spent hours – literal hours – debating who should get which room in the villa, asking Grace for floorplans and photos of every angle, every piece of furniture and art on the walls. She must have been royally sick of me. But needs must and it'll be worth the work to keep everyone vaguely happy.

'You're in this one,' I say as we get to a door. 'There's a garden terrace that's only shared with the next-door room, so you can get some peace and quiet if it gets too much.' My point is underscored by yet another poolside roar, although slightly muffled this far away.

'Shared with whom?' my mother asks.

'Scott and I are next door,' I point down the hallway. 'Scott won't use the courtyard but I wanted to be able to read in the morning without all the other distractions.' I don't need to say that the 'other distractions' are the Coopers. This little slice of secret garden paradise will be my safe haven from the others: you can only access it from the two rooms so there's no chance of anyone interrupting my peace.

'Sounds perfect, poppet,' my dad replies as he opens the door. 'We'll just unpack and freshen up and then I suppose we should go and be sociable.' He says it like it's the last thing in the world he wants to do. It probably is; it's not like Dad ever wanted to tie our lives to the Coopers'. Funny how for so long I was grateful he eventually supported my marriage, but now I wish he'd put his foot down and made more of an effort to keep us apart. I always did what he told me – eventually anyway. I would have listened.

5

I leave my parents to sort themselves out and head towards the kitchen. It's probably about time for a drink, I'm feeling far too sober considering I'm meant to be on holiday.

The kitchen is like something from a science-fiction movie – or one of those TikToks that claim everyone in China is living in 2050 given the sheer number of gadgets they have. Everything is white, a brilliant glossy white that bounces light around the room, and the counter tops are covered in little machines designed to do jobs you didn't even realise needed doing. A mini chopper. A knife-sharpener. A pod-coffee maker – actually there are three and I have no idea what the differences between them could possibly be. There's even a cocktail maker that you pop a pre-mix bottle into and then the machine will shake or stir or do whatever it needs to end up perfectly served like you're in a fancy bar somewhere.

Grace is standing by one of the counters. 'Everything OK?' she asks, briefly looking up from the enormous bag of ice sitting in front of her.

'Perfect,' I tell her and offer up a smile.

'Great,' she replies as she swings the ice down and drags it towards the freezer. She moves with the kind of ease that comes from a job repeated over and over again, day in and day out. This job must keep her fit too; the ice must weigh a ton and she barely breaks a sweat as she tips it into the cooler at the bottom of the freezer. 'There's a dispenser,' she tells me, 'which can give you either cubes or crushed ice for drinks.' She motions to the control panel on the front. 'And you can also get it to make snow cones. There're syrups in the fridge for flavour, including a sugar-free one.'

'Lovely, thanks.' I feel like she wants me to say something more, that she's waiting for something. Am I meant to be more enthusiastic and ebullient about the villa? Or is this a test? Are there things I'm meant to ask her, things any normal person might but that in my stress to stay in character I just don't have the mental capacity to even consider? Shit. The silence is getting really long now. I really need to say something. Anything. I open my mouth to speak but she beats me to it, evidently bored of the awkwardness rapidly infecting the room.

'Right then. Well, everything's set up for pre-dinner drinks. And the catering team will be here in...' she trails off as she checks her watch. 'It's just gone six now, and they'll be here around seven-thirty. The food will all be prepared per your instructions last week, just the meat and fish to cook on the barbecue on the terrace.' She picks up a tray of empty glasses. 'There's another drinks fridge on the outside terrace, I'll just take these out.'

'Great.' I don't know why I can't seem to string a sentence together in her presence.

'Cool.' She narrows her eyes at me, just for the briefest of seconds, but it's enough for me to clock. I'm going to need to be more careful around her. 'I'll be next door if you need anything.

Just press the buzzer.' She shifts the tray to one hand and uses the other to point at the panel by the kitchen door. It looks more like the command centre for a small space rocket than something that belongs in a Grecian villa.

My father walks into the kitchen and Grace almost drops the tray. 'Good afternoon, sir,' she mumbles as she tries to recover her composure.

Dad merely nods in her general direction before shooting me a look that says *who is this weirdo fumbling in the kitchen?* I want to tell him not to be rude, he does have a bit of a tendency to ignore people he considers to be 'staff'.

'Please let me know if there is anything I can do for you, sir.' And then she spins on her toes, so quickly the glasses almost go flying a second time, and practically runs from the room.

Dad shakes his head as he heads towards the fridge. 'She's a little...' he gropes for the word, but then his attention is over-taken by an already open bottle of his favourite Sancerre chilling in the door of the fridge. 'Don't tell your mother,' he says with a conspiratorial wink as he pours us both a large glass. He likes to joke that Mum is some kind of dragon breathing down his neck about all manner of petty infringe-ments, but she pretty much treats him like everyone else does, with a touch of trepidation and a dollop of deference.

As I sip my Sancerre, I contemplate Grace's reaction to my father. Not that I'm surprised she's nervous around him. She has access to Google and knows exactly who my father is purported to be, even though no formal charges have ever been brought against him.

I remember the day I discovered what my father really did. For a job, I mean. The day my whole world cracked like an egg and all the insides ran out.

I perhaps wasn't the most astute child in the world ever. But, then again, we're primed to think the things our family does are normal, aren't we? Don't we all think everyone else lives just like us when we're small? But, anyway, I didn't realise until I was thirteen. Before then I assumed my dad worked in finance and that all the men who would come to the house with their cash and apologies were just clients who let Dad sort out their monetary problems. We even had some stationery with a fancy printed letterhead I used to sketch pictures on. And, in my defence, it wasn't like my father discussed his business over the dinner table with me at the time, he wasn't asking my advice over my fish fingers before ballet class.

But then, when I was thirteen, a new girl turned up at school and we became besties almost overnight. I think I had a bit of a crush on her if I'm totally honest. I'd never really had a bestie before; sure, I had friends and was part of a bigger group of girls who were just kind of normal – you know, not in the cool crowd, but not right at the bottom of the social strata either – but then Arabella changed everything overnight. She was a year older – repeating year nine because she'd got in a bit of trouble and been kicked out of her last school – and she was so effortlessly chic I wanted to climb inside her skin. And I was the one she chose to make friends with. My heart nearly exploded.

'Come to mine this weekend,' she told me at the end of her first week. It wasn't a question. She didn't need it to be a question, she already knew I'd follow her to the ends of the earth. I had it bad. 'And get in your father's stash, yeah?' That part was kind of a question, but more of a dare than anything else.

I'd just nodded and skipped home. Dad had one of those retro bar globe things in his office where he kept his stash of whisky. The next day, I turned up on Arabella's door with a bottle of Macallan.

She laughed when she saw it. 'Whisky?' She raised an eyebrow and stuck out a hip as she said it.

'My father's stash,' I mumbled, face flaming red. How had I got this wrong?

'Oh, sweetie,' she replied, her voice warm and sticky like honey. She took a step backwards and looked at me, head cocked as if I were an experiment on a petri dish in science class. 'You have no idea, do you?'

We dumped my overnight bag in her hallway and went for a walk to the park behind her house, arms linked and heads so close our hair tangled together. 'What do you think your dad does?' she asked.

'What, like for a job? Ummm... something boring in finance.' It was the standard line, the same one I heard him tell strangers at parties and when he took me to dance competitions.

'Oh, sweetie.' And then she told me everything. About the empire the Wilson clan had built over generations. About how they were a huge importer of recreational drugs and had a whole team of suppliers selling their products to the wealthy citizens of south London.

I didn't realise, back then, that Arabella had singled me out because of my father. It wasn't the first time it would happen, but I didn't realise that second time either.

Not until much, much later, when it became abundantly clear that Scott Cooper had sought me out for the Wilson name; desperate to form an alliance between our families and thinking the easiest way would be through my teenage infatuation.

6

I leave my father surreptitiously drinking a second large Sancerre and go to get ready for dinner. My family has always liked the evening meal to feel like a formal affair, all of us sitting around a table laid with the best cutlery, the dinner service my grandmother bought my parents as a wedding gift, wine drunk from crystal glasses. Tonight it feels like there's even more at stake than the usual Wilson leaning towards ceremony. After all, my father does like to remind the Coopers of his pedigree, likes to ensure they realise the Wilsons have been in this business for generations, making money hand over fist for so long we're practically aristocracy. Peter Cooper used the money he made to buy his kids flashy cars. My father used his to buy a veneer of legitimacy and then leveraged it to secure his kids the very best education possible. 'It's all about class, sweetheart,' he told me once. 'Never about money.'

So, anyway, that was a long way of saying I'm about to go and slap on some fresh makeup, whack my hair into an updo and put on a slinky navy maxi dress. The dress was a total boon, it looks amazing on, but feels like you're wearing the most comfortable lounge outfit in the world. And it was in the sale. Which was the best thing because it meant I could add a few more pennies to the escape fund.

But when I get to my bedroom, I find Tori coming out of it. 'Chloe!' she exclaims when she sees me. 'There you are. I was looking for you.'

I can see the guilt etched into her features. She wasn't looking for me, she was up to something. 'I was in the kitchen,' I say, keeping my voice level. But I allow an undercurrent to seep into my words, one that says *you didn't exactly look very hard*. 'Did you need something?'

'I just wanted to know what you were wearing this evening. Are we dressing up?' Her smile widens further, but if she thinks that'll distract me from the fact she blatantly just tucked something into the back pocket of her shorts, she's wrong.

Should I confront her? Or shall I pretend I didn't see, let her and her kleptomaniac tendencies go ignored, for tonight at least? I know her and she'll only have pilfered a lip gloss or hair clip or something else equally trivial. I choose the easy life and let it go. 'I was just going to pop on a dress and maybe a bit of makeup,' I tell her.

She nods. 'Sounds like a good plan. I should definitely freshen up, I look like such a state.' She does this funny twisty thing with her face. She thinks it makes her look self-deprecating. In reality it only makes it clear she knows she looks almost as far from a 'state' as it's possible to get.

'See you in a bit then,' I reply and give her a pointed look until she moves out of the way of my doorway.

'Great, yes. See you,' she replies as she does this little side-step, I assume to avoid me being able to see whatever might be bulging in her back pocket.

I can tell immediately that she took the new Benefit mascara I bought as Jack dragged me through the huge duty-free shop at the airport. A flash of annoyance ignites but I squash it down. It really doesn't matter; I only bought it because everyone else was buying something and it isn't like I don't have any others with me. I catch sight of myself in the bathroom mirror over the basin; why do I already look slightly sunburnt and blotchy? My face is going to need a lot of TLC to make me look even vaguely presentable. I reach into my makeup bag for the Natasha Denona concealer I rely on an unhealthy amount – it's perfect for disguising hangovers and the stubborn bastard spot that keeps appearing on my cheek like some kind of witch's boil – but my hand brushes something square.

What the hell? A tiny slip of paper has been tucked into the side of my makeup bag. I pluck it out, treating it with the kind of reverence you might save for something that's about to explode in your face. My gut tells me it just might do so.

I KNOW WHAT YOU'RE CAPABLE OF.

I drop the note and step back from the vanity, eyes darting around the room as though looking for the person who stashed the note. It's written in block capitals, each one so neat it almost looks typed. Was this what Tori was doing in my room?

A cold sensation settles in the pit of my stomach.

Does she know what I'm planning?

Once the shock of finding the note wears off a little – and I've necked a miniature bottle of champagne to settle my nerves, thank God for the in-room mini fridge – I start to think a little more clearly. The only person who could possibly have sent this note is Tori. She was obviously planting it and then decided to take a little souvenir because she just can't resist helping herself to other people's stuff.

You know, when I think about it, she's been looking at me funny all day, like she knows a secret but won't share it. I thought it was just her trying the whole sisters-in-crime thing, but what if I'm wrong? What if she's watching me, checking for cracks in my story of the perfect marriage? But that's ridiculous. How could she possibly know? It isn't like I've told her anything. And even if she did think my fairy-tale relationship with her brother is a sham, why would she think my solution to marital woe was murder? Occam's razor would not swing in that direction; divorce maybe, but not a hitman lying in wait.

Although she does love a passive-aggressive note: like the comment in lipstick she left on the mirror at the place we stayed for my hen party. And didn't I tell her the story of my mum when I was little? Like literally last week I was telling her that. My mum, bless her, used to pop little notes in my lunchbox – this is before Daddy packed me off to boarding school to learn to be a lady – to make me smile at break time. All like, 'you're a star' and 'love you to the moon and back'. It was sweet. Obviously, I didn't appreciate them at the time – I was a bit of an ungrateful bitch if I'm honest, which I'll admit may have played a little bit into the decision to send me to Chelsham Park – but with hindsight it was adorable.

It's definitely Tori's MO to take something that should have been a sweet little memory and twist it into a fucking threat. The audacity of her.

This holiday was meant to be the perfect alibi. But if Tori knows, then who else might she have told? And what will she do next week when the plan reaches its final conclusion?

I need to find out what she knows. Or what she thinks she knows.

This is a disaster.

I need a gin.

7

I decide not to bother with too much makeup, just a few dabs of concealer to cover up the worst of the red splodges and a slick of mascara – applied with a curse under my breath that it isn't the new Benefit one, obviously. After twisting my hair into a sleek bun – yes, I know a messy bun is better but the ballerina in me can't bring myself to do one – and throwing on the miracle dress, I'm ready to head out to the terrace. I need to keep an eye on everyone, but for now my priority is Tori.

My anger at my sister-in-law flares for a moment. Why the hell did she have to leave a passive-aggressive note and make me question everything? The anger fades, replaced with a squall of fear churning in my guts. Because, what if she does know? What if she heard something, saw something? What if I've not been as careful as I think I've been?

I count to ten to try to steady myself and then open the door into the hallway. *It's all going to be fine*, I whisper under my breath. If I say it out loud it has to be true. Right?

But, before I have time to head out onto the terrace, Rob and Farah arrive. Rob is my baby brother. Now, you know earlier I mentioned my mother's quiet melodrama? Well, let's just say that my brother inherited the melodrama part. In spades. With fucking bells on. Only his brand is anything but quiet, it screams its presence from every rooftop until all the dogs in the area howl in reply.

Rob and I share an awkwardly stiff hug in greeting, and then Farah leans in to give me an altogether less awkward kiss on each cheek.

'Good journey?' I ask.

'The *flight* was acceptable,' my brother replies and throws a look at Grace who is hovering in the background.

I can only assume that the transfer didn't go quite so well, but I'm not going to kick that particular nest – Rob will only moan for at least ten minutes and I can't be arsed to listen to him.

Instead, Rob finds a new topic. 'That wall around the villa?' He pauses for a moment. 'Have the team checked it?'

'Of course.' Does he think I've never been away before? Fuck's sake. The team he's referring to is a couple of Mr Cooper's men, a small security detail to make sure nothing happens while we're sunning ourselves on the private beach or by the infinity pool.

'It looks a little low.'

'It's fine,' I correct him.

He makes this small noise of disagreement. He always does this; looks for an argument and then, when you rebuff his attempts, he'll do this 'hmmm'. I think it's simply to give himself time to think of a new thing to be upset about. And I'm right. 'I don't like how cold it is in here.'

Now there's a surprise. I take a breath. 'Well, it's roasting hot outside so the air-con's on.'

'Hmmm.'

'Did Baby Luke settle OK with your parents?' I ask Farah. Baby Luke – the 'Baby' always used so no one accidentally confuses the one-year-old with my sixty-two-year-old father – has been deposited with Farah's family so Rob can enjoy a week of rest from his apparently stress-filled life. Although how stressful being the de facto heir to the Wilson fortune can possibly be, I don't know; he's literally guaranteed a job for life no matter how badly he fucks up.

'Yes thanks,' she replies, her eyes flicking to the idiot she tied her life to when she got pregnant. Or at least that's what I assume – why else would she have married him? It certainly wasn't for his sparkling wit and unbridled charm.

I show Rob and Farah to the kitchen and point out some of the key features, all the while braced for the next thing he'll decide is wrong. He opens the fridge and peers inside. And there it is, staring him in the face. Or rather *not* staring him in the face. Because of course there's no oat milk inside.

'I need oat milk,' he shouts at poor Grace, who'd followed us to the kitchen. 'If I drink cow's milk I will literally die!'

He will not die. He is – and I'm being generous here – maybe a tiny bit lactose intolerant, he might get a little tummy ache. But Rob will never let the facts get in the way of a good meltdown.

Farah on the other hand is actually human. I make a beeline for her now, just to bask in her reflected normality. She's always kept me at arm's length, I've never got to the bottom of why, but I'll take her slightly frosty demeanour over the rest of the lunatics in the asylum.

'What are you waiting for?' he almost screams at Grace, so loudly she physically blanches. I guess that temper of his still hasn't burnt out at all. Dad was convinced marrying Farah would temper him, but it almost seems to have had the opposite effect. 'You need to go and get me some oat milk.'

Jesus Christ, I wish he'd chill out about the oat milk.

'How about you nip to the shop and I'll show them which room they're staying in?' I suggest to Grace. She smiles thankfully at me and slinks away. I make a mental note to up the amount we leave as a tip at the end of the week, she's going to earn every penny.

'I thought there were staff,' Rob says as soon as Grace has disappeared around the corner. 'Like plural. People to make sure we could actually relax on this trip. You have no idea how stressful my life is.' I want to punch him in that overly privileged pretty little face of his.

'There's a concierge. That was Grace, who you just dispatched like a maid.' I try to keep my voice neutral, I've tried calling Rob out over his shitty behaviour many times but it only makes him even more petulant, if that's possible. 'And someone will come and cook for us if we request it.'

'But no staff?'

'You really want a load of people sniffing around and listening into every conversation?' Sometimes he really is a total idiot.

Twenty minutes later, Farah comes to find me on the terrace. I've finally poured myself that large gin and tonic I've been craving, but I hand it straight to her instead. 'You look like you could do with that,' I say with a small smile.

She takes a large swig and a beatific look passes over her face, turning her features into a mask of pure bliss. Goosebumps bloom across her arms. Well, there were at least three measures of gin in there. 'Thank you,' she says and then takes another gulp. 'I think I might just kill him this holiday.'

She sounds so serious for a moment I'm caught suspended in time, as if she's opened my brain and looked directly inside at the blueprint of my plans for my own husband. But, of course, she's just being hyperbolic. No one actually ever kills their husband.

'Is the room OK?' I ask, turning away from her to fix my own G&T.

'It's perfect,' Farah says.

I wait for the 'but'.

'But.' There it is. 'Rob wanted a room with steps out to the pool.'

I bite back a laugh. Like Rob deserves one of the prime rooms. Idiot. 'Well, I gave that one to Peter and Libby.'

'I know.' She rolls her eyes and drains the rest of the glass. 'Rob wants to ask them to swap.'

'Ha!' It's out of my mouth before I can stop myself and I clap my hand over my lips.

'I know, I know,' Farah says. 'Rob is going to ask and then offer to play them for it.' She sounds weary. To be fair, I lived with Rob for years and I know just how exhausting he can be. I can only imagine how much more irritating he is when you also have to think about keeping a small baby alive.

'What game?'

'Poker.'

'Ha!' I don't bother to cover my mouth this time. 'Libby will kick his arse. *Again*.'

'I know.' Farah shrugs her shoulders. Last Christmas, Mrs Cooper took almost twenty grand off my little brother. Apparently, her poker prowess is where the origins of the Cooper empire come from; Libby was once a pro and has lifetime tournament winnings of over five million dollars. She has a sister, Aubrey, who acted as her manager and is now one of the most important people in the Cooper organisation – actually maybe *the* most important person. Rumour has it that Libby fronted the money and Aubrey provided the brains to expand the Cooper operation in the early days, enabling them to break onto the next rung of the ladder.

'Just don't let him do anything stupid.'

'Guess I'd better have another gin then,' she says drily.

'I think I'll join you,' I reply as I hear a commotion in the distance. It's the Cooper clan descending on the terrace for drinks. The evening is about to begin and I need to get my head into gear.

Right then, game face on. Let's make sure everyone believes I'm happily married and completely overjoyed to be hosting the extended family for a whole week.

This isn't hell, it's paradise, I repeat to myself three times, although it's going to take a miracle to make me believe it.

8

The Cooper family congregate on the terrace. Libby looks cool and elegant in a flared-leg black jumpsuit. Mr Cooper, on the other hand, is wearing khaki cargo shorts and a crumpled linen shirt, unbuttoned so we can all get a delightful look at his hairy beer belly. I take another gulp of gin. My father is going to love this, he won't be able to help himself from making a few barbed comments.

It starts the moment my parents step onto the terrace. 'Glad to see you made an effort this evening, Peter.'

Mr Cooper – I still can't actually think of him as Peter, even after all these years – pauses while he openly appraises my father. Dad's wearing a pair of tan-coloured slacks, a crisp white Ralph Lauren shirt tucked in and with the sleeves carefully rolled to the middle of his forearm. He's completed the look with a baby blue linen jacket held over one arm and a pair of deck shoes. He looks like he's walked off the page of a 'how to dress on holiday' article in SAGA magazine. A sentiment that may be shared by Mr Cooper.

'Well, I guess all fashion sense finally evaporates over sixty.'

Mr Cooper is three years younger than my father and still a few months from the big 6-0.

'Taste is universal.'

My mother-in-law breaks the atmosphere with a compliment of Mum's dress. 'This tropical print is just divine, Erin,' she says, reaching out a hand to gently brush the fabric. 'Now then, shall we have some champagne?'

I step forward, a bottle already open in one hand, the other holding the stems of a collection of flutes.

Tori is watching me. Again. I can feel the way her eyes follow as I move across the terrace playing hostess, topping up glasses and making sure everyone is getting suitably well lubricated. This is the role I always play at gatherings and parties, making sure everyone else is happy. It used to drive me mad that no one else thought to take the initiative and left it to me to do, but now I realise that it makes it so much easier to avoid any serious conversations. I also need to spend a lot less time with my bastard husband as I flit from person to person, but am still able to keep up the charade with a sneaky pinch of his bum every half an hour as I pass him.

Tori follows me to the kitchen as I go in search of more ice. What the hell does she want? Or is she just trying to figure out if I saw the note yet?

'Everything OK?' I ask her.

She stops and just kind of stares at me. 'You tell me,' she replies, the words loaded.

For just the tiniest second, I wonder what she'd do if I did tell her. If I told her every detail of my plan to kill her big brother and walk away as if I'd had nothing to do with it. Am I going to spend the rest of my life wanting to blurt it out?

'I'm kind of busy,' I say instead, motioning her to move out of the way of the huge fridge. I extract another bottle of champagne and concentrate on opening it.

'You should get Scott to help more,' she says.

'Yeah, 'cause that's going to happen.'

'But, if you're so in love, wouldn't he want to be by your side?' She reaches across me to open the fridge and remove a bottle of water.

I pause. It's such an odd thing to say and I have no idea how to respond.

'Or is some of your whole "loved up" thing just an act?' she asks quietly as she twists the cap off the bottle.

'Of course not.' But I answer too quickly and I hear the lie hanging in the air between us. She's so dangerously close to the mark and I feel a shiver run down my spine despite the heat of the evening.

'Ten years is a long time.'

'Yep,' I try to sound a little more enthusiastic, after all, it is now over ten years since our first date.

'You'd get less for murder.' She waits for a moment and then laughs. She has a full laugh, almost sensuous. But, yet, it doesn't sound like a joke. 'Well, as long as it wasn't pre-meditated.'

Pre-meditated? Like hiring someone to do it for you?

Shit, shit, shit. The watching. The note. The barbed comments.

She knows.

Of course she knows.

But how can she know? I mean, come on! How could she possibly know? It isn't like there is any trail. No evidence. Not even a hint of it.

No. She cannot know.

So why is she looking at me like that?

I head back to the terrace with her following behind me like a predator stalking her prey. I beeline towards my husband, coiling around him like a snake. He flashes me a look. It's one that says a million things: *what the hell are you doing? Are you drunk? My parents are here. Your parents are here. I'm literally trying to have a conversation with my sister's boyfriend.*

'Hey sweetie,' I say, pulling him even closer to me. 'Just wanted to tell you that I love you.' I pout a little, the kind of flirty pout of the newly infatuated. I turn slightly to face Tori's boyfriend who's sitting next to Scott. 'Hi Jack.'

'You OK, Chloe?' he asks, tilting his head as he looks at me.

'Just a little too much wine and sun making me giddy,' I reply and let a small giggle erupt from my lips. I'm not drunk, but it feels like this is the way someone on holiday would act. And, later on this evening, when Tori says something to Jack about how she thinks there is something going on in my personal life, he will tell her that I was drunk and silly and very obviously manhandling my husband like a horny teenager.

I need to use dinner as an opportunity to mop up some of the alcohol; it's one thing to act a little pissed, but quite another to actually allow myself to become sloppy and careless.

The catering staff turn up at exactly seven-thirty and soon the scent of flame-seared steak is wafting across the terrace, making my mouth water in anticipation. I have designed the menu for this evening to include all the foods my darling husband adores; prime grade tomahawk steaks, jacket potatoes slathered in butter, whole cobs of corn with the edges caramelised on the barbecue. A huge bowl of Caesar salad – minus the anchovies – with enormous croutons.

'Butter!' exclaims my brother. 'Caesar dressing?' He huffs

loudly until everyone at the table turns to look at him. 'What?' He demands. 'I can't eat this shit.'

Now, in all fairness to Rob, he can't eat these things, or at least not in large quantities. But he always has to kick up a fuss about it. You'll remember earlier in the kitchen with the whole oat milk thing? Even though I always make sure there are options for him. In fact, I can see a member of the waiting staff approaching now with a French salad and a lactose-free butter alternative for his potatoes.

My mother stiffens as Rob continues to bitch and moan, even after his options have been delivered. I catch Mum's eye and offer her a look of solidarity. It's going to be a long evening.

At least the paternal dick swinging is paused as we eat. Watching my father and Peter Cooper circle each other is like watching a young upstart lion trying to size up the leader of the pride. My father followed his father into the family business set up by *his* father's father. The Wilsons trace a pedigree through at least three generations, stretching back through time to the beginning of the last century and an import business established under a banner of legitimacy enabled by the First World War. Daddy was born into this life and it is all he's ever known. And he's bloody good at it, ruling his kingdom like a FTSE 100 CEO, a smooth machine delivering results year after year and making us very rich in the process. Very rich and totally untouchable – the police have never even so much as knocked on the door to our home.

Mr Cooper, on the other hand, is an opportunist. He saw a gap and he decided to fill it, and – albeit grudgingly – I have to admit he did alright. In the beginning at least. But the most difficult thing in this industry is to keep what you have and that is not my father-in-law's strong suit. He's too ruthless, too scrappy, too inconsistent. And he doesn't care who gets hurt along the way. Which just isn't how you do business, everyone knows that. It's also a sure-fire way to get caught and my father has always worried that one day the Cooper luck will run out. It only needs one charge to stick and the whole empire will collapse like a house of cards.

But, in the end, the little barb that ignites the tinder of a full-blown argument between the two men is something so innocuous it's laughable. But at least we've finished eating by the time it happens.

'I see, Luke, that you're still wearing the old Patek Philippe,' Mr Cooper says to my father, glancing pointedly at his wrist.

'It was my father's.'

Mr Cooper wrinkles his nose. 'Surely you can afford to buy yourself your own watch.'

My father opens his mouth to speak but then closes it again. I can see the anger bubbling beneath the surface, even if Mr Cooper might not be able to recognise the tell-tale signs. Like the vein now throbbing in his neck and the slight twitch in the corner of his mouth.

'I bought this a few months ago.' Mr Cooper lifts up the sleeve of his shirt to flash the monstrosity of gold around his own wrist. It looks like it must weigh a ton. 'Solid gold Rolex Sky-Dweller,' he says with pride. 'Any idea what that kind of timepiece actually costs?'

'I assume you're about to enlighten me,' my father replies.

'Fifty grand.' Mr Cooper nods a few times, as if we might not believe him. 'Fifty grand. What do you think of that, eh?'

Now, it might look understated with its white face and black strap, but I know what the Patek is worth. My brother has had his greedy eyes on it for years and constantly updates me. It's a 1984 'Padellone' and would fetch over three hundred grand if my father was to sell it. Which he won't. He also won't tell Mr

Cooper the value, because of course that would be gauche. 'Mine is a family heirloom,' he says instead.

'Yeah, but come on, it isn't a Rolex.'

'I don't want a Rolex,' my father says quietly.

'Everyone wants a Rolex, mate.'

There's a soft intake of breath from my father. He *hates* it when people call him mate. 'I am not your mate.'

Mr Cooper laughs, a big hearty laugh that ricochets around the terrace. 'Calm down, yeah. I'm not one of your minions.' He looks at Scott as if to say *what is this guy on* and then returns his gaze to my father, head cocked ever so slightly. It's an invitation, I've seen him act like this so many times over the last ten years.

My father picks up his wine glass and takes a slow sip. 'You wouldn't last five minutes in my organisation.' His voice is level, his words clear and well enunciated.

'You fucking what?' Mr Cooper stands up abruptly, toppling his own glass and sending a spray of wine towards Tori, who shrieks as if it's acid about to burn her skin.

Mrs Cooper and my mother share a panicked look. The situation needs to be de-escalated and quickly, both of the older men are stubborn bastards who will refuse to step down of their own accord.

It's my mother-in-law who comes up with the brainwave to save the day. 'Let's play some poker, eh?' she says, sliding a deck of cards from her handbag.

'Small stakes only,' I add. I really could do without massive debts being added to the tension.

'That isn't how you usually play,' Tori leans closer to me to whisper in my ear.

Fuck. I think this holiday was a terrible idea.

9

It's almost midnight when I find the pair of them. They're sitting in the big swing chair looking out over the dark sea, the inky sky a mass of pinprick stars. For a second I wonder if Tori and Jack are taking some *ahem* 'couple time', but no. Thankfully.

They've obviously been drinking, and the occasional chink of glass on teeth suggests they're still going strong. For a moment I'm jealous they can be so carefree. They don't realise I'm here, in the shadows, shoeless so I make no sound as I walk around. The perfect spy on their conversation. Not that they seem to care who hears.

'I tell you there's something weird about her,' Tori says and I stiffen. I could leave them to their bitching, but I need to know who they're talking about – is it me?

'She's just the concierge. She's fine. Harmless.' Jack's words are a little slurred.

'You're kidding?' The ropes of the swing squeak a little as she shifts her position. 'She's a nut job. Didn't you see the way she was looking at my father?'

'All I'm going to say about that is your father can be a pretty intimidating man.'

Jack isn't lying when he says that. Mr Cooper looks like a thug and acts like one most of the time too. Grace was freaked out when she met my dad so I guess it makes sense that Mr Cooper would terrify her too.

'She's still weird,' Tori replies. I notice she doesn't try to defend her father, even though I've heard her justify his behaviour a million times before. Perhaps she's finally realised that she is just as much a pawn as all the other girls who help make the Coopers so much money. Although I doubt it. Self-awareness has never exactly been Tori's strong point.

The pair fall into silence for a while, the bottle passing between them.

'And don't get me started on Chloe,' Tori says. I can hear the eyeroll in her voice.

'What's your sister-in-law done now?' Jack sounds like this isn't the first time they've had this conversation. How often *does* she bitch about me?

'You don't see that either? Fuck's sake Jack, you have to be more observant.'

'Sorry.'

'You're meant to be another pair of eyes for me.' I can imagine the way she's pouting as she says the words.

'Sorry,' he repeats.

'She's acting funny.'

'Funny, like how?' Jack sounds kind of bored, like he can't be arsed to have this conversation.

'Fuck's sake. We've talked about this.'

'Yeah, but you don't really think—'

She cuts him off. 'Yes, Jack. I do think.'

'You're nuts, Tori. Come on, we need to get up early so let's call it a night and head to bed.'

I leave before they spot me and decide to head to bed myself. I just can't do this any more, keeping up the pretence is starting to grate on me and I know I'll screw it all up soon. Plus, I've been up since four this morning, no wonder I'm shattered.

I debate just slinking off and not even saying goodnight, but I know I need to pull off this one final performance. So, I gird my loins and approach the table on the terrace where my brother is still playing poker with the rest of the Coopers. And still losing. I dread to think of the amount of debt he's accruing. Oh well, perhaps they'll let him off all that next week, I doubt it'll be at the top of their priorities once their firstborn son lies cold in a box.

For once my mother isn't fussing over Rob and trying to get him to stop. It's almost as if she's given up. Given up trying to get him to be a functioning adult. Given up worrying that his actions will come back and bite him hard on the bum.

I slide into the seat next to Scott. 'I might go to bed,' I whisper in his ear.

'Cool,' he replies.

'You going to join?' I deliberately make eye contact with Farah as I say it. Ha, let her think I'm making a pass at Scott like a dutiful wife.

'I think I'll stay up for a bit,' Scott replies. After all, I have already told him there wouldn't actually be any sexy time this evening.

I make my excuses and wish the rest of the table goodnight.

My shoulders relax as the tension flows from me the further from the terrace I get.

The bedroom is stuffy so I open the patio doors fully,

desperate to get some fresh evening air inside. The scent of rosemary wafts from the terrace and I pause for a moment to breathe it in.

There's a mini fridge in the corner of the room. I already decimated it earlier but I crack it open just in case. It's been replenished with more miniature bottles of champagne and even a bar of ION chocolate. I smile as I take a bite, the sweetness creamy on my tongue. Everything's coming up Wilson. I've even started to think of myself using my maiden name; I can't wait to be a Wilson again and shrug off the grubby cloak of the Cooper name.

I suppose it's time to tell you exactly why I'm going to kill my husband and why I have absolutely zero remorse about what is to come.

Are you sitting comfortably? Right, then. Let me begin.

I've already told you the story of how we met. How I was going to break up with him in favour of a rather delicious snowboarder named Sébastien. But then there was Rosie's accident just a week into the new term and none of that mattered any more. Scott was there for me. My rock. My constant. Ours was a love built on the foundation of a tragedy. It was almost Shakespearean.

It was also a lie.

There was no accident.

I didn't mean to read Scott's message from an old mate. Brandon was someone he'd hung around with back in the day, a hanger on, a guy who thought he was all that until he got caught dealing speed and was sentenced to three years at Coldingley. He moved up to Manchester when he was released and tried to turn over a new leaf, even met a nice girl. Cut Scott and his cronies from his life. But no one ever actually gets out of this game, and there was no way Scott was going to let him walk away anyway, not with everything he knew.

So, Scott has a thing. About control and secrets and making sure he knows everything in my life. I hate it, always have, but I used to think it was kind of cute too. Like it meant he really did care about me. It was just another blood-red flag I should've seen. Anyway, it means we have our messages open, you know, so when it comes up on the screen as a notification you can read the first line or two.

We were watching TV; *The Traitors* to be exact. Scott paused the show to nip to the bathroom and left his phone on the arm of the sofa. I saw it flash up with a message and absentmindedly scanned it.

> My missus is preggers. Wants to name the girl Rosie.

Then another message came in from the same guy.

> After what we did. Can you imagine…

After what they did?
A third message.

> I still remember the look on her face when she realised she was going off the roof of that fancy school.

I ignored it. Pretended to be playing Candy Crush on my own phone when Scott came back into the room.

He scooped up his phone and scanned the messages. I made sure I didn't react, made sure he'd think I hadn't seen.

'Get the show back on,' I said and snuggled into him.

I have no idea what else happened in that episode. All I could think of was that message.

Rosie hadn't fallen.

She was pushed.

My husband killed my best friend.

And that is why I'm going to kill him.

Fair is fair after all.

DAY TWO

TORI

10

Apparently, the shopping here is iconic and not to be missed. Which is why Jack insists we leave the villa at the literal crack of dawn to head to Nammos Village, this amazing shopping area and an absolute must-do on a trip to Mykonos.

'But it's so early,' I tell him, putting on that slightly whiny voice I know he hates.

'It's eight thirty,' he replies.

Bastard. It's so easy for him. All he has to do is have a quick shower, throw on a pair of shorts and a t-shirt, and splash on a bit of aftershave. He doesn't even have to do his hair as the shoot he did last week cropped it into a buzz cut. I've been up for two hours already to make sure my hair looks perfect, my makeup is just the right level of natural while being anything but and I've tried on three different outfits to nail that island nonchalant elegance. I eventually settled for a gorgeous Zadig&Voltaire dress in a deep khaki colour with a delicate pattern of embroidered butterflies. The lace trimming gives it that nightdress vibe as it sweeps to about mid-calf. The only downside's the quantity of commercial grade tit tape needed to prevent a wardrobe malfunction. But the end result is to die for. I slip on a pair of slightly battered sandals to complete the 'just rolled out of bed' look. Perfect.

'Damn,' Jack says with a whistle between his teeth as I emerge from the bathroom and give him a twirl. 'You look hot, girl.'

I give him a quick curtsy and remember to look a touch embarrassed; he loves it when I'm a tad humble. Hang on a sec. 'Ummm... what are you wearing? Is that...?' Yep. He legit is wearing a pair of Stone Island shorts.

'Just making sure I blend in this holiday,' he says when he realises I'm pointing at the massive logo on his thigh.

My brother wears Stone Island. But he's a chav and a drug dealer. I'm assuming you already knew that bit about Scott? He's exactly the type of person Stone Island was invented for, all toxic masculinity and beating the shit out of anyone who gets in your way. But Jack is more of a chino shorts and maybe a nice form-fitting polo shirt kind of guy, someone who likes a cocktail and gets his nails done and has an obsession with skincare.

'Why can't you just be yourself?' I ask him.

He bursts out laughing. 'Yeah, that's great advice, coming from the queen of the shifters herself.'

The insult smarts a little. Like, I know I adjust my behaviour a bit around different people, but everyone does that, don't they? Why wouldn't you want people to like you? But this is taking it to a whole new level. 'Stone Island, though?' I raise an eyebrow.

'Shall I change?' He turns to face the mirror, twisting and turning to get the best possible angle of himself. 'I should change. Yeah, I definitely should. What was I thinking?'

I stay quiet, he doesn't want my input, not really. He looks at his watch – a neon yellow Swatch that he adores and I appreciate even more after that weird showdown between Daddy and Mr Wilson last night. 'I'll make us late if I change though.'

'It's fine,' I tell him and pick up my phone to scroll Instagram while he somehow manages to spend another half an hour getting ready.

Jack drives, and I'm in such a good mood I even allow him to take the roof off the convertible that the villa concierge sorted for us. The wind in my hair will only add to the overall look. After all, Mykonos is *the* place to be seen and you never know who might be out and about; this shit is important.

The car is cherry red with cream-coloured leather seats that feel soft as butter beneath my fingers. Perhaps I can convince Daddy to buy me one when we get home? But then I squash down that thought. I need to do this on my own. Claw my way to the top without anyone else's help; it's time for independence.

Well, from tomorrow anyway.

I pull the black credit card from my bag. Jack flicks his eyes to it from the road in front of us. 'Daddy's?' he asks with a waggle of his eyebrows.

'Of course,' I reply. My father has always been generous; he doesn't even suggest an allowance, but I'm careful not to take the piss too much. I know the limits of the Cooper family, even if Daddy would never admit to them.

I used to think he was just being a sweetheart and making sure his baby girl didn't have to want for anything. Now I think it's a combination of things. A desire for me not to ask too many questions. The need for me to continue to model and give him access to my friends and colleagues. And guilt. Guilt because what happened to Markus was partly his doing, even if he didn't actually do it himself.

I'll be free of him soon. But first I'm going to get myself a banging new wardrobe upgrade. It's all well and good to have principles, but it's better if you can look fabulous while you have them.

It turns out I was right about it being basically the middle of the night. We leave the car with the valet and walk through the village. I mean, it's called a village but it's purpose built to look like a fancy resort, dotted with exclusive boutiques. All the best brands are here, but everything is closed.

'Fuck's sake, Jack.' I turn to look at him.

He puts his hands up. 'Sorry. I didn't realise this place was so...' he trails off, but I can see the edge of something xenophobic running through his brain. Remind me again why I put up with this man? Besides the obvious good looks, impeccable taste in clothes and career pedigree that helps me get into all the best industry parties, of course. 'Mrs Wilson said we should come early so there weren't all the queues.'

I give him *the look*.

'I thought it was good advice,' he adds.

I stifle a yawn. Not because I'm physically tired. But because I'm tired of all this. The mental drain of this life is exhausting. I pull out my phone and spend less than thirty seconds ascertaining the shops don't open until eleven and so we have almost two hours to kill. 'Well, what do we do now?' I raise an eyebrow at him so he realises this is his problem to fix.

In the end the boy does good and manages to secure us a breakfast table at the Nammos restaurant right next to the beach. It's so wonderfully Instagrammable and I make the most of it. We order a fruit platter – well, you don't want to be bloated when you're about to head to the LUISA Boutique, do you? They might have that Alaïa dress I've been dreaming about, the bright pink one with the fringing.

'You remember last night?' he says as our food arrives.

'Um, you might have to be a little more specific.' My tone is sarcastic. He likes to do this, just assume I can see inside his brain and know what the hell he's talking about.

'When we were on the swing. You were talking about your sister-in-law?'

I'm going to admit that I'm not the best drunk in the world. I tend to have a little too much and then my memory gets patchy, the evening disintegrating into snapshots of conversations and locations. I tend to try to style it out though, I mean no one needs to know I can't remember stuff. And it isn't like any of it has any real importance anyway. The best way is to stay quiet and let the other person fill in the details. It's amazing how much people don't listen and so, if you let them talk, they'll do all the work for you.

'You were saying she was acting off, like there was trouble in her and Scott's marriage,' he adds and suddenly it all clicks into place and the memory unlocks, unfurling like a sail in front of me.

'Yep,' I reply, bringing my glass to my lips so he'll fill the silence and tell me even more. How much did I actually share with him last night?

'That was it. It just made me think, that's all.'

Oh. Now I see it. The puppy dog eyes. He's taken my comments about Scott and Chloe and somehow made them about *our* relationship. I put down my glass. 'We're nothing like them, you know.' I try to keep my words soft. 'We're special. Different.' The same thing I always tell him to try to shift the conversation away from the fact he thinks we should get married.

'Promise?' He looks so hopeful.

'Promise,' I confirm and he breaks into the goofy smile he

reserves only for me. Oh, and the other people he fucks behind my back. But every relationship has its flaws.

We order another round of sparkling waters – even though I'm gagging for a sweet and creamy frappé – and I try to angle the conversation back to the marital troubles of my big brother and his ice queen wife. Every day is better when it's filled with gossip.

'So, do you think there's something odd there? With Chloe?' I ask.

Jack contemplates the question for a few moments. 'I mean, she's always been a bit highly strung.'

This is true. 'But you weren't getting a *vibe* from her?' Vibe is such a great word, it can do a lot of heavy lifting in a gossip session.

'I don't really know why you're getting so obsessed with this,' Jack replies.

I'm not obsessed. I'm interested.

Chloe has plans to kill my brother and I need to understand why.

11

We get back to the villa mid-afternoon, laden with bags full of glorious things. Daddy's black Amex lies exhausted in my handbag, begging for a break.

A blast of icy cold air hits me in the face as I push open the main front door. 'What the fu—'

'It's freezing in here,' Jack says over me as he steps inside.

'What's going on?' For a moment I go into panic mode, but then I force myself to take a breath. It's just cold. Everything is fine; the panel for the security system is flashing all green.

'Let's find the others and see what's happened.' Jack takes the rest of the bags from me and motions towards the kitchen. He follows me down the corridor.

Chloe's brother Rob and his wife Farah are in the kitchen, wearing matching hoodies as they wait for the kettle to boil. 'Air-con's on the fritz,' Rob tells us. He says it like he's person-ally offended about it. I don't know him that well – it isn't like we'd normally socialise – but he seems like a major douche. Plus, he has that whole wandering eye thing, which makes me want to slap him. 'Just making some tea to warm up. We were having a siesta and when we woke up it was like we'd been transported to Siberia.' He says 'siesta' with a Spanish accent; doesn't he realise we're in Greece?

'OMG that sounds hideous.' I twirl a piece of hair around my finger and adopt the dumb model persona I often tend towards when I'm with people I don't know well. At this point it's kind of become a default and it comes with the added bonus that everyone thinks you're also blind and deaf so they don't care about censoring themselves around you. You'd be amazed at some of the things I find out this way. 'Any idea what the issue is?' I ask.

Rob just shrugs. 'No clue. Feels like the house is trying to kill me. First no oat milk and now this.' Chloe thinks we're like sisters and tells me all kinds of stuff about her extended family during our cosy heart-to-hearts. I remember her saying Rob had a flair for the melodramatic and she certainly isn't wrong.

Farah – who Chloe says is a fool for putting up with Rob's shit, even if he is Baby Luke's daddy – rolls her eyes and pours boiling water into two mugs. 'Would you like some tea?' she asks me and Jack.

'No thanks,' Jack replies as he strides towards the fridge. 'You know if the air-con in the gym is fucked too?'

'No idea.'

Seems like Rob doesn't know very much. But then Chloe walks in, at least she'll have more of a clue.

'It's fine. Just one of the sensors on the control panel playing up,' she tells us. 'The engineer will be here soon.'

That woman is here, the one who picked us up from the airport. Grace, I think her name was, to be honest I wasn't really paying attention, I was too exhausted from the flight. She's wearing denim shorts and a cropped white vest, a red bandana wrapped around her hair. On the face of it she looks like she's simply dressed practically, like she could personally chuck a tool belt around her waist and get her hands dirty, even though all she seems to be doing is directing other people. But if you dig a little deeper...

The shorts have a rope tie at the waist, they're from this season's Citizens of Humanity collection – I spotted the logo on the white leather jacron when she turned round. These are expensive. Like, really expensive. Over three hundred pounds a pair. And the vest is properly seamed, so not something she picked up from Next or wherever you'd expect someone like her to shop. I have no idea what a villa concierge gets paid, but I highly doubt it's enough to buy Citizens of Humanity or pay over fifty quid for a vest.

I open my mouth to say something to Jack, but then I close it again. I know everyone thinks I'm paranoid, that I see patterns where there are none. That maybe I need to think about seeing another therapist, getting another prescription to try. I've always wondered where the lines are. Between paranoid and careful. Between observant and nosy. Between connecting the dots and just making shit up.

It's probably nothing. Grace could have a rich boyfriend. Or maybe being a villa concierge is really lucrative in a way I don't understand. Or she could have a sister who works in fashion and gets her a great discount or even freebies. It could be nothing. It's probably nothing.

'I love those shorts,' I tell her.

'Oh, thanks,' she replies and smiles. But there's a flash of something in her eyes.

'Where are they from? I might get myself a pair.'

'Oh. Um. I can't actually remember,' she screws her nose up and I notice the freckles smattering her nose. She's kind of pretty in a really wholesome, farm girl next door, kind of way.

She could probably get some catalogue work if she sorted out those eyebrows and dropped a few kilos. I lean forward a little, like I'm pretending to read the label. 'Oh, they're Citizens of Humanity.' I act surprised. I mean, I am surprised, but I mean surprised in terms of only just noticing. 'They must have cost you a fortune.' I make sure I'm using my 'I really like you, honestly' voice I tend to reserve for the other models and people I'm forced to make nice with constantly.

'Oh. My old flatmate,' she replies and I can tell she's grasping for an answer. 'Umm... she worked in retail. Killer discount.' She grins.

It doesn't add up.

I leave it for now, it's too cold to stay inside the villa anyway and so I head outside onto the terrace, turning my face to the sun the second I'm out of the shade. Now that's more like it. I was born for the heat and I do everything I can to spend as much of my life in warmer climates. Who wants to live in rainy Croydon anyway? No offence if you're from Croydon; but then again you'll probably know what I mean better than anyone.

'You're not going to put your purchases away?' Jack hurries up behind me to ask.

'I can't stand the cold. Can you do it, sweetie?' I stick my bottom lip out like a spoilt little girl.

He agrees instantly, as I was sure he would, the lip thing gets him every time. 'Sure, baby.'

I head closer to the pool, regretting coming straight out here and not stopping to get changed into my bikini first. Mummy and Daddy are here so I can't exactly go skinny dipping. That would definitely not go down well. Although it might perk Mr Wilson up a bit. I know he's a big deal and all that but he's such a bore, like he's half dead already.

Well, if I can't go swimming, I may as well have a drink.

'Darling,' Mummy calls from the other side of the terrace area, where she's reclining on a huge white daybed. 'I could use a top up, if you're making.' She rattles her empty glass in case I didn't realise what she was asking.

'Of course, Mummy.' I affect a sing-song tone. I might say it was Daddy's credit card I was using today, but I know it's Mummy who's really in control of the purse strings. 'Vodka, lime and soda?' I don't know why I'm even bothering to ask, she's drunk the same thing for as long as I can remember.

'With lashings of ice,' she replies with a wink. Like I'd forget the ice.

There isn't any in the little bar area next to the barbecue, just a dribble of water left in the bottom of the ice bucket. Which means I'm going to have to go back inside the villa.

I brace myself for the onslaught of freezing air as I step into the kitchen area. But it's already a few degrees warmer than earlier; hopefully that means the engineer is sorting it out. I hear the rumble of a male voice from the hallway and poke my head around the corner to take a look. There's a guy with his bum sticking out of the little cupboard in the hallway, his trousers slung so low I can see more of his arse crack than I'd like. Which I would like to be zero – this is not some Greek Adonis, this guy looks like he barely bothers to wash and certainly hasn't hit a gym in the past decade.

'The engineer,' Grace tells me, pointing towards said arse crack. It's a bit unnecessary, who else could he be?

'Well, fingers crossed,' I reply and hold up both hands to show her.

She gives me a thumbs up and I duck back into the kitchen to get Mummy more ice.

You remember what I said about people assuming I'm deaf as well as dumb? Well, I hear Grace and the engineer talking in the hallway and they are making no effort at all to keep their voices down.

'There's nothing wrong with it,' he tells her.

'But the villa got freezing.'

'Sure. Someone had a little fiddle with the settings.'

'Oh. Why would they do that?'

'No idea.' I can hear the shrug in his voice. 'But they had a play around with some of the other settings too.'

'The other settings?'

'Like the alarm.'

'Oh.'

Hmmm. Who would want to mess with the alarm system? And why?

I take Mummy her drink, a virgin one for myself in my other hand. The ice cracks as I walk.

Very interesting, this whole alarm business. I mull it over as I sip my lime and soda. Very interesting indeed.

12

I'm woken up by my head nodding forward, causing me to bolt upright as if I've been shot. My neck aches and I rub it as I look around, trying to figure out if anyone saw me. I hate people watching me sleep, it makes me feel all itchy and gross. I mean, what if I snore or scrunch my face up in such a way that it gives me a double chin?

I think the sun might have gone to my head a bit. Plus all the travelling yesterday and then staying up so late. I can't even remember going to bed, to be honest, but I think it was past two. Although I am on holiday, so surely no one would judge me if I went and had a little nap, would they?

Mummy looks up as I clamber out of the fancy deck chair I dozed off in and I mime going to sleep with prayer hands tucked under my cheek. She gives me a thumbs up. Daddy doesn't even look up from the magazine he's reading; I can see from the way he's folded it that it's actually more of a brochure on private yachts. I'm not sure we have yacht-money – my kind-of-friend and fellow model, Natasha, just married this super loaded guy and his yacht was multiple millions – but I guess

Daddy wants Mr Wilson to think we do. Oh well, it's nice to dream and he isn't hurting anyone.

Just as I'm about to walk into the kitchen, I hear hushed voices inside. Interesting. I hang back, trying to listen to what secrets are being shared.

'Are you sure?' says a woman. I think it's Mrs Wilson.

'The engineer was clear.' That is definitely the concierge with the fancy denim shorts.

'Well, I'm sure it's nothing.'

'Someone tried to tamper with the alarm system.' Grace – that was her name, right? – sounds worried.

I hear Mrs Wilson take a deep breath inwards. 'There's a lot of paranoia in this villa. A lot of people who worry far too much and are so hyper vigilant they see shadows around every corner. I don't want the men to worry about something so trivial, OK? So, let's just keep it between ourselves. No point setting everyone off in a panic.'

'I think Chloe needs to know. She was the one who made the booking.' Grace is insistent.

'Listen, Chloe is one of the worst. She'll overreact. Insist on cutting short the trip. There will be a whole load of drama over nothing.'

'Why are you so calm?'

Yes, why are you so calm, Mrs Wilson? She normally looks like she's teetering on the edge of a meltdown; although I guess being married to Mr Wilson must be a pretty nerve-wracking experience.

'I've been married to Luke for over thirty years. I've seen everything there is to see, a lot of which would make your mind boggle.' She laughs a little. It sounds genuine. She really is calm. I'd like to be like that one day.

'You're sure?' Grace asks.

'Positive. Now, why don't you be a darling and come help me with my dress for this evening? It got terribly creased on the flight over.'

I wait until they leave the kitchen before I stroll through, acting as if I heard nothing. Well, it was hardly important, was it?

Jack joins me for a nap but tosses and turns for about half an hour before announcing he's going to work out in the gym attached to the villa instead. He's got a shoot next week and so can't relax his regime for even a single day while we're away. I, on the other hand, only have beauty shoots for the rest of the month. Serendipity – this brand I do a load of work with – are bringing out a new range and I'm booked as one of the key faces of the campaign. It's super exciting, and everyone knows that for beauty shoots you don't want to be too lean. So, I've got plenty of time to relax while we're here in Mykonos. You know, I think this might be one of the first times I've been able to eat and drink what I like for more than a day. It's kind of exhilarating. Is this how the rest of you live?

I've not been able to sleep either and I'm feeling a bit restless, devoid of purpose. I don't like it. Perhaps I should go for a swim? Get a few laps in to work off some of the energy fizzing through my veins. And so, armed with a large glass of tropical fruit juice, topped up with a load of ice and a metal straw clinking against the sides, I make my way out onto the terrace.

Chloe is out by the pool, in that same spot in the corner she bagged yesterday, sunglasses covering half her face.

'Hi Chloe,' I call out across the corner of the pool.

She waves lazily from the sun bed.

I was fourteen when she started dating my brother and I thought she was a goddess. So mature and sophisticated with her fancy leather riding boots and her glossy ponytail. Now I realise she was just like every other slightly horsey teenager at that fancy school, but for a while all I wanted was for us to be friends.

Oh, who am I kidding. That desire never left, I've followed her around like a bad smell for a decade now. But all this time I had no idea who she really was, what she might be capable of. She thinks she's clever, that no one would possibly suspect what she's really up to. But I know all the details of her plan. Except for the most important one: *why* does she want Scott dead? And then there's the biggest question of them all: what am I going to do with that information?

Fuck it. I'm going to talk to her. 'Hey,' I say as I walk over to her, glass in my hand like a shield.

'Hey.' Her reply is clipped. She doesn't want me here.

'So, how's things? You having a good time?' The words sound lame to my own ears. I dread to think what they sound like to her.

'Of course,' she replies smoothly. The inference is clear, why wouldn't she be having a good time?

'Cool. I just...' I wrack my brain for a way to segue into a topic that might help shed some light on the whole situation. But I come up blank. She's staring at me, waiting for me to say something. 'What time are we heading out later?' I blurt out. OK, it won't give me answers to the questions I'm so desperate to ask, but at least she might stop giving me the same look she normally reserves for people she thinks are absolute idiots.

'Seven.'

'Great. And the transport's all booked?'

'Yes.' Her tone is clear. Of course she's fucking booked transport to take us to ELIAS. Which was my choice, I've been banging on about it for months as it's meant to be the best restaurant on the island and literally everyone goes there.

'Great,' I reply.

She slides her glasses back up her nose and picks up her book, the conversation over. Or at least it is from her perspective. I wonder what she'd do if I just stayed here, hovering next to her? 'Where's Scott?' The question is out of my mouth before I really think about it.

She sighs loudly and puts her book back down. 'Probably in the gym. Where's Jack?' Her words are clipped, part bored and part wanting to show me just how dumb a question it is by turning the table to the whereabouts of my own partner.

'Also gym,' I reply.

'Not joining them?'

'Week off. You're not working out?' This whole conversation is excruciating.

'No. We thought perhaps I should lay off the cardio.' Her tone softens. 'Apparently a bit more of a fat store is preferable if you're thinking about starting a family.' Her hand sweeps over her lower belly.

For a second I wonder if I misheard her. Did she really just imply her and Scott were trying to get pregnant? 'Oh wow,' I manage to get the words out with a stutter but they sound too high and too over the top in my ears. 'That's great news.'

'Thank you.' She smiles and picks up her book once again.

'I'll leave you to it,' I say and motion to the paperback. Then I hurry away, straight to the kitchen and the ice-cold bottle of vodka in the freezer. Enough of the fruit juice, I need something much stronger.

There is no way she is planning on having a baby with my brother. No way in hell. Unless she's trying to get knocked up before she kills him? No, that doesn't make sense. But it's interesting. The fact she's prepared to lie about it, and so blatantly to my face – means something. Very interesting indeed.

I measure three fingers of vodka into a glass and then tip in a tiny extra for good luck. The clear liquid burns the back of my throat and makes the hairs on my arm stand up on end. Jesus, that feels good and I close my eyes as the alcohol hits my bloodstream and sends a rush of warmth through my limbs. Despite the family business, I don't take drugs. I'm sloppy enough with a few drinks in me, I'd be a total nightmare if I started on the harder stuff. So, vodka will have to do.

The baby thing is utter bullshit, but why is she lying to me about it?

And how can I get to the truth on her motive to murder my brother?

13

I decide to pop my head around the door of the gym to see what Jack and Scott are up to. You'd think the two of them would have nothing in common, but they actually really get on. Or perhaps it's just that when you put two guys who think so much of themselves together, they will inevitably compete and that feels like bonding to them?

Jack primarily models for Vuori – athleisure wear for men who don't work out but who think they'll look like they do if they wear the right shorts and tees. As a result, he's honed a very specific physical aesthetic. He's tall, six foot two to be exact – and a genuine six two, not a five ten who adds a few inches that no one but him actually cares about. And with excellent muscular definition, broad shoulders, small waist. Oh, and this super peachy butt that does something to me I can't explain. Which might have something to do with why I keep him around.

I've already said he cheats, haven't I? Although *is* it cheating if I give my tacit agreement by not actually giving a shit? He's fun to be around and when I'm with him I don't have to think too much; it's just... easy. And, so what if it isn't some great love story? I had that once upon a time and then it went to shit.

Anyway, Jack and Scott are having a pull up competition in the gym. Shirts off, sweat dripping. A round of friendly back slaps after each attempt. It's almost sweet. But they aren't chatting to each other and sharing secrets, like about how my brother and Chloe are trying for a baby. That's what I want to know right now. I decide to leave them to it, it's a total bust on the gossip front. Boring.

I have a little wander around the villa, but it's pretty quiet. It seems like most people have retired to their rooms to start getting ready for this evening. I stressed a few times last night that ELIAS is more than just a restaurant and there is actually a dress code. Daddy had better not turn up in that disgusting shirt again, I love him dearly but no one needs to see that much of him when we're eating. Still, maybe it being quiet means that everyone is actually preparing themselves to be presentable this evening. ELIAS is the kind of place where you post the menu and then the food to Instagram, film a few reels for likes and shares, and round off the experience with some group shots of the table looking like they're having the best night imaginable to make everyone back home jealous of the perfect life you're living. I don't want to have to spend forever cropping people out of the photos if they've not made enough of an effort.

I'm kind of shocked Chloe agreed to us all going to ELIAS; it's absolutely not her kind of place. It's like the mecca of influencers and Chloe doesn't do the whole social media thing. She's never said it to my face but I can tell she thinks she's too good for Instagram. I thought she'd shoot me down and then I'd have to bitch for a while before sneaking out with Jack like a pair of naughty teenagers. I was almost looking forward to that aspect, although we would've been rumbled the moment I posted about it, there's no chance I'd have missed the opportunity to get a new profile pic against the infamous wall of flowers outside the entrance. So yeah, I don't really understand why she agreed to a night out at ELIAS. I mention that to Jack as we get ready.

'Perhaps she just knew you'd like it,' he says as he walks to the patio doors and lights a cigarette. He's naked and I allow myself a few moments to enjoy the view.

'Hardly,' I scoff. It isn't Chloe's style to do something she thinks other people might enjoy. There'll be an entirely selfish reason for this outing. She plays the game of being selfless, but I'm not fooled at all.

'Perhaps she just wants to get out of the villa for a few hours?' He holds out the cigarette for me to take a drag. I gave up last year after a casting director told me I needed to be careful about fine lines, but the odd drag on someone else's doesn't count. I hold the smoke in my lungs for a count of five and then breathe out, my head spinning in that delicious way after a hit of nicotine.

'It's definitely sus.'

He takes the cigarette back and laughs softly. 'What is your obsession with her?'

I don't want to have that conversation again. I'm not obsessed with her. I take the cigarette back and grind the butt into the ashtray. Jack's hand skims my waist as I bend over. I could do with a distraction so I turn towards him. 'Shower with me?' I ask with a raise of my right eyebrow.

'I thought you'd never ask,' he says as he grabs my hand and pulls me towards the bathroom.

* * *

At exactly 7 p.m. two cars pull up in front of the villa. Chloe catches my eye and gives me a smug little smile that says 'See, I really did book transport'. It feels a little unnecessary if we're honest. She should maybe be a little nicer to me as well, given what I know about her.

We pull up outside ELIAS to see a huge queue snaking down the hill. It's full of wannabe girlies in sparkly bikini tops and too short skirts, waiting their turn to pout in front of the wall of flowers in white and shades of blue that ELIAS has become famous for. They won't be dining here. I'm not being a bitch but there isn't a hope in hell they could afford to. Plus, everyone knows that you have to take the picture *after* you've eaten, with the twinkly lights embedded in the wall showing their full glory, and a branded doggy bag to prove you're a diner and not just a tourist.

'Table for Cooper,' I tell the concierge at the door. He's like a Greek god, all tanned skin and smouldering eyes and a fitted white shirt that shows off every carefully honed muscle in his back. I glance at Chloe and see her eyes flare for a moment as she takes him in. Interesting. Maybe my sister-in-law isn't a total ice queen after all.

The place is packed, full of everyone who's anyone. Mykonos is the playground of the rich and beautiful and it seems they have all descended on ELIAS for the evening.

I spot some friends at a banquette in the corner and head over to say hi. Scott follows me. Of course he does, he always wants to meet my model friends.

'This is my brother, Scott,' I tell Hilda who, judging by the short white veil she's wearing is on her hen party.

'Ah,' Hilda replies. 'The famous Cooper brother.' She appraises him like a cat as she shakes his hand.

'It's a pleasure to meet you,' my brother says. 'And please let me know if there's anything you'd like to get the party started.' He twerks his eyebrows.

Interesting. He's just confirmed my suspicions over why he agreed to this ridiculous holiday. He's trying to expand the empire and the party island of Mykonos could be another jewel in the Cooper crown.

We finally make it to the table – of course I had to stop to have a quick chat with a few other people I kind of know, especially when I realised one of them was live-streaming. Chloe hands me a menu, her face like thunder.

'Can we please order?' she demands. 'Apparently the wait is over an hour for food.'

'Perfection takes time,' I remind her. Now, I've heard kind of mixed reviews about this place if we're being honest. A lot of talk on the down low that the food isn't all that great, but it does look fantastic. Which is the most important thing, you don't come to a restaurant like this to actually eat.

I order the lobster ceviche. It will come presented on a huge plate with edible flowers, delicate scoops of basil sorbet and intricate parmesan crisps. The photos will be insane.

'How do you know Hilda?' Scott asks when the waiter leaves the table.

'Work,' I reply. But then I wonder... 'She's friends with Rosie,' I add, focussing my attention on Chloe. She's good, too good to show much of a reaction. But even she couldn't hide the flare in her eyes and the almost imperceptible tightening of her grip on her knife in her right hand. Interesting.

'Rosie?' Scott asks. He had zero reaction to the name, not because he's a good actor but because to him it means so little.

Chloe's eyes drift to her husband and her knuckles turn pale as her grip tightens further.

I don't actually know a Rosie but it isn't like they can check.

'Laura's sister,' I say with conviction. 'You met her last year.' The lie seems to stick as Scott doesn't ask anything else.

But now I have my answer.

Chloe knows what really happened to Rosie all those years ago.

I heard the truth from a friend of a friend of my brother's. And only because he didn't realise I was listening to him shooting his shit. It's a valuable skill to learn, to listen but not appear to be interested at all. The best way to get gossip and even better when they don't realise who you really are.

But this was beyond that. This was a man bragging about how he knew someone who knew someone who was friends with the great Scott Cooper. 'He's a fucking legend,' the fool was saying. 'I mean, like a literal fucking legend. Stone fucking cold, man. Kill you if you cross him.' He was telling everyone who would listen about how much respect he had for the Coopers. 'He just don't give a fuck. Do anything to get what he wants. Fuck, man. Killed some girl to get close to his wife. How fucking sick is that?'

The idiot fanboyed for another half an hour. Going on and on about how amazing he thought my brother was. I almost let slip who I was, but managed to keep my secrets. My head was full of that particular brag. That Scott killed a girl to get close to his wife.

Rosie.

Rosie and Chloe were best friends at school. Until Rosie fell off the roof in their final year. I remember it. There was this huge *thing*, everyone mooning around the town in their school uniforms, black ribbons in their hair.

Chloe kept coming over after that and I'd always find strips of black ribbon in the bathroom I had to share with Scott. It was everywhere. Like a constant talisman. Scott took to tying it in Chloe's hair for her, playing the supportive boyfriend, the shoulder to cry on, the constant in her life. She fell for him. Hook, line and sinker.

But it was all a lie.

He killed Rosie.

Killed Rosie to get close to her.

I look at her now, dressed in a plain navy halter dress, hair swept into a chignon, the soft light of the restaurant casting long shadows on her features. How does she sit there with him? Sit there with his hand on her knee making suggestions that she's planning on having his baby?

I know she's planning on killing him.

But what is she waiting for? I would have killed him the moment I found out.

14

Dinner is an interesting affair. And when I say interesting, I mean more that it gives me a great opportunity to get a bit more intel on all the different dynamics at play here. Obviously I know my own family, I've been tolerating the constant family dinners and need to keep up the public appearance that the Coopers are just one big happy bunch. It looks chaotic to outsiders, but trust me that the whole family dynamic is carefully curated. It's all orchestrated by Mummy; nothing she does is accidental, even if no one else realises it.

The Wilsons, on the other hand, are an altogether different prospect. I've spent a bit of time with them over the years, Chloe and Scott have been together for more than a decade, but it's mainly been big events that have brought our two families together. Like weddings and stuff. I hate weddings: an entire day when it is seriously frowned upon for anyone other than the bride to be the centre of attention. I don't want to steal the limelight, you have no idea how much happier I'd be to blend into the background, but I just... well, I just don't. And then I take shit for it, even though it isn't my fault.

Mr Wilson is a formidable presence, the kind of man you just can't help but be impressed by, even if you didn't also know his pedigree and the size of his empire. I know Daddy's jealous of him, and would desperately love to ooze that same kind of class. He's not bad looking either, in that silver fox kind of a way that Patrick Dempsey rocks.

Mrs Wilson, Erin, doesn't say a word over dinner. In fact, except when she was talking to the concierge, I'm not sure I've heard her say more than a handful of sentences since we all arrived yesterday. It's almost like she's mute, unable to speak. Or perhaps Mr Wilson has spent so long talking for both of them that she just doesn't bother any more.

Rob, Chloe's brother, is a dick. A proper self-entitled little shit who thinks the world owes him a living. He keeps looking at me, a smirk twisting his face, tongue occasionally poking out to lick the corner of his mouth. It makes me want to go and have a shower, but I'm used to men like this and I move a little closer to Jack, using him as a human shield. It's useful to have a boyfriend in situations like this. Rob's wife is a sweetheart and she should one hundred percent drop his ugly arse and find someone who deserves her.

Mr Wilson holds court over the table and I can feel Daddy seething as Mr Wilson orders champagne for everyone. 'Tonight's on me,' he says, looking Daddy directly in the eye.

'Oh no,' Daddy replies. 'Tonight is on me.'

There's a pause as they both size each other up.

'No no,' Mr Wilson raises both hands. 'Trust me, I've got this.' He offers a smile, one that feels laced with something that leaves a bitter taste in my mouth. I have a bad feeling about this evening, like a storm is brewing. Which quite frankly isn't fair as I've been looking forward to coming to ELIAS for months and months and it's going to get ruined.

I nudge Jack. Hard. My elbow makes contact with his ribs, causing him to make an 'Ooof' sound. 'What the hell?' he whispers into my ear, his hand rubbing his side.

'You need to pay for tonight,' I tell him under my breath, keeping my eyes on Daddy and Mr Wilson.

'What? This place is extortionate.'

'I'll pay you back.' Jack is moderately successful as a model, as in he books enough work to justify calling himself a professional. Not enough to actually pay for rent and bills, and certainly not enough to pay for a big group at ELIAS. But Jack is also not shy about spending other people's money.

Jack huffs and scowls. I nudge him again, even harder this time.

'Fine,' he whispers. 'Now then,' he says loudly, getting the attention of the rest of the table. 'This evening is on *me*. As a thank you for inviting me on this wonderful trip with you all.' Jack beams and the atmosphere shifts, the approaching storm diverted. 'Was it the Perrier-Joüet you ordered?' He directs this at Mr Wilson who nods in reply. 'A fantastic choice. How about we also get in a round of Palomas?' He turns to look at Daddy. 'I believe they're your favourite?'

Damn, he's good. When he wants to be at least. My father smiles. 'Perfect,' Daddy tells him.

Crisis averted, I go back to my primary hobby of people watching. Actually, people watching isn't quite right. I'm not just watching. People analysing might be better. Even if Jack normally says I'm people judging. My main focus is Chloe, of course. What I want to know is why she organised this holiday? All this playing happy families is just weird. Right?

I watch her drink champagne and eat dainty little loukoumades doughnuts and laugh at something dumb Rob says and squeeze Scott's knee. None of it makes any sense.

Jack goes to the bathroom and bumps into some model friends of ours on his way back. I hold my breath and cross my fingers, hoping he'll behave himself and not destroy all the goodwill he literally just made by offering to pay for the evening. Once again, he manages to fail me. But I pretend not to notice, we'll talk when we get back to our room later. Besides, I still have to record content for my socials.

'We need to get some photos,' I tell everyone as another round of drinks is delivered to the table. This time they are a range of different flavoured margaritas and all the vibrant colours will look fabulous in the pictures. I even take a few more arty shots with the drinks as the focus, the background blurring into a mass of colour and light. Perfect. I want to tell Rob to suck in his gut but I hold my tongue. I can always just crop him out later.

Just before midnight, there's a general murmur about how late it is from around the table. It's actually still early, but I have to remember that not everyone is mid-twenties. Jack asks for the bill and I sneak a look at the total as the waiter slides it discreetly towards him. He whistles under his breath – not that I can blame him, it's over seven grand – but I ignore him. Daddy will end up paying in the long run anyway.

Erin Wilson pauses at a table on the way out of the restaurant. Everyone else in our party carries on walking towards the exit, but I lag behind to see who she's talking to. It's a group of guys I don't recognise, although one of them does have the prettiest pair of bright blue eyes I've ever seen on a man. I take a quick photo of him on the sly, pretending to be checking my phone. Erin drops down a few inches, her lips mere centimetres from Pretty Eyes' ear. I don't hear what she says, but he nods in agreement.

Erin straightens up. 'Have a lovely evening all,' she says to

the table at large and then hurries to catch up with the rest of
our group. What the hell was that all about?

We get back to the villa and everyone heads off to their
respective bedrooms. I want to get another drink and spend an
hour on the terrace with Jack discussing what I saw in ELIAS
with Erin and the man with the pretty eyes. But then I
remember Jack's in my bad books. And, to be fair, I'm far more
in the mood for a fight than a gossip.

'I saw you, Jack,' I tell him the second the door to our
bedroom closes behind us. I stride over to the mini fridge and
grab a baby champagne.

'It wasn't like that,' he blusters and tries to act like it was
nothing.

'You couldn't keep your hands off her, touching her arm, the
back of her chair. It was so fucking obvious.'

'But you know I love you, Tori,' he says, his voice affecting
that pathetic little whine that sometimes – if I've already had a
few glasses of wine – makes me relinquish my anger and
forgive him for embarrassing me with his philandering ways.

'In front of my family, Jack.' My words are tinged with fury.

'Oh.' He pales slightly. He's been busted.

'Daddy saw you, for fuck's sake,' I hiss.

'But baby, I—'

'I don't want to hear it,' I interrupt his excuses. 'You made
me look like a fool in front of my family and now you'll have to
reap the consequences.'

'Consequences?' He seems surprised that his actions might
finally come back to bite him in that peachy bum of his.

'I can't just forgive you, can I? I can't just say it's all OK.
You'll have to sleep on the sofa.'

'No.' He looks stricken. 'You can't.'

'Yes, I fucking can.' I drop my voice. 'You did this, remember?' And then I raise my voice, shouting loudly enough that everyone else in the villa will be guaranteed to hear, even though they've all already gone to bed. 'You can sleep on the beach for all I care!'

'But... but...'

I just stare at him. It isn't like he actually has a defence, is it?

'Fine,' he says. 'There're two spare rooms. I'll sleep in one of them.'

'No. The sofa.' I'm adamant. He needs to be seen to be in the dog house. Everyone needs to know I kicked him out of our room.

The thing is I don't care even one tiny shit what my father thinks. But I'm keeping up appearances. And Daddy would think I would be mad at my boyfriend for chatting up other women right in front of my face. In truth I couldn't care less. I've spent my whole life in the shadow of other people's expectations. I'm done. But I'm still trying to figure out a proper plan for my escape. I need to find a way to leave the Cooper machine behind; until then I have to perform the role I've been playing for all these years.

15

It turns out the villa has the most obnoxious intruder alarm known to man. Which I discover when it starts blaring at 2 a.m. just as I'm finally getting into bed. For fuck's sake! I've had enough of today. But nooooooo, I now have to get dressed again and stand on the terrace like a fool while one of Daddy's men sweeps the house.

Movement by the patio door almost gives me a heart attack as I'm pulling on the khaki Zadig&Voltaire dress I wore to Nammos this morning. 'Jesus Christ,' I shout in his face as I open the door. 'What the hell are you doing, Jack?'

Anger flashes momentarily across his face. 'Coming to check you're OK.'

'Right.' Well, that is kind of sweet. Unless... 'You didn't set it off, did you?'

'The alarm? No. But when it went off, I ran here to make sure you're alright.'

'Is it real?' A shiver runs down my spine. My first thought was an inconvenience, like a drill or something. But what if there's a reason for the alarm? It's gone two and we've been out all night. No one would schedule a drill now, certainly none of Daddy's men would be that stupid anyway. You should see Daddy when his sleep is interrupted; it's not a pretty sight. But alarms don't just go off by themselves.

Someone has tried to get into the villa.

In the middle of the night.

The protocol is to gather on the terrace, which is open to the sea but cut into the rock on the other sides, like a naturally forming panic room. Personally, I feel like it just gathers us together like fish in a barrel, but I keep that thought to myself. I've always been accused of overreacting. And, right now, I'm struggling to keep my fear in check.

'It'll be fine,' Jack whispers at my side. But the way his eyes are darting around the space suggests he doesn't believe his own words.

Chloe looks ashen, sitting in the corner, a sarong wrapped around her shoulders.

The Wilsons join us. They were obviously still awake as Erin is in full makeup and her uncrumpled appearance stands out against the rest of the family, who are in varying stages of zombie transformation.

Ethan and Mikey, two of Daddy's best men, conduct a full sweep of the villa. It takes them a good twenty minutes before they return and Ethan announces that it looks like a false alarm.

'What exactly does that mean?' Mr Wilson demands.

'Umm...'

'Just be clear. What does false alarm mean?'

'We couldn't find any sign of a break in.' Ethan is sweating, from the heat or the stress of being interrogated by Mr Wilson, I'm not sure.

Mr Wilson turns his attention to Daddy. 'And you think

that's satisfactory, do you?' His tone suggests he does *not* think it's satisfactory.

Daddy stands up, making sure to use the extra three inches he has over Mr Wilson to best effect. He doesn't even flinch. 'I trust my men.' There's a subtle accent on the 'my': *my* men, not *your* men, and *where* are your men exactly?

'You promised me you would have security under control for this trip.' Mr Wilson doesn't raise his voice, but it's clear he's pissed.

'And I do. My men have swept the villa and there is no threat.'

Mr Wilson glances towards Chloe and then to me. 'And you're prepared to gamble my daughter and your own on that?'

The mask my father wears cracks for a moment, just long enough for me to see that perhaps he does actually care about me after all. In his own twisted way at least. But then the shutters come back down. 'Yes.'

Daddy makes an announcement to the rest of the group that it was a false alarm and we head back to our rooms. 'Are you still going to make me sleep on the sofa?' Jack asks.

I shoot him a look. One that says, *What do you fucking think?*

'Fine,' he replies and huffs again. The huffing is really starting to grate on me.

I flick on the light to my room and something skitters into the corner. I jump backwards into the hallway, heart hammering. What the hell was that? Is there someone inside? My fingers move to my bag like a reflex, curling around the hilt of the small knife I keep stashed in there. Other people might say I'm paranoid. But better safe than sorry.

With the blade held out in front of me, I push the door open again and edge over the threshold, breath held so I can hear any movement. But the room is quiet, almost too quiet.

There's a pair of Jack's trainers by the door and I use them to prop it open. Always keep your escape route clear.

I look under the bed, lifting the edge of the sheets carefully with one finger. Nothing. Onto the wardrobe, piled high with dresses and bags from today's shopping spree. Nothing. Into the bathroom. This is where an intruder would be hiding if this was a slasher film. Which I love by the way, even if they don't exactly help with the whole 'thinking the worst possible outcome in every scenario' thing. After all, isn't it better to understand what you might be up against?

The bathroom's empty and I feel my shoulders start to relax. Maybe I just imagined the skittering?

But then I hear a grunt from by the door and I'm back inside the room, knife in front of me, huge strides towards my assailant. Always attack first. Don't wait to see if you might be the prey; you always are unless you're the predator.

'Jesus!' my assailant shouts as I lunge at him. He twists out of my range. 'Tori. It's me.'

I look up at him, his features coming into focus as my brain catches up with who it really is. 'Mikey.'

'Glad to see you putting my advice into practice,' he says with a grin and a pointed look at the knife I'm still brandishing.

'You scared me.'

'I apologise. I just wanted to make sure you're OK. Where's Jack?' He says it like he hasn't already seen that I've sent Jack to the sofa. Mikey's never tried to hide his disdain for my boyfriend.

'I heard something in the room,' I say by way of explanation for the whole knife waving thing.

Mikey immediately snaps into business mode and ushers me into the corner while he sweeps the room. He's far more thorough than I am and I make a mental note to do better myself next time. Once he's satisfied there's no one hiding in here, he checks the patio door. 'You should keep this locked,' he tells me. 'Air-con on and door closed.' He says the last sentence like a parent to a naughty child. He's told me all of this before, more than once.

'Jack must have left it unlocked.'

'And Jack is a fool.'

I can't exactly deny it.

'I'll stay for a while, OK?' Mikey says as he takes a seat on the sofa in the corner of the room. It isn't a question and I'm grateful to have him here.

Mikey started working for Daddy about a decade ago and I was totally infatuated by him when I was a teenager. He's not actually that attractive – he has that classic ex-boxer look with the crooked nose and penchant for a bomber jacket – but there's something about him that women are drawn to. He's always treated me like a kid though, a little girl he must protect at all costs, even teaching me self-defence.

An hour later and the intruder alarm goes off again. This time I know it's definitely not a drill. And I don't believe it's a false alarm either, not judging by the look on Mikey's face.

This time we're all even more dishevelled when we congregate back on the terrace.

Erin arrives on her own.

'Where's Luke?' Daddy asks her.

'Where do you think?' she answers, keeping her eyes on the floor to avoid looking him in the face. She moves over to her daughter and whispers something in her ear.

Chloe stands up. 'My father wanted to conduct his own sweep,' she announces, saying the words Erin is apparently too timid to say herself. 'Since this is the second alarm this evening.'

I wait with my heart in my mouth for more information. I hate this. I hate not feeling in control of the situation, not knowing if there's a threat or it's just a dodgy wire somewhere in the system that's setting off the alarm.

Mr Wilson arrives fifteen minutes later, with Grace the concierge in tow. She's got her hair pulled back into a ponytail and for a moment I think I recognise her. Not from here but from another time. She probably just looks like someone I once knew.

'Grace is going to look at the alarm system as it seems to be malfunctioning.'

Grace nods, but she shoots a look at Chloe. There's something going on here. Something that's being kept from the rest of us.

16

When the alarm goes off for the third time, we once again congregate on the terrace. It's half past three and sleep is looking less and less likely. I grab a bottle of tequila from the kitchen on my way through.

'Beach?' I ask the rest of the kids. I know we aren't technically children, but I mean not Mummy and Daddy or Mr and Mrs Wilson.

There is a round of shrugs and then a murmur of agreement. Scott grabs a bottle of whisky from the terrace bar. 'Can't stand that shit,' he says, motioning towards the Jose Cuervo in my hand. He has always had this thing where he acts like he's above me, even though we both know he has the least discerning palate you've ever met. Like he will literally drink bootleg shit from the depths of Eastern Europe – I had to call an ambulance for him once after I found him passed out in the bath.

We spread blankets over the sand as the sound of waves lap a metre away from us. It's gorgeous out here, the air cool and crisp with a hint of salt. I pass the tequila to Jack and watch him take a swig before he passes it to Chloe.

'Have you forgiven me yet?' Jack asks, leaning in so the rest of the circle can't hear.

'Are you sorry?' I reply.

It's dark but I can still tell the look he'll be wearing. Of course he isn't sorry; if he was he wouldn't keep doing it. 'You know I am,' he lies.

'In that case you're forgiven.' It's a game and we both know it.

'Good.' He snuggles in closer. 'And are you going to apologise for having Mikey in our room?'

He's had this weird thing about Mikey for months. 'He was just making sure I was safe. You know, because I was on my own.' I add the last bit pointedly.

'I guess I deserved that,' he replies.

'We should play something,' Farah says. 'I feel like I barely know you all. How about Truth or Dare?'

'Never Have I Ever,' Jack counters. 'Much more fun and, besides, I cannot be doing with thinking of dares at this time in the morning.'

'We need cups,' Chloe points out, ever practical. 'Or how will everyone drink together?'

'Ta da,' says Jack, as he reveals a stack of red plastic cups. 'I came prepared.' Jack loves this game. Where someone says a sentence and then you have to drink if you have done the thing they describe. I guess it's the perfect game for someone with zero shame.

'Is it weird to play this with family?' I ask.

'Probably,' Rob replies as he sloshes tequila into his cup. 'But I already know all my sister's secrets so we're good.'

I watch as Chloe shoots Scott a look that says Rob one hundred percent does not know very much at all.

'Alrighty then,' Jack says. I guess he's become the master of ceremonies of this particular game. 'It's Never Have I Ever time!' He leans over to me, his lips touching my earlobe. 'You wanted to know what is really going on with everyone? This is your chance.' Then he sits back up and gives me a wink.

Sometimes I hate him. Other times I love him.

'I'm going first,' Jack says. 'Obviously.' He makes eye contact with each person around the circle. 'Now then, have we all got drinks?' He waits as everyone raises their cups towards him. 'Cool. I'll go first.' He pauses as if he's thinking for a moment. 'Never have I ever had lewd thoughts about someone in this circle.' He flashes a grin and takes a gulp from his cup.

The others groan. 'No fair,' says Farah. 'We're all couples.'

'Maybe I just wanted to get everyone drinking?' Jack replies. But I can tell from the way he says it that he'd actually forgotten about the whole couples thing. Rob watches me as he drinks, making it clear he isn't thinking lewd thoughts about his wife. Gross.

Jack catches the look and I feel him stiffen slightly next to me. 'Never have I ev—'

'You did it last time,' Rob interjects.

'Fine,' Jack replies with a shrug. 'You crack on.'

We go round the circle, each person raising a 'never have I ever'. They are mainly banal and quite frankly I'm getting a little bored. Jack obviously feels the same way because he interrupts Chloe, who's about to raise hers. 'Never have I ever,' he says, his tone mischievous. 'Been to a strip club without my partner knowing.'

Now I do not care one tiny bit if he goes to a strip club, there are far bigger things to get upset about. But Rob takes a drink and then looks guiltily at Farah. 'It was my stag do,' he tells her when he sees the look of thunder cross her face. She is not happy, not at all. 'Oh, come on,' he says, 'it was harmless fun.'

'You promised me you wouldn't,' she says as she stands up and brushes the sand from her skirt.

'It's not that big a deal.' He sounds a little more desperate now. I'm inclined to agree with him, but you shouldn't ever judge someone else's relationship, I know that only too well after the number of 'friends' who have waded into mine.

'It is a big deal. To me anyway. You promised and then you lied and now you decide this is the time for me to find out.' Her voice is level, but it's that kind of controlled tone that makes you realise she's mad as hell. I wouldn't want to be Rob right now. She turns and walks away.

He watches her go. 'Should I follow her?'

No one answers and there's an awkward few moments of silence before Jack claps his hands together. 'Right then, more drinkies.' He grabs the bottle of tequila and makes his way around the circle, topping up outstretched cups.

A rustle behind us causes me to jump, my hand instinctively reaching towards my shoulder bag and the knife concealed inside.

'Scott.' It's Daddy. 'We need you up at the villa.' It's a command.

'What about me?' I ask.

'Not you, sweetheart.' He doesn't add *this is a guys thing* but he really doesn't have to.

Jack leans in to me. 'Bingo. Now you can get more from Chloe with Scott gone.'

He's right. This could be the perfect opportunity. I'm not sure if you know this yet, but Mummy is brilliant at poker and she taught me how to play when I was a little girl. The secret?

You don't play your cards, you play the other people sitting around the table. And really all you need to do is figure out who's lying. Chloe isn't going to tell me what I want to know. Or not on purpose anyway.

'Never have I ever discovered my spouse's deepest darkest secret,' I say, keeping my eyes on Chloe. She doesn't drink. But I can tell she wants to. Ha. She definitely knows what he did. No one asks another question, so I take the opportunity to go again. 'Never have I ever wanted someone dead.'

Jack takes a gulp of tequila next to me. 'I mean, who hasn't?' he says to the rest of the circle with a grin. 'It isn't like you'd actually do it though.'

Chloe says nothing. Her tell is nothing more than a tiny flare of her nostrils, so subtle I bet even she doesn't realise she does it.

Interesting. Very, *very* interesting.

The tequila runs out and we start to make our way back to the villa. It's almost five in the morning and I desperately need to get some sleep before I pass out. Soon it's just me and Chloe outside our respective rooms and I take the opportunity.

'So, here's what we're going to do.' I take a breath, just enough time for her to wonder exactly where this is about to go. 'Tomorrow, we're going to the spa at the Mykonos Grand. Just the two of us. A sisters' day out, if you will.' I give her a slow smile and watch the way her eyes crease at the corner as she pulls an involuntary frown. 'And then, when we're all safely wrapped up in our robes and the rest of the world is shut out... well, then you're going to tell me everything.' I take a step backwards to appraise her reaction more fully.

Her nostrils flare and guilt skitters across her features, just for a moment before she tamps it down. She's good, my sister-in-law, I have to admit. But she isn't *that* good. 'Everything? I have no idea what you mean,' she says.

'Of course you do.' I turn and walk down the hallway to my own room. At the door I spin to face her again. 'You're going to tell me all the details of how you're planning to kill my brother.'

And then I pull the door open and slip inside the cool of the room, leaving her open mouthed in the corridor.

DAY THREE

CHLOE

17

Fuck. Fuck. Fuck.

Did Tori really just say that?

Or did I imagine those words through my fug of exhaustion and tequila?

How can she possibly know? This cannot be happening. But it is happening. She was clear as day in her accusation, no question there at all. But how?

And, perhaps more importantly, why doesn't she seem to care? She seems more interested in the details than horrified by the potential outcome.

My bedroom is empty as I slip inside, my brain racing.

Shit, shit, shit.

I comb through every conversation we've had in the past few months, my mind snagging on anything that might be important, anything that might suggest I've somehow let slip about my plans. But I come up blank. Tori and I spend a lot of time together so I've been super careful with everything I've said recently. I like my sister-in-law, but she can be a bit of a liability: hardly the ally I'd want for a murder plot.

Not to forget that Scott is her brother. The Coopers are one of those 'blood is thicker than water' families, who think the name is everything and promise – more regularly than is strictly necessary – to die for each other if it comes down to it.

It's all a farce though. I know that Scott chased away Tori's previous boyfriend. He told me it was because he was no good for her. 'He wants her to retire from modelling. To give up on her dream,' he told me one evening.

'Does she actually like modelling?' I'd asked. She never seemed to be particularly into it for herself, it was their Uncle George who'd always encouraged her career.

Scott took a step back from me like I'd said something totally out of order. 'Are you serious? Of course she does. It's every girl's dream.'

He'd been so resolute in his argument I hadn't bothered to point out that I'd never had any desire to be a model. He would only have twisted my words and made some kind of comment about me not having some of the prerequisites. He'd made a few comments around that time about my weight and I'd been pretty salty about it if I'm honest.

Anyway, the boyfriend had been dispatched under this pretence that it was in Tori's best interest, even though it was obvious something else was going on. That there were other reasons for getting rid of him.

Not that it worked, he came back a day later with a diamond and a promise of marital bliss.

That was the last time I saw him.

I'm not saying Scott killed him. I know for a fact that he's still alive – I may have done a little Instagram stalking, mainly because when I found out how ruthless my husband was, I realised this wouldn't have been far outside his MO – but he hasn't set foot anywhere near London since that day.

I wonder if Tori knows what her brother did? Perhaps I could use that to buy her loyalty? But, no, it's a stupid idea. Despite the fact that Scott treats her like shit, she thinks the sun shines out of his arse and nothing I can say is going to change that.

So why didn't she sound more... upset? If she really thinks I'm going to kill her brother, surely it would have more of an impact?

What am I missing here? The question rattles round my brain as I slip into bed. Scott is still somewhere with his father and brother, some kind of Cooper family emergency, but I can't enjoy the peace and quiet.

How does Tori know? And what might she do with that information?

* * *

I wake up in the morning and for a moment feel a sense of absolute calm. A gentle breeze flows into the room from the patio, moving the voile curtains lazily. The scent of coffee hits me: despite all our problems, my husband demonstrates occasional flashes of sweetness and this morning he has left an espresso for me.

I knock it back in a single gulp, bitterness hitting my tongue and making me grimace. Delicious. My synapses fire.

And then I remember.

Tori knows.

Tori wants us to spend the morning together.

Tori knows. Oh, I already said that.

I have a cold shower, hoping the icy water will help me make sense of the bizarreness of last night. It doesn't help. I'm just left with even more questions. I try turning the water to scalding hot, but still to no avail.

There is only one solution here; I'm going to have to go to this spa with her and find out what she thinks she knows. And convince her she's losing her mind, that it's just her paranoia, that she should go back to that therapist she was seeing last year.

Yes. That's what I'll do. I stare at myself in the mirror as the steam begins to clear. There are deep bags under my eyes and my skin is almost grey. I look like shit. What great joy that I need to spend the day in the company of an actual model.

I'm not a great lover of spas, which I know sounds batshit. I mean, who doesn't like spas? But I find myself getting too hot, or too cold. Or itchy. And there are people watching you in a state of half dress. And it isn't like I can relax while I'm getting a massage. I mean, I don't relax at the best of times, I've always been pretty tightly strung. My mum used to call me Viola when I was little because I was so taut, like a string tightened a little too far. But, in a spa, with someone touching me, how can I relax?

Plus there's the forced proximity, the person whose job it is to pamper you. The weird dichotomy of that. I've never felt good about people working to make my life even easier, it feels off to me.

I mentioned it to my mother-in-law, Libby, once and she was horrified. 'But they are there to do a job. That is what they do. If you don't let them because of some misplaced feeling you don't deserve their efforts, then how do they pay their mortgages or feed their families? You don't do them favours by being some kind of conscientious objector.'

'But—' I'd tried to explain myself but she cut me off again.

'Take the massage. Or the drink. Or whatever. But treat the

people who serve you like they're people. Tip them well. Sing their praises to your nice friends so they build up a client list of other similarly good customers. That is how you help them.'

I sigh. I'm still not sure which of us is right. But I guess today I need to suck it all up and go to the spa.

How else am I going to find out what the hell Tori thinks she knows?

I take a deep breath and reach into my makeup bag to try to sort out my face at least a little before heading out. My fingers brush the corner of a folded piece of white paper and I unfurl it to read the words written so neatly.

I SEE WHO YOU REALLY ARE.

Hang on, didn't I throw this away? I peer at the slip of paper, is it the same one as before? Or did that say something about what I was capable of? Which means... What does it mean? It was Tori who left the last one, but why is she leaving cryptic messages one moment and then asking me straight to my face about my plans for my bastard husband the next? None of it makes any sense.

I tuck it into the pocket of my shorts. I'm going to take the bull by the horns and demand Tori tells me what the hell she thinks she's up to. And then deny, deny, deny. *Of course I'm not planning on killing Scott.* I repeat the words into the mirror, but even I can see the lie painted across my face. And one thing I know my sister-in-law is a master at, is spotting a lie.

Fuck. Fuck. Fuck.

This is bad. Very, *very* bad.

18

Grace has organised a driver for us, and so Tori and I sit in silence as the arid landscape slips past the window. I desperately want to ask her about last night but I need to bite my tongue until we're in private.

The spa is inside the Mykonos Grand hotel, a temple of whitewashed walls, marble floors and the occasional pop of brilliant blue. The place is full of attractive young women like this place is the literal fountain of youth. I'm not even thirty and I feel fucking ancient, most of these girls can't be much older than twenty-one – it's like the waiting room for auditions to be Leonardo DiCaprio's next girlfriend.

Tori takes a few pictures, turning the camera on herself and pouting into the lens with the hotel logo prominently in the background. Her fingers fly over the keypad as she uploads them to her socials, no doubt with a flurry of hashtags attached. I don't really do social media myself and have no desire to constantly post pictures of myself or details of where I am at any given moment of the day.

I'm kind of surprised that the Coopers allow Tori to be so

blatant on Instagram. I think back to last night at the alarm constantly going off. I know all about the need for security, you don't grow up as a Wilson without understanding these things. One of the reasons I was sold Villa Bougainvillea was the high wall and attention to detail on aspects like the state-of-the-art alarm system. But I was always taught that the best defence is anonymity; if no one knows who you are or where you are, then you can't become a target. But then here's Tori literally posting our exact location to the whole world.

'Hey Tori?' I ask. 'You haven't posted stuff about the villa, have you?'

'The villa?' It's clear from her tone that she's wondering why the hell I would think to ask the question.

'Yes. Like anything that someone could use to figure out where it is.'

'I've said we're in Mykonos.'

'Yes, I get that. But I mean something that could pinpoint exactly where the villa is. Like the name or anything.'

She takes her sunglasses off her head and slips them into a case before throwing it into her bag. 'I'm not an idiot, Chloe. I know what I'm doing. I prepare my posts when I'm out but I don't actually upload them until we're leaving. No need to encourage a stalker to turn up at dinner. And I only post about where we've been in public; I know not to give away details of where we're actually staying.' She sounds kind of pissed that I asked. Perhaps she isn't as dumb as I thought.

'Of course. Sorry. Just checking.'

'Whatever. Come on,' she says, linking her arm through mine. 'Let's go find this spa and have our little chat.'

I read the advertisement board outside the spa. Apparently this place has been designed to 'optimally utilise the glorious natural light aligned with the Cycladic architecture in white &

blue shades', which I guess just means it will feel quintessentially Mykonian. So far, so not too horrendous. Plus, apparently, a lot of the treatments are done outside with a view over the sea and that does sound almost pleasant. If only I wasn't here with Tori, just waiting for her to announce my fate.

I should be more worried. I know I need to take this seriously. But somehow it just doesn't feel real. Like how can Tori possibly have guessed what I'm up to? The whole thing is just bizarre, like an out of body experience or a bad trip.

The poster promises 'a complete sense of all-round wellbeing'. That feels rather a bold claim given my current state of mind.

'I booked you in for a Mykonos Glow facial,' Tori tells me as we push open the door and enter the quiet hush of the spa's reception area. 'Apparently it's great for tightening and firming the skin.' She flashes me a smile. 'It'll make you look years younger.'

There's no malice in her words, it's like she's simply being honest. Brutally honest. I'm twenty-nine and I look... well, I look my age. I know there is some weird discourse doing the rounds about how young or old people of my generation look. But I'm doing OK – no Nicola Coughlan to be sure, but OK.

'Welcome to the Althea Spa Retreat,' a stunningly attractive woman dressed in a simple navy shift dress says in the perkiest voice I think I've ever heard.

'Althea was the Greek goddess of healing,' Tori tells me with the smug tone of a student who finally did some studying.

'Cool,' I reply and pick up a pamphlet about thalassotherapy. Apparently, I can rejuvenate my mind and body with the powerful healing properties of seawater. It doesn't sound too bad if I'm honest, and it finishes in the pool where hopefully Tori and I can finally have that conversation. But first I'll have to make it through the facial my sister-in-law so kindly picked out for me.

There's a window in the treatment room and I stare out across the sea towards a smudge on the horizon. 'That's the island of Delos,' my therapist tells me as she prepares the gloop she's about to spread across my face. 'Huge concentration of cosmic energy,' she says like that's a fact and not honest to God woo-woo. 'It's where Apollo was born. He was the god of light.'

I make some non-descriptive noise to show I'm at least half listening.

'You really need to relax,' the therapist tells me. But I can't relax. If anything, I can feel the tension building inside me. This is getting ridiculous. I need to know what Tori thinks is happening.

'Relax,' the therapist tells me again.

But inside I can feel the scream building.

Finally, our facials are done and we're escorted to the steam room to begin our thalassotherapy journey. And, finally, I'm alone with Tori. Where do I begin? How do I start this conversation? My mind is blank, grasping for words that aren't materialising.

Tori inspects her nails and then turns to face me. 'So?'

'So?'

'So, start at the beginning. I told you I wanted to know everything.'

What does she already know? That's the question and the one I've been turning over since dawn and then all morning as I've been poked and prodded in the name of being pampered. 'Everything?' I ask. I'm fairly sure this an exact repeat of the conversation we had in the hallway of the villa in the early hours of this morning.

'Fuck's sake, Chloe.' She throws her hands up in exasperation.

Maybe this is the key to getting her to spill what she already knows, just getting her angry.

'I don't know what you're talking about.' I play innocent.

'You know exactly what I'm talking about.' She pauses and takes a deep breath in before releasing it slowly, closing her eyes for a moment. 'I need you to be honest with me.' Her tone has returned to normal, or even more measured than that, the emotion taken out. She glances around her as if to make doubly sure we're alone and no one has managed to sneak into the blue tiled steam room. 'I'm on your side.'

I drop my voice to match her. 'What side?' I'm curious now.

'The side where people pay for what they've done.'

I tilt my head to one side and appraise her. 'And what have they done?'

Her eyes bore into mine. 'Blackmail. Extortion. Turning young girls into mules. Forcing them into sex work.'

'And what else?' I ask softly.

'Murder,' she whispers. 'And not just your friend Rosie.'

19

'What do you know about Rosie?' I ask.

'Scott killed her.'

She knows. But *how* does she know?

The thought hits me like a bolt of lightning from Zeus. Is this all a trap? She's Scott's baby sister; did he put her up to this? Is this my husband's way of finding out if I know the truth about Rosie? Is Tori doing this for him? 'And how do you know that?' I ask her.

But, before she can answer, one of the therapists opens the steam room and tells us it's time to move to the thalassotherapy pool.

The pool is built into the side of the cliff, jets churning the water into white foam, the scent of salt heavy in the air.

Once again, we're alone. 'Tell me about Rosie,' I demand.

'Scott killed her.'

'So you said. But what else?'

She leans back and turns her face to look at me. 'She was your best friend. I remember she came to the house once. I was, what, fourteen? I thought she was the most gorgeous woman

I'd ever seen. That hair! Like she was Ariel come to life on land.'

I can't help but smile at the memory of Rosie. She really did look like a mermaid with her waist length wavy hair. She was performing in a school play just before Christmas and for reasons I can't remember now had dyed her hair bright red. Like post-box red. She thought it would wash out, but it was permanent. Our house mistress went ballistic, but it actually looked amazing. And Rosie definitely had the sass to pull off the look.

'He was jealous, you know,' she continues. 'Scott. He hated that you had this best friend and didn't want to spend every hour of every day with him.'

Scott has never liked me having friends. It's not that he forbids me from having them – not explicitly anyway – but he's found so many ways over the years to manipulate the circle of people around me to the point I don't really have anyone who's just mine. My job is super corporate and no one socialises outside of work, so the people I spend my free time with are wives and girlfriends of *his* friends. Or my sisters-in law: Tori and occasionally Farah, when my brother isn't around. Shit. I don't think I'd ever really thought about it like that before. If I'd decided that all I would do is divorce him, I'd be left with noth-ing. With no one.

'And then you came back from Christmas break and told him you thought maybe things wouldn't work out between you. Oh my Goooooood,' she elongates the word. 'He was so angry that night. He went out and battered the shit out of some random guy in town. Put him in hospital for over a week as far as I can remember.'

I swallow the guilt at the thought someone got beaten up just because of me.

'It wasn't your fault,' Tori says quickly when she sees the look on my face. 'It's all on him. Anyway, after that he didn't leave his room for two days. I could hear him pacing up and down, Mummy kept screaming at him that he'd wear out the carpet.' She pauses for a few moments and turns to look out at the Aegean. 'He finally went out, I heard him leave at about 11 p.m. but I didn't really think much about it. I mean, he was always coming and going, it wasn't like Mummy and Daddy gave him a curfew or anything, he was twenty-one by then, hardly a baby like I was.'

We're interrupted again by one of the staff. 'Everything OK for you?' she asks.

'Perfect, thank you *so* much,' Tori says, all charm and light like she flicked a switch.

'Great. Just shout if you need anything.'

And then she's gone and it's just us again and I'm both desperate for Tori to continue and horrified at what I'm about to hear.

'I was at school the next day and by lunchtime it was all anyone could talk about. The girl who fell. Such a horrible accident. So tragic.'

They are all the words I remember being used at the time. It made me think they could be talking about anyone; it wasn't my Rosie they meant, it couldn't be. She was too vibrant, too alive to die.

'He'd got one of his friends to text her, pretending they wanted to meet up with her,' Tori tells me.

This is a new bit of information, something I've been wondering. How did Scott get Rosie up onto the school roof in the first place? 'Which friend?' I ask.

'Chris,' Tori tells me.

'Oh.' That makes sense. A lot of the girls had a thing for

Chris. And it finally explains something the police said to me back then. They asked me if there was a chance Rosie was meant to meet a boy and he didn't show up. If perhaps that might have influenced her behaviour. Like they thought she jumped off the roof because she got stood up.

'Scott lured her up to that roof. And then he pushed her off.' She meets my eyes as she says it and I can see the pain and the fear there. She isn't lying. She isn't trying to trap me. She believes her brother actually did this.

'He did it because I dumped him,' I tell her, trying not to cry.

'He did it because he's an evil bastard who will do whatever it takes to get what he wants.'

She stands up, water dripping off her skin and sparkling in the sunlight. She looks like the image of Althea on the spa poster as she stretches. Then she moves to the edge of the pool, balancing on the side as if she might throw herself into the sea below at any moment.

'Do you know how old I was when I started to model?' she asks.

'Fifteen, wasn't it?' I remember telling Scott that I thought she was too young, that the modelling world would eat her up and spit her out. He laughed at me, told me I was overreacting, that she'd be fine.

'I hated it,' she whispers. 'Hated being the centre of attention, hated the way everywhere I went people would size me up, judge me. Hated the creepy old men and the bitchy old women.'

'So why did you do it?' I ask. The question is genuine but she snorts derisively.

'Why? You think I really had a choice? You think anything has *ever* been about what I want?'

I know how she feels. It's the same for me, like I've been taken for a fool and I'm only just waking up to the full impact of the deception. 'Can you break away?'

Her smile is sad and goes nowhere near her eyes. 'I already tried that.'

'You did?' I'm surprised. Scott never so much as hinted that Tori was unhappy, let alone that she wanted out of the whole industry.

'Oh yes.' Her fake smile drops. 'I met Markus and all of a sudden I realised the life I could lead, if I was free from them, from all the bullshit.' There's an edge to her voice. Markus is the ex-boyfriend who got chased out of town but it feels like there is far more to this story.

'What happened?'

'My wonderful brother and my godfather decided to take matters into their own hands.'

'They didn't kill him.' The words are out of my mouth before I can stop them.

'No.' She raises her hands a little. 'And I know therefore what they did was nowhere near as bad as what happened to Rosie. But still... they smashed the fingers on his left hand and told him if he ever came near me again they'd go after his family.'

'His left hand?' I mime picking up a violin to confirm the importance of it being his left, the fingers he would use to coax beauty from the instrument.

'He can't play. All that talent and hard work just...' She mimes throwing dust into the air. Markus was first chair violin with the Munich Philharmonic. My husband didn't kill him, didn't take his life. But he did take his music: his career, his joy.

I stand up and move next to Tori, placing my hand gently on her shoulder. She sags slightly, as if the memory of what happened is a physical weight she must bear. I turn her to face me and look at her. It's time for me to make a decision. To decide which side I really think she's on. She could be lying to me, this could all be a made up sob story to extract information from me. If I get this wrong... well, I don't really want to think about what my husband would do if he found out what I'm planning.

'So, what's next?' I ask her softly.

'You're going to tell me how you're planning on killing him,' she replies. Then she lifts her eyes to meet mine and stares straight into my soul. 'And then I'm going to help you.'

20

A shiver runs down my spine as I see the look in her eyes.
There's a quiet anger there. Actually, it's more than anger. It's
rage. A pure, unadulterated rage that has been simmering for a
very long time. She means it.

I don't say anything. Not yet. I need time to think about
what this could all mean. For me. For her. For the plan that I've
been working so hard to create for months now.

One of the spa therapists comes to tell us that the experience is over and leads us to the dressing area. I still don't say
anything and neither does Tori.

'You're both so quiet,' the therapist says in her perky voice
that tells of sunrise yoga and green smoothies. 'You must be so
relaxed.' She laughs and Tori joins in.

'Honestly,' Tori tells her, laying her hand on the therapist's
arm. 'You have no idea. I feel a-maz-ing.' She trills the final
word.

Minutes ago this woman was telling me how she wants to
help me kill her brother. And now she's laughing and joking

with the therapist as if none of that had happened. I shiver once more; I think perhaps I still don't know Tori at all.

We get dressed and retire to the bar area. It's quiet; well, it isn't quite midday yet and the only people around have taken seats on the patio. We take a table inside in the furthest corner. I can't risk someone overhearing.

'Can I get you ladies a drink?' the waiter asks, all of his attention on Tori. Not that I'm surprised, she's wearing a sundress with a neckline slashed to her navel and a pushup bikini top. For someone who apparently doesn't like the lime-light, she's very good at attracting attention. Sorry. That was bitchy of me. Well, bitchier than I'd like to be. It's just hard not to feel like you pale into the background around her.

Tori picks up the drinks menu from the table and flicks through it. She turns to me. 'Are we drinking?' She puts a heavy emphasis on the word 'drinking'.

I just nod in reply. I'm planning on picking whichever cock-tail looks to have the highest alcohol content. My world has tilted on its axis and I don't even know which way is up any more. A drink might be the only thing that helps to right the ship.

'Good, I'll have a Japanese Long Island,' she tells the waiter and then hands me the menu.

I glance at the ingredients of a Japanese Long Island. Vodka, gin, rum, sake. Sounds perfect. 'And the same for me, please.'

We wait until the cocktails arrive, neither one of us speak-ing, both lost in our own worlds. I have no idea what she's thinking. But all that is going through my brain is how much to tell her about my plan. I believe her story about Markus and so I don't really think she's one of Scott's spies, but the whole 'enemy of my enemy is my friend' thing is bullshit. She could still be a massive problem to me.

The Japanese Long Islands are a pale, almost cloudy, white colour and garnished with cocktail cherries and a slice of lime. I take a tentative sip and enjoy the sweetness of the rum on my tongue and the burn of so much alcohol at the back of my throat.

'Please signal if you need anything else, ladies. I'll be just over there.' The waiter motions towards the bar.

'Thank you, Christos,' Tori says with a smile. I think she's flirting, just a tiny bit, enough to make him feel special but not enough that he might misconstrue the situation and think she's genuinely coming on to him. It's a subtle art and one I've never mastered. Not that I've spent much time practising if we're honest about it. I'm going to have to learn though. Once I'm free of the Coopers and living my brand new life as far away from them as possible. I'm not even thirty, there are so many years ahead of me, so much catching up to do of all the time I wasted in my twenties married to such a beast.

I take another sip of the Japanese Long Island and weigh up my options one final time. But, when I open my mouth, a question I hadn't even been thinking comes out. 'Why do you trust me?' I ask.

'How do you mean?'

How do I mean? 'Well,' I begin, I'm thinking as I speak, obviously my subconscious has been musing over something but my conscious brain is trying desperately to catch up. 'Well,' I repeat, 'You've told me a lot about your brother. My *husband*.' I emphasise the title. 'How do you know I won't go to him and repeat our whole conversation?'

She laughs and takes a long pull on the straw in her cocktail. 'Your *husband*,' she mimics the way I said it, 'killed your best friend, tricked you into marrying him and then has treated you like shit for over a decade.' She laughs again. 'I really don't think that is where your loyalties lie.'

She's right. But still. 'I thought blood was thicker than anything for the Coopers?'

'Hahaha.' This time there is no humour in the laugh. 'Perhaps to my brother. But Scott destroyed my trust when he took Markus from me and everything from Markus.'

I pause and stare at her over the rim of my glass. I'm not sure she actually answered my question so I try one more time. 'Why do you trust me?'

She huffs and sets down her glass, before leaning forward a little to rest her elbows on the table. 'Here's the thing, Chloe. I don't trust you. But I also don't care any more. I want Scott to pay for what he did and I think you're my best chance to help make that happen.'

It sounds like the truth.

'Can I trust you?' I ask her in return.

She runs her tongue across her lips and assesses me. I feel myself shrink slightly under her gaze, as if she's staring straight into my soul. 'Chloe. We're in a mutually assured destruction scenario.' The words sound alien coming from her tongue; I've always assumed my sister-in-law actually is the stereotypical dumb blonde, but I think perhaps I underestimated her and it's just a persona she puts on, like Paris Hilton. 'You cross me and I will fuck you. You can trust me exactly as much as I can trust you.'

I don't need her help to kill him. The plan is already in train, unstoppable. But I do need her allyship to get away with it. Mutually assured destruction indeed. I think it's the best I'm going to get.

I take another sip of my cocktail and then realise it's almost finished. I wave towards the waiter and he comes scurrying over. 'Another one of these, please,' I ask him and turn to Tori with a raised eyebrow.

'And for me,' she replies and takes a final slurp.

I wait for the next round to be delivered.

And then, once the waiter has returned to his position by the bar, I turn slightly to face Tori more fully. 'Next week,' I tell her.

'Next week, what?'

'When we're back home. That's when it'll happen.'

She nods. 'How?'

'I have no idea.'

She furrows her brow in confusion. 'What do you mean you have no idea?'

'It's all organised.'

'You hired someone?' Is that awe or disappointment in her voice?

'I can't risk doing it myself.' Only a fool would even think to put their own sticky fingerprints on a murder scene if it was at all avoidable.

'But don't you want to...' she trails off. 'Don't you want to be the one who... you know.' She raises an eyebrow and makes a motion with her right hand, which I think is a reference to that movie where she stabs him in the head with an ice pick.

'This is better,' I assure her.

'This is *bullshit*,' she hisses, forcing me to move backwards from the force of her words and the spray of spittle.

'It's the only way.' I try to remain calm. This is how you get away with murder: with a cool head and impeccable planning.

'No. He needs to suffer for what he's done. To you. To me. To so many others I can't even name.'

'He'll suffer.' I could make certain stipulations within the contract.

'But he won't know it was us.' She sticks her bottom lip out like a pouty child who isn't getting her own way.

'It has to be this way.'

'No.'

I'm starting to get bored of this. 'It does, Tori.' I use my best school prefect voice, the one I used to use to keep the younger girls at school in line. 'It's done. There's no way to change it.'

'What do you mean, "it's done"?' She mimics me.

'The contract is signed. The details agreed. I have no way to stop it now. No way to contact the people who will complete the job.'

'No.' She's vehement. 'No.' Her knuckles turn white as she increases her grip on the glass in front of her. I wonder for a moment if it might shatter. 'No,' she repeats a third time and then snaps her head up to look me dead in the eye. 'He has to know it was us.'

* * *

Tori and I have lunch at the hotel, a light feta salad on the terrace overlooking the sea. We barely talk and there's no further mention of Scott. I can see that she's seething though. Seething and scheming and it terrifies me. I might have under-estimated her intelligence over the years – even though, in my defence, she is the one creating that alternative persona, so maybe it was less me being judgy and more her being manipu-lative – but I am clear about how stubborn she can be. Once she's set her heart on something, she will fight to get her own way. And she won't fight clean.

As soon as the waiter has cleared our plates, Tori calls for a car to take us back to the villa. I settle the bill and meet her outside the front of the hotel. I need to get back to the others so

I can spend the afternoon working on my tan and pretending to be madly in love with my shitbag husband. And I want to keep a close eye on Tori. There's a very real possibility she will try to take matters into her own hands and wreck everything in the process.

Surely she wouldn't try to kill him herself?

Not even Tori would be that stupid.

Would she?

21

The front door of the villa is slightly ajar as we pull up. I push it fully open, movements tentative as if I'm waiting for a bomb to go off at any moment. The interior of the villa is quiet as we step inside. Too quiet.

'The alarm's off,' Tori notes as she closes the door.

She's right, the electronic screen for the anti-intruder system is dark. I'm instantly alert. Has something happened while we've been out?

I hold my fingers to my lips so Tori knows to shut the fuck up and pull out my phone. The screen glows brightly in the gloom of the hallway, no sunlight penetrating through the thick stone walls. I haven't had a missed call or a text message to tell us to stay away. 'Check your phone,' I hiss at Tori, my eyes darting around the space to check that no one is hiding in the shadows. She turns the screen to show me. She has over a hundred Instagram notifications but no messages or missed calls.

I slip out of my shoes and motion for Tori to do the same.

'You think there's someone here?' she asks.

'Shhh.' *Jesus Christ woman: do you want to get us killed?*

She shoots me a contrite look. You know, for someone who's normally so paranoid about everything, she seems remarkably calm in this moment where there could *genuinely* be something wrong.

I never thought I'd have to do this to her, but I need her focussed on the potential threat here. Otherwise she's a liability. 'Tori,' I say quietly, but with that same school prefect edge I've used before. 'Get a fucking grip. This is serious.'

I watch her face as her emotions rearrange themselves. First, she's shocked I spoke to her like that. Then a little pissed. On to uncertainty. Then, finally, the fear settles under her skin. There. That's better.

I cast around me, looking for a weapon. There's a bronze statue of Artemis with her bow on the side table in the hallway. I take a few steps and pick it up. It has a bit of a heft to it and might just do in a pinch. At least it's better than nothing. I turn to look at Tori, she'll need something—

Oh. She stops me mid-thought. She's holding a knife. An actual knife. One of those flip ones the kids carry, except hers has a gorgeously ornate handle. There's an ease to the way she brandishes it, as if it were an extension of herself. As if she's done this before.

'What the—?' I start to say, but stop myself. Now isn't the time.

Instead, we creep down the corridor, me with my statue and Tori behind me with the knife. I should probably swap positions with her, she seems like she might actually have half a chance against a surprise opponent whereas I'm probably screwed.

All the doors are closed, but Grace did tell us to do that to make the air-con more efficient. My father-in-law made some comments about how he didn't exactly need to worry about the electricity bill and Grace took him down. 'It's not about money,' she'd told him, keeping her voice soft so he didn't think he was being schooled. 'It's about making sure there's a planet for the future.' Mr Cooper doesn't believe in climate change.

The air hangs heavy, the silence absolute as we continue to move through the villa. I'm trying to keep my panic at bay, trying not to picture all the terrible things that could have happened.

Eventually the corridor opens out into one of the central lounge areas. It's deserted. No sign that anyone has been in here recently. It's eerie. But there's also no sign of a struggle, no broken glass or objects knocked off a shelf.

I push open the door into the kitchen, inch by inch in case that's where an ambush is lying in wait. But there's nothing, no one.

'Now what?' Tori whispers behind me.

It's a good question. There's no one inside this part of the villa and no one has tried to intercept us. 'Terrace.' I decide and turn to look at her. She nods to say she's on board. 'We've got this,' I tell her, even though I don't think we have this, at all, not even one tiny little bit. But I need her strong.

She waves the knife in my direction as if to agree with me, but in truth she just makes me nervous, she really does look like she wouldn't be afraid to use it.

We position ourselves by the back door, ready to run or attack or whatever the situation may require of us. I make eye contact and nod, raising an eyebrow in question. *Are you ready?*

She nods back. *Ready.*

I swing the door open in a quick motion and am blinded by the sun. A roar greets us. It's coming from the pool area. Fuck!

There really is something happening. Another roar and there's the sound of a loud slap.

'Get in!' The words are almost screamed. A voice I recognise. My brother. 'Flush, baby,' he shouts.

'Is he...?' Tori whispers.

'Playing poker. Certainly sounds like it.'

'With them?'

It's clear the 'them' she's talking about are our unknown assailants, come to wreak havoc on our apparently perfect little holiday. 'I don't know.' I start to creep round the corner so we can see what Rob is doing.

'Jesus Christ,' I say under my breath. Rob isn't playing with an unknown group of bandits. He's playing with Mrs Cooper.

'Why the fuck are you skulking around?' he asks when he sees me. 'And is that a statue you're brandishing?' He scoffs at the sight of my makeshift weapon.

'We thought...' I trail off. 'The alarm is off.'

'Yeah,' he replies with the same irritating tone he used to use when we were little. 'So what?'

'The front door was ajar. So, we thought something had happened.'

He smirks. I want to punch it off his stupid face. Why does he still have the power to make me feel like a fool, even though he's proved himself to be far more worthy of that moniker so many times over the years? 'I left the door open for the technician. Aww. Did you think we were under attack?' He's a patronising shit.

I'm not going to put up with this. 'The door was open, the alarm was off, the villa was silent. What the hell were we meant to think?'

'Calm down, sis. Jeez. Overreact much?' He laughs. 'Anyway,

the alarm's off because it keeps blaring. It happened twice this morning while you were out so we disconnected it. No biggie.'

'You did what?' If I sound incredulous it's because I am. Our father didn't raise us to live in fear, but he did raise us to take reasonable precautions.

'Libby and I were getting distracted by the alarms.' He shrugs. As if playing poker was a good reason to throw caution to the wind. 'And I need to win back some of my losses from the first night.'

'We can't not have an alarm.' I know I sound like a whiney brat, but it's the truth.

'That Grace woman is calling someone out to look at it again. Hence why I left the door open for them.' He picks up the deck of cards, obviously done with this conversation.

Mum and Dad walk past. I hate to tattle on my brother but this is serious. 'Dad, did you know the alarm got switched off?'

Concern flashes across his features. 'No.' He glances at Rob. *Do you know about this?* his look asks.

'It's nothing, Dad. It'll get fixed later.'

'He left the door open for the technician. The front door. Wide open.' The whiney brat in me comes right to the surface.

'You're an idiot,' Dad tells him. Then he turns to Mum. 'I suggest you call the concierge and find out what's happening.' She nods and scuttles off to do what she was told.

Five minutes later and the poker game is back in full swing. Scott has come to join in and the level of competition between him and my brother is bordering on the ridiculous.

Grace is striding up the terrace towards us. She looks a little nervous. 'So, the alarm company promised me someone this afternoon, but now they're saying they need to send one of their more senior technicians. He'll be here tomorrow first thing.'

'Tomorrow?' Dad asks. 'Why not today?' My father is used to people doing what he wants immediately.

'He needs to come from the mainland,' Grace explains.

'We're leaving it switched off,' Rob says, barely looking up from his cards. He's holding a pair of tens. It's not the worst hand he could have.

'Yeah, fuck it. It was giving me a headache,' Scott adds. He's holding an ace and an eight of spades. 'We'll be fine. We have Mikey and Ethan.'

Tori looks at me. She's pale, probably from the adrenaline rush of our skulking through the house looking for potential murderers. She slips the knife into the pocket of her shorts.

I'd already decided to stay close to her today to keep an eye on her, but now she has the knife, I'm not letting her leave my sight.

22

The afternoon passes without event, just the pool and the sun and the sense of dread rushing towards me like a juggernaut. Tori sunbathes close by, saying nothing and pretending to be engrossed in the biography of a celebrity I've barely heard of. I really should try to stay a little more up to date with the gossip columns.

The air begins to cool as afternoon passes into the early evening. Part of me thinks we should go out for dinner, get away from the villa for a few hours. But I've organised something special for the evening and it's far too late to cancel. Besides, it's the perfect nod to my perfect marriage.

I debated a vow renewal ceremony for this week. Just imagine it: the gorgeous villa, me in a huge white dress pledging my love to my husband all over again. And then... BAM! Next week he's dead and what a total fucking tragedy. But let's be fair about it, you've met Scott now, you know he's hardly the vow renewal kind of guy. Part of me never even thought he'd propose, I thought I'd be 'serious girlfriend' forever. Then suddenly he was down on one knee with a diamond ring. I thought my heart would burst at the time. So pathetic. So, anyway, not a vow renewal. But I have recreated elements of the wedding. And this evening we will be eating our wedding menu.

I chose it the first time round because it's Scott's favourite and I wanted him to be happy. Personally I'm not a fan but I was so willing back then to give up a part of my own identity for him. Vomit inducing I know.

The chef arrives just after six to set up and get everything ready. It's still a surprise for Scott, but he's started to ask a few questions about what exactly we're eating so he can figure out which wine to decant. He never used to drink wine, and especially not red wine. Until about a year ago when he suddenly announced we were going to learn more about it and – and I quote here – 'learn how to appreciate it properly'. Such a wanker. He never used to be pretentious but I think the last year or so, with his dad giving him more responsibility for the family business, has really gone to his head.

'We're proper adults now,' he'd told me. 'We need to make sure we can blend in with the other grown-ups.'

The 'we' in that sentence was doing some seriously heavy lifting. I've been drinking chianti with Sunday lunch since the age of about eleven and allowed champagne on special occasions since I was old enough to lift a flute.

I thought for a while he'd met another woman, someone he was desperately trying to impress. For a few days I'd been desperately heartbroken, reading his messages, following him around like a stalker. But it wasn't another woman. It was a man; some old-Etonian he'd met at this golf club open day and who he was hoping would agree to sponsor his application. It was almost pathetic. In the end, the old-Etonian refused to help him, and so Scott went for the old-fashioned approach of threats and blackmail. He's been a member of Oaksmere golf club for nine months now, but the other clientele haven't warmed to him. They can smell desperation a mile off.

Anyway, I get ready for dinner and then hang around the chef, sipping a glass of champagne as he preps the potatoes to go with the pre-cooked centrepiece he bought with him, now resting in the kitchen. Mum pulls me to one side when she sees us. 'Is that a beef wellington I saw?' she asks.

I nod. 'We had it at our wedding.'

'Yes.' She pauses as if weighing up what more to say. 'I remember the wedding.' There's concern in her eyes. 'But why now?'

'I just wanted to do something nice for Scott.' I flash her my best 'wedded bliss' smile. We've never been close, Mum and me. Or at least not since I was a teenager. Before that we'd do loads of stuff together but since I was about twelve all I wanted to do was spend time with my father.

She holds my gaze for a few moments. 'I love you, sweetheart,' she says eventually, her voice tinged with something almost melancholic. 'You can always talk to me.'

'I know,' I reply, keeping my voice light. We don't really do all this 'deep and meaningful' stuff. 'Love you too.' And then I walk away feeling a little unsettled.

* * *

There's a brief moment as the wellington is served when Rob looks like he might kick off about his dietary requirements for about the billionth time this holiday. But another waitress arrives with a special lactose-free one for him and he's stopped in his tracks.

'We haven't had this for ages,' Scott says as a piece is sliced for him. 'Mum,' he turns to her, 'didn't we have this for your fiftieth?'

'We had it for our wedding breakfast,' I tell him, leaning in close so I can whisper under my breath.

'Did we?' he looks confused. I want to punch him in the face.

'Yes.'

He shrugs. As if it means nothing at all that he can't even remember what we served to our guests on the most important day of our lives as a couple.

'I think this one is better though,' Mr Cooper says, cramming a huge forkful into his mouth. I watch him chew for a few moments, as unable to drag my eyes away from the sight of masticated meat as a rubber-necker passing a car accident. 'The one at your wedding was a little on the dry side.'

The one at the wedding was prepared by one of the best chefs in the country. It was most definitely not on the dry side.

'I couldn't believe you were too cheap to go with the wagyu,' Mr Cooper says, pointing his knife towards my father.

'Wagyu is no good for a wellington,' Dad replies, his words clipped. We debated that at the time. Of course we did; it wasn't as if the only daughter of the Wilson family was getting a cut-price wedding.

'Wagyu is the best money can buy.' Mr Cooper is adamant, this isn't something he thinks is open to debate.

'For steak maybe. But it's too rich for a wellington, puts the flavours out of balance.'

'Whatever. All I'm saying is that when *my* princess gets married, only the best will do.' He uses his knife to spear some of the meat and his teeth chink against the metal as he transfers it to his mouth.

Mum puts her hand on Dad's arm. He narrows his eyes at

her, a warning look, one so brief you might miss it. But he does unclench the hand holding his knife and take a slow breath. Then he picks up his wine glass and takes a deliberately languid sip. *You're a fool and I won't rise to your jibes*, he says without uttering a word.

The rest of the dinner passes without incident but I can feel the start of a throbbing headache, a ball of pain building behind my right eyeball. I think it's stress. I excuse myself from the table to get some ibuprofen from my bathroom.

I bump into Jack in the kitchen. He looks shattered. I rattle the ibuprofen in his direction. 'Need some?' I ask.

He nods gratefully and shakes out two of the small white tablets, stuffing them in his mouth and swallowing without the need for any liquid. It's something I've never been able to master, having to swill my own down with almost a pint of water to stop myself from gagging.

'Do you know what's got into her?' he asks, leaning against the kitchen counter.

'Who?' I ask. But it's a pointless question; of course he means Tori but I want to draw him into the conversation so he'll spill as much detail as possible.

'She's driving me up the fucking wall.' He runs his hand across his face. 'Did she talk to you earlier? In the spa?'

'About what?' I ask. My heartrate is starting to rise. What has she told him about this morning?

'Anything. Anything that might explain why she's a nervous wreck this evening.'

'Maybe the alarm thing?' I suggest. 'We thought there'd been a break in when we got home.'

He stares at me for a moment. 'You know, it's the kind of paranoid shit I'd expect from Tori. It isn't the first time. She rang the police last week because she was convinced someone had climbed into the house through the third storey window.' He raises an eyebrow at me. 'But I thought you'd be more sensible.'

'Jack.' I try to keep my tone neutral. 'Do you know what my father does? What Peter Cooper does? Scott?'

'Yes.' He sounds defensive.

'But, do you really?'

'Yes.' But this time there's more of a question there.

'You know they're crime bosses. You know they are involved in drugs.' He nods, even though I was stating the facts and not asking questions. 'But you know this in some sort of abstract way, as if they were movie characters. But you don't *really* know, do you?'

He shakes his head.

'You see the glamorous side,' I continue. 'The parties and the cocaine and the women and the cocktails. But you don't see the other sides. And you certainly don't know the dangers, the rivalries, the people who would do anything to take the power and wealth from my family, from Tori's. If you did, you wouldn't think we were overreacting.'

He looks chastised. 'Alright. Fair enough. But I don't think that's why she's acting strange. She's been in an odd mood this whole holiday. On edge. Grumpy. Distracted. Did she not talk to you at all this morning?'

'Not about anything specific,' I lie.

'I think it has something to do with her family, but I don't know what.'

'I'm sure everything's fine.'

He looks down at his hands. 'Would you do me a favour?' he asks softly. 'Take her out. Like a girls' night or something. She's been desperate to go to Elysium. See if she'll open up to you over a vodka or two. I'm worried. She keeps clamming up on me but I need to know she's alright. She's normally so open with me. Tells me everything.' His eyes meet mine.

I could ignore him, tell him I'm too busy for a girls' night, make up an excuse.

But then what? He'll push and push and push with Tori and eventually she'll break and tell him everything about Scott. And then everything about me. My perfectly constructed house of cards will come tumbling down.

I take a deep breath. 'Alright,' I tell him. 'I'll take her out.'

'Tonight?' He makes this weird little face. I think he's trying to be charming but it just looks like a grimace.

I take a deep breath. Tonight? For fuck's sake. 'Fine,' I reply through metaphorically gritted teeth.

His face breaks into a grin. 'Thank you,' he says. 'You're a star.'

The door opens and in walks Farah.

'Perfect timing,' Jack says to her, more animated than I've seen him all week. Has he taken something, beyond the ibuprofen? Probably, knowing him. Which makes it even more imperative to stop him pestering Tori. I can't have Jack stumbling around shooting his mouth off to anyone who'll listen to him when he's high.

'Why?' Farah looks more than a little confused.

'Chloe and Tori are going on a girls' night. You should go with them.'

For fuck's sake. Farah coming along for the ride is the last thing I need. But I can't say that. 'Great idea,' I say instead. 'We're going to Elysium. You up for it?'

'Tonight?'

I nod.

'Well,' she says. 'I guess anything beats watching Rob lose even more money to your mother-in-law. And I haven't been out properly since Baby Luke was born.' She glances at her watch. 'It's just gone nine. What time are you thinking about heading out?'

I have no clue. This isn't my idea. I'd far rather stay in and get an early night. Or perhaps take a nice big glass of wine and a book onto the terrace outside my room and get a few moments of peace. But I guess we don't always get what we want, do we? 'An hour?'

'Perfect. I'll go tell Rob.'

Shit. And I'd better go tell Scott. Who will be pissy about it. Not for any good reason, but just because he's a prick.

'And I'll tell Tori. She'll want a bit of time to get herself made up,' Jack says. He stops next to me. 'Thank you, you're such a good person,' he whispers in my ear.

If only he could see inside my mind and the darkness within.

Then I doubt he'd get within ten feet of me.

23

I decide to bite the bullet and just tell Scott while he's still sitting at the dinner table amid the carnage of the beef welling-ton. 'Tori, Farah and I are going clubbing later,' I tell him, as if this was normal.

'No.' He doesn't even look at me as he says it.

I feel a ripple of nervous tension cross through the rest of our families and steal a glance at my mother. She averts her gaze, the same way she always avoids eye contact if there is a potential argument. Unless it's one she will be the centre of, then out will come the tears to curry sympathy before the conflict has really begun.

Now, I have a decision to make here. I can argue in front of the whole family, create a real atmosphere, one that's awkward for everyone else involved. But then, when Scott dies next week, they might have an image in their heads of this night. They might think back and wonder if maybe that argument was a sign of a deeper rot in our marriage. They wouldn't be wrong, of course, but that's hardly the point. Or, alternatively, I can take the argument away and have it behind closed doors.

I think I've fucked up here. Whatever I do, this will leave a stain on the night. I should've played this differently. Shit. I'm so stressed about Tori that I've screwed up the one job I had this week. All I needed to do was convince everyone that Scott and I are madly in love. I can feel myself starting to scramble, like I'm on the edge of a cliff and my feet are slipping over the edge, unable to find purchase. *Get your shit together*, I admonish myself.

So, I laugh softly as if this is a private joke between us, then paste a smile across my face and prepare to gently ask my bastard of a husband if we can talk privately. 'Let's—'

'Hey bro,' Tori interrupts as she appears at the edge of the table. 'I'm stealing your wife tonight.' She states it as fact, as something that is definitely happening with no possible alternative. 'You're not going to be a dick and insist on some "couple's time" are you?' It isn't really a question. And the lewd way she says "couple's time" makes her own father blush slightly.

Is this my saviour? The woman who somehow *is* actually going to help me get away with this? Perhaps this is the role she is meant to play here. Help with my alibi. Build the narrative. Smooth the edges so we both get what we want and no one ever suspects. If she can keep that ornate-handled flip knife to herself, that is.

Scott looks up at her. Jack obviously told her about the plan to go clubbing and she's already changed. I can only describe her outfit as a scrap of sequins, just enough to avoid an accusation of nakedness but with the genuine possibility it was plucked off a child's doll. She looks sensational. I tamp down the jealousy that threatens to overtake me. I know the truth of the work she undertakes to look the way she does – not that she wasn't also blessed with good genes, but no one's genes are *that* good – and I have zero desire for that level of commitment.

'You'll need an escort,' my husband says eventually, sounding resigned about the situation but also all kinds of pissed off. I've avoided a public argument but he's going to give me hell later.

'We're not in Bridgerton,' Tori says and laughs. 'Imagine what the Ton would think of this outfit.' She sweeps into a curtsy and narrowly avoids flashing her underwear. If she's even wearing any.

'You know that isn't what I mean.' Scott's anger is barely concealed.

'Yes, brother dear. We'll take Mikey.'

Scott opens his mouth to say something but then closes it again. I can see the anger rippling beneath his skin. He has told me 'no', but he will have to give a better reason to the family than just being a controlling prick who enjoys fucking up my plans for the sheer fun of it. He can't even make a safety claim any more, not if we take Mikey with us. He's been part of the Cooper team for years, even though I've started to wonder if there's something between him and Tori, something the family would definitely not approve of.

'Right then,' says Tori with a beaming grin. 'It's all settled.' She looks from Scott to me. 'Jesus!' she exclaims and wrinkles her nose, taking a tiny step back from me.

I instantly raise my hand to my hair, brain whirring through the possible list of things about me that have obviously disgusted her so much. I can see myself in the mirror behind the dining table. I don't look *that* bad. 'What?' I ask eventually, hating the way my voice catches like I really care about her opinion of me.

'What? What? Oh sister-in-law, that outfit just will *not* do. No no. Not at all.' She reaches out a hand to me and flaps her fingers. 'Come with me. We need to make you a little more presentable.'

I follow her meekly from the terrace and into the cool of the villa.

I've never really been a girlie girl. I've never really understood what I'm meant to do with all the various different types of makeup, never known what style of jeans are in fashion or how to pull off a statement necklace without feeling ridiculous. Don't worry, this isn't one of those 'I'm not like other girls' claims; you know, the ones where the girl will claim she's different and therefore somehow superior. I would *love* to know about makeup, it would be amazing to look in the mirror and feel glamorous and gorgeous and actually comfortable in my own skin.

At school I was into sports and horses and was happiest in the ubiquitous leggings and sweatshirt combo we all wore, hair scraped into a ponytail or braided tightly against my skull. At home, I only had Rob for company while Mum and Dad buggered off on yet another holiday so he was hardly much help. And I've never really had many female friends to learn this stuff from. I used to think it was because other girls didn't really like me, but then I realised how insidious an impact Scott has had on my adult life. The way he has systematically moved me away from any potential female friends to leave me lonely and bored. And, therefore, resultantly desperate for his attention and prepared to forgive him for a huge range of red flags that should have sent me running for the hills years ago.

Anyway, Tori teaches me more about makeup in five minutes than I've known my whole life.

'You look bloody fantastic,' she says with a little squeal as she reveals my new face to me in the mirror. She isn't joking. I really look good. My eyes are smoking and sultry, rimmed in kohl to make them almost almond shaped, a deep brown eyeshadow the perfect shade to make my green eyes pop.

Tori reaches for a hairbrush and somehow turns the slightly frizzy sun damaged nest on my head into a sleek waterfall.

'And now for the final piece of the jigsaw,' she says and motions towards her closet. It's overflowing, she must have hit the shops at Nammos seriously hard yesterday, she certainly didn't have that much in her suitcase.

'None of your clothes will fit me,' I tell her. She's tiny and I prefer Jaffa cakes to hip bones.

She cocks her head to one side and considers me, one eyebrow raised. I resist the urge to cross my arms over my chest and suck my stomach in even further. 'Hmmm...' She has the perfect opportunity to say something bitchy under the guise of being honest like she normally does. But something has changed in her since the spa this morning. She may just be keeping me on side, of course, but it feels as if a camaraderie has been forged between us and so the catty little comments have dried up. If I'm honest, it's a bit disconcerting.

Suddenly she spins on her toes and strides towards the wardrobe. She flips through the rail of dresses in primary colours, scrutinising each before flicking to the next. I spot the dress she mentioned before, the one in the same gorgeous teal colour as my bikini, but she moves past it with little more than a cursory glance. When she makes it to the end, she pauses. I knew she wouldn't have anything that fit.

'Oooh.' She sounds animated and turns to look at me. 'You have a black bandeau bra, right?'

I nod.

Her eyes narrow. 'And black briefs?'

I nod again.

'Sweet.' She digs into the suitcase at her feet. Despite the full rail of dresses, there are even more clothes still stuffed inside it. 'Ta da,' she exclaims and then throws a piece of black fabric towards me.

I unfurl it to discover a slinky black dress in a semi-sheer lace. It feels almost like liquid in my fingers. 'Ummm...' Is she really suggesting I wear this with a bra and knickers underneath?

'Um, what?'

'It's just... it's a bit revealing.' I grimace.

'That's why you wear a bandeau and briefs.' She says it like it's so obvious.

'Just this and underwear?'

She throws her head back and laughs. 'I wear it with a thong and nipple flowers.'

'Oh.' I don't quite know how to reply to that if I'm honest.

'Just trust me, OK. It'll look fucking amazing.' Then she walks over to me, grabbing something from the dressing table as she approaches.

'What are you doing?' I ask as she brandishes whatever it is in my direction. It looks suspiciously like the eyeliner I bought myself at Gatwick, did she steal it when she left the second note? I decide now is probably not the time to get into it – she's already played her hand that she knows my plans and so her little messages hold zero importance now.

'That dress needs a little more.' She motions for me to close my eyes and begins to add more kohl. 'You're going to look sexy as hell.' Then she slaps me on the bottom. 'Now go and get ready. I wanna get going.'

Back in my own room I find the bra and briefs. I'm still not convinced about this outfit, but I don't think I have any real choice in the matter.

The dress is lighter than air as I pull it on and it snaps to the curves of my body.

Jesus, I almost whistle under my breath. Tori was right. This dress is fucking amazing. It hugs in all the right places, the pattern on the lace so gloriously asymmetric that it somehow forces the eye to keep moving over the fabric. With the hair and makeup, I look... well, I don't look like me. But in a very good way.

'No. Absolutely not.' Scott is standing at the door staring at me. His eyes flash fire.

Perhaps I haven't been entirely honest with you. I don't just hate my husband for what he did to Rosie, or for all the ways he's manipulated me over the decade since.

I'm terrified of him.

I thought about leaving him. Trying to walk away and simply leaving all this shit behind me.

But he would never allow it.

Kill or be killed. It's the only way.

I take a deep breath before I turn to face him. *One more week.* 'Hi Scott.'

'What the fuck are you wearing?' He takes a few steps towards me and I can't stop from shrinking into myself. He has never been violent towards me. But I have seen the savagery this man is capable of and I know it is only a matter of time.

'It's Tori's,' I reply.

'You look like a whore.' He spits the word into my face and I'm forced to recoil.

'Actually, she looks like a fox,' Tori says, coming up behind her brother. She reaches round him to grab my hand and pull me to her. 'Come on, we're going.'

'Not in that,' Scott almost growls.

'Yes, in that,' Tori insists, dragging me down the corridor toward the front door.

'We'll talk about this later,' he calls after me, each word dripping with a cold anger that chills me to the bone.

24

I can hear the music and feel the reverberation of the bass before we even get out of the car. I've spent the twenty-minute journey trying to compose myself after that run-in with Scott and the thinly veiled threat he left hanging in the air as we walked away from him. *One more week. One more week.* I repeated the mantra over and over until my heartrate returned to normal.

Tori strides straight up to the bouncer, ignoring the line of other people queuing to get into Elysium. She acts like she owns the place, as if it's a simple fact that she wouldn't have to wait like everyone else.

The bouncer looks at her, his gaze travelling quickly down her body and then back up. He doesn't even check the list on the clipboard in his hands, just motions her towards the door, which swings open as if by magic. She blows him a kiss and Farah and I hurry to catch up with her.

'Wow,' Farah says as we slip inside the cool of the building. 'How the other half live,' she adds with a hint of awe in her tone as she nudges hips with me.

'Insane,' I reply. 'The way the door just opened.'

'I'd have been schlepping to the back of the queue if I'd been on my own.'

'Me too.' Now, Scott's name will get me the VIP treatment in clubs across South London and Surrey, but that always means an awkward moment where I have to tell the bouncer my name and then twerk my eyebrows in a way that suggests they need to think a little harder about my surname being Cooper and what that might mean for them. I don't usually bother. And it isn't like I go clubbing often enough to care either.

'No one would be sending you to the back of the queue in that dress,' Farah says. 'You look incredible.'

'Thanks.' I feel my cheeks flush pink. I've never been very good at receiving compliments, especially for the way I look. Actually, scrap that last part, for anything at all. I can still remember the crawling embarrassment from the standing ovation my ballet class gave me for being the first to land a double pirouette when I was about nine.

A man in the tightest white t-shirt I've ever seen appears at Tori's elbow. I can only assume he's going to lead us to the fancy VIP area. I'm proved right as he leads us up a short flight of stairs and then onto a mezzanine. It's like being on an observation deck, looking down onto the heaving dance floor. Everything up here is designed to set us apart from the crush of club-goers beneath us. Air-con blasts, turning the air around me icy cold, even though I can see sweat beading on the people down below.

'What are we drinking, ladies?' he asks as we sit down on the sprawling sofas.

Tori looks from me to Farah and back to me. 'Let's start with a round of Pornstar Martinis.'

He grins and I notice just how perfect his teeth are. 'An excellent choice.'

We drink and dance and I can feel the tensions of the day melt from my shoulders. I'm almost having fun and believe me I'm as surprised as anyone. We drink some more.

Over the rim of yet another Pornstar Martini – which are absolutely delicious by the way – I look at these two women, brought into my life through marriage and not through my own choices. My brother's wife. My husband's sister. That's all I've ever thought of them as: extensions of the men in my life. But I was wrong.

They are brilliant, wonderful women. We have another round of Pornstar Martinis, this time chasing them down with shots of something called a Purple Haze, alcohol burning the back of my throat and raising goosebumps on my arms.

We laugh and chat and point out hot guys and even hotter girls. At one point we head to the main dance floor and prance around to 'Espresso'. A few moments later I find myself demonstrating that perfect double pirouette from ballet class all those years ago. Farah claps like I've done the thirty-two fouettés from Swan Lake. I drop into a deep curtsy and almost fall over as I rise back out of it. Tori grabs me to haul me upright, face split into a beaming smile.

We return to the VIP lounge to catch our breath. The guy in the tight white t-shirt with the perfect teeth brings us yet another round of cocktails. I'm drunk but happy.

Farah excuses herself to use the bathroom. As soon as she's gone, Tori stands up and then plonks herself next to me on my sofa. 'Promise me,' she stage whispers in my ear, 'we can still hang?' I lean back a little and look at her. Her face is a picture of earnest expectation.

'Of course,' I reply. Perhaps one day – when I've spent the

suitable amount of time in mourning, of course – Tori and I could actually be friends. Going out like this on weekends could become something that's part of my life. I'm only twenty-nine. There's still time for me to go out and have fun, dance on tables, drink amazing cocktails and maybe even find a handsome stranger for the evening.

'Promise?' she asks again. Her eyes are glassy, she's definitely had too much to drink. But, then again, I can hardly talk.

'Brownie's honour.'

'You were never a *Brownie*?'

Of course I was. I was a nerdy kid who took ballet and had a pony. Of course I went to Brownies as well. But I don't burst Tori's bubble. I want her to think I'm cool and the kind of person she might actually want to hang around with again.

She holds out her little finger. 'Pinky promise.'

I wrapped my own round hers. 'Pinky promise.'

'Even after Scott is gone?' There's a hint of something in her voice, a vulnerability.

I look around me. 'You can't say that!' I don't think anyone heard but there's no need to take risks.

'What?' She looks so innocent. 'Oh, you mean because we're going to kill him.' Her eyes roll a little in her head. She's definitely had too much to drink.

'Shhhh!' *Jesus*.

'He needs to die.' She's adamant.

'Yes,' I say softly.

'I hate him, you know.' The sudden venom makes me turn to face her.

'Next week,' I tell her. 'Next week it'll all be over, I promise.'

'I need to be there. I need to watch.' The venom intensifies. It's like a switch has been flipped, her anger and pain cascading from her in a wave.

'We've talked about this, Tori. There's a plan, OK?'

She pushes me away and stands up on shaky legs. Damn, when did she get this drunk?

'You have to let me in.' She points a finger at me.

'Just sit down, Tori,' I say, conscious she's starting to draw attention to us.

'Promise me.'

'Tori, please.' Heads are turning in our direction.

'Scott has to suffer. I need to make him suffer.' She almost screams the words.

Shit, shit, shit. I look behind me and find Mikey is already striding towards her. Fuck. Did he hear that? Did he hear the words flying from her mouth?

'Oopsy,' Mikey says as he catches her in his strong arms. 'I think we've had a little too much, haven't we?'

Tori turns into his bear hug. Her shoulders shake as she begins to cry. I'd forgotten what a messy drunk she can be. At my wedding she got shitfaced on champagne and passed out in the toilets.

'She'll be OK,' Mikey says to me over her head. 'I'll get her home and then come back for you.'

I nod in agreement and sink back into the sofa.

I look up to find that, in the meantime, Farah has slipped back into her seat opposite. She's staring at me, a puzzled look creasing her features.

How much of Tori's outburst did she witness?

We have another drink, sipping our cocktails slowly. The fun atmosphere has been broken and Farah keeps glancing at her watch as the minutes tick down to Mikey coming back to get us.

I study her discreetly. How much did she hear? A sick feeling crawls in my stomach. Is it all over? Will Scott die next week and Farah turn her finger to point at me? Or would she just dismiss it as drunken ramblings?

'I thought she might have learnt to hold her drink by now,' Farah says eventually.

'Yeah,' I reply. I need to tread carefully here. Find out how much she heard but without incriminating myself further. 'She went from happy to psycho in five minutes.'

'She'll have passed out in the car.'

Oh shit. I hadn't thought about that. What if she doesn't and she's sitting there telling Mikey everything? *Fuck! This is a total nightmare.*

'Can we join you?' I look up to see two smartly dressed guys looming over us.

'Sure,' Farah says before I can object. Normally I would simply dismiss men like this, show them the diamond on my finger and throw a withering look in their general direction. But now I'm scooching down my sofa to make room for the one with the blue eyes.

What's done is done and I have no idea how to recover the situation. And what else can I do except pretend that everything is fine and Farah and I are just out having a bit of fun?

'Cheers,' says the taller of the two men, handing me a cocktail and then clinking his own glass against mine.

'Cheers,' I reply. Perhaps this is the distraction I need? It certainly beats heading home to face the wrath of my husband who has had a few hours to stew in his rage.

25

I wake up to daylight filtering through my still closed eyelids. The sound of a curtain flapping in the breeze. *What the hell?* The last thing I remember is sitting in the VIP area of Elysium chatting to Farah and those two guys. A black hole yawns after that point.

What happened?

Why can't I remember anything?

I crack open one eye. The curtain is the same one as in my room at the villa.

OK. That's good. I obviously made it home.

There's a smell in the room. Like... I struggle to figure out what it is. It's almost metallic.

I swing my legs out of bed and stretch. I'm just wearing the bra and briefs I had on last night, the dress obviously discarded somewhere. Probably the bathroom.

My head is throbbing, my mouth dryer than the Sahara. I raise my hands to rub my face.

What the fuck?

My hands are red.

I look down. My torso is red. Smeared and browning at the edges.

Fear grips me. Is that blood? Am I hurt? But there's no pain. I breathe out slowly, trying not to let the panic consume me. And then I list the facts to myself:

I have no memory of how I got here.

I am covered in blood.

I don't think I'm harmed.

OK. Think this through.

It isn't my blood. But if it isn't my blood...

I push myself to standing and begin to turn, inch by inch, to look at the rest of the room.

He's lying on the left-hand side of the bed. A deep wound across his neck the source of the blood seeping into the sheets as it pools around him.

Scott.

I close my eyes and count to five under my breath.

One... two... three... four... five...

But, when I open them, he's still there, lying flat on his back, skin grey. How long has he been dead? Is there a way I can tell? I don't know.

Did *I* do this? I hear a whoosh in my ears and steady myself against the dresser before I pass out. Did I come home to find my husband in a rage and was forced to kill him in self-defence? Was *I* the one in the rage? My head throbs, like someone is taking a drill to my brain. Did I just break and say fuck the consequences and kill him in our bed?

I take a gulp of air. *Get a grip,* I tell myself. Why would I kill him? He's going to die next week and I'm going to get away with it. I have a plan; it's clean and beautiful. This is so messy, so... well, obvious. The moment someone sees this they will assume I killed him. What else could people possibly think?

So, what happened between me being in the club and waking up here? It's been... I glance at the clock on the wall. It's nine in the morning. OK, so about seven hours have passed since my last memory. That would be more than enough time for me to have come back here, had a blazing row with Scott and slit his throat.

I look around the room for any other signs, clues about what happened in the missing seven hours. There's no sign of a struggle. No sign that he came at me and I defended myself: I doubt he'd be lying perfectly prone in bed with his head resting on the pillow. I have to be honest and say it doesn't *look* like self-defence. It looks like he was asleep when his throat was cut. That's the only real explanation for the position of his body.

OK. So... A flash of inspiration hits me. Where's the knife? If it was me, if I was the one who did this, then surely the knife is still in here? I pad around the room looking for it, leaving an alarming trail of bloody footprints across the floor as I go.

The aroma in here is getting worse. Actually, perhaps it's not just blood I can smell any more, the stench of metal over-layed with something altogether more... I don't know how to describe it. Except that it triggers a more primal part of my brain. It smells like death.

I'm sure I read something once that there's a reason dead humans are the literal worst stink in the known universe to other humans. It's a primitive warning sign of danger; if you smell it, you run. We don't recoil at the smell of other dead animals, not until they start to rot and that's just nature's way of telling us the meal has gone bad and we should look elsewhere for sustenance.

Shit. I'm blabbering.

Disassociating.

Whatever you want to call it. I need to focus. First, I need to find the murder weapon.

There's nothing under the bed. Or in the bathroom. The ghost of myself stares back at me in the mirror. I look like shit. Well, more accurately, I look like an extra in a Scream movie; all pale skin and crazy hair and blood smears, standing in my underwear. I meet my own eyes in the mirror expecting to see horror reflecting back at me. But, instead, I see an eerie blankness. Like none of this is actually important. I drag my eyes away, unwilling to stare deeper into the abyss of my own soul.

I peek out of the doors to the terrace. Nothing.

Back inside a shiver runs through me. I pull the patio door closed to shut out the breeze.

There is no knife. So, either I hid it somewhere last night, losing it in the dark pit of my lost memory. Or I wasn't the one who killed him.

But, in that case... who did? And where was I when it happened?

There's a knock on the door and it startles me from the almost catatonic state I've drifted into.

In a panic, I look around the room. There is blood everywhere.

Caked under my fingernails.

In my hair.

On the floor and the walls and the ceiling.

Not to mention an actual dead body lying on the bed.

Another knock. Fuck, fuck, fuck.

'Who is it?' I call out.

'Tori,' comes the reply. She sounds perky.

Shit. 'Umm... I'm in the middle of something,' I call back, my voice shaking. I sound guilty as all sin.

'You OK?' There's an edge of concern in her voice.

'Fine.' But I sound anything but fine.

'What the hell's going on?'

'Nothing. Everything's good. I promise. Just in the middle of something.' I cross my fingers that it'll be enough to make her walk away.

'I'm coming in,' she announces and the handle squeaks as she turns it.

'No,' I all but scream as I throw myself towards the slowly opening door, my full weight knocking it closed again.

'Are you hurt? Has something happened? What the hell?'

'I'm fine. I'll be finished in a few minutes. Just—'

But my words cut off as the door begins to move open again, my feet slipping on the tiles as I try to retain enough purchase to push back against the force.

'Chloe, move away from the door.' She sounds seriously pissed off. 'I'm coming in. You know you're weak as shit and I'll win this fight.'

I try to stop her but she's right, I'm no match against her.

The door opens.

'What the—'

She stops mid-sentence as I grab her hand and pull her inside the room, slamming the door behind her and twisting the lock. Why didn't I lock it before? I could have avoided this situation.

'Is that...?' Her voice trembles as she points to the bed.

'Yeah,' I whisper.

'You killed him?'

'No.'

She turns to me, her eyes flashing fire. 'You killed him.' This time it isn't a question, it's an accusation.

'No. I woke up and...' I trail off and just motion towards his prone body.

'You killed him.' She's starting to sound like a stuck record.

'No—' I start, but then I give up my denials and look at her. She seems kind of chill. No sign of panic or disgust or any other normal response to finding your brother murdered in his bed. Did she really hate him so much this would have so little impact on her?

Or... did *she* kill him?

Did she come back last night, seething with rage, veins full of vodka. Take that pretty knife she carries. Decide that she wanted to be the one who killed him. Took her opportunity before I could take mine?

There's another knock on the door. Tori's eyes meet mine, and now I can see panic in her.

'What do we do?' she asks softly.

I put my finger to my lips. We've locked the door. Whoever is knocking can't just get inside. We can wait them out.

Another knock. This time a little more forceful. 'Chloe?' It's Grace. 'Are you in there?'

Tori looks at me in panic.

'We need her help,' I say softly.

'Help? What are you talking about?'

'To clean up. Get rid of the body.'

'We need the police,' Tori corrects me.

'No,' I reply quickly.

'Is this some weird Wilson rule?' she asks with a raised eyebrow.

'Of course not. My family is clean.' *Cleaner than the Coopers*, but I don't add that last bit.

'And so we have to act like any other clean family who find one of their own dead on holiday. Call the police, get a death certificate and take his body home.'

She's right. In a way. But still. 'No. They'll think it was me.' I say it like it's a fact. A foregone conclusion.

'But...'

I need to stop her thinking the police are even an option. They are bound to think it was me; I'm literally covered in Scott's blood. What are Mykonian prisons like? Something tells me I really don't want to find out.

'We need her,' I tell Tori. And then without waiting for her to say another word, I stride to the door and unlock it.

DAY FOUR

GRACE

26

You wouldn't believe some of the things I've seen working at Villa Bougainvillea. The kind of shit people get up to behind closed doors. And especially the kind of people who don't think of 'the staff' as being actual real human beings who might have an opinion on their terrible ways. I've seen a ton of weird sex stuff too. The wealthy are so often deviants, people who think the normal rules don't apply to them and get their kicks in increasingly bizarre ways. I guess if your whole life is spent with people telling you 'yes', you end up with a very warped sense of normality.

But this is the first time this summer that I've been dragged into a room and shown a dead body. Actually, not just a dead body, one that has very obviously been murdered. What the hell am I meant to do with him?

'Is that Scott, umm, Mr Cooper?' I ask.

It seems the safest question. Learn the facts. Understand what's happening. Figure out a solution. That's the rulebook of every good concierge. Tori nods. Chloe shifts her weight from foot to foot and refuses to make eye contact. She is literally caked in his blood.

'And did *you*...?' I address this to Chloe. Let's be honest here, she *is* the most likely culprit.

'No,' she whispers.

I just about stop myself from saying 'Oh really?' in her face. 'What happened?' I ask instead.

'I don't know.' This time she does look at me. I take the opportunity to stare into her soul.

I've always been exceptionally good at reading people. It's one of the other reasons I'm so good at my job. What do I see when I look at Chloe? I see a woman on the brink of breaking down. A woman thrust into a situation she doesn't quite understand. A woman who needs help.

I've never been able to resist a damsel in distress, it's a bit of a blind spot for me but I'm working on it.

I look between Chloe and Tori. 'Do you want me to call the police?' I ask, because that is what *should* happen in this situation.

'No,' Tori says quickly, her eyes darting to Chloe. 'They'll think...' she motions to the carnage in the room and then to Chloe.

'So, no police?' I ask it like a question. And it is. I'm asking what the hell else they want me to do.

Tori stares at me. She's obviously sizing me up. Trying to decide if I can be trusted. If I would actually do what she's about to suggest. If there is really any chance here that there's a way out.

The younger Cooper child is a total spoilt brat. She's lived one of the most ludicrously charmed lives and still has no sense of just how lucky she is. I've met so many young women like her. Daddy's girls who become models or influencers or minor actresses. Who go on to marry rich men and simper in the background, spending money they didn't earn on shit they don't need. Looking down their haughty little button noses at the rest of us.

Although there is one thing this particular spoilt brat has that many like her don't. She has balls. She is genuinely looking at me right now as she waits for me to realise that she's asking me to help Chloe get away with murder. And not just by keeping my mouth shut either. It's pretty obvious that she wants help of a far more practical nature.

OK. So, I'm going to level with you. I'm guessing you're wondering why I'm not totally freaking out. Why I'm even considering helping these strangers get rid of a body and then cleaning up their crime scene for them. I mean, it's fucking batshit, right?

Yep. So, here's the truth. I know Chloe was planning on killing her husband next week.

And how do I know? Because that is why they – as in the Coopers and the Wilsons – are here this week, at the villa. At *this* villa. It's all part of the service my company offers; we don't just get rid of the problematic people in your life, we also make sure you get away with it. The family holiday to cement the idea of Chloe and Scott's perfect marriage was my idea. And then I've spent the last four months working at Villa Bougainvillea to build enough of a background for myself that none of the rest of the family would suspect anything.

My job this week is to make sure Chloe doesn't do something stupid before the hit next week. I should probably use the past tense because she has done something stupid, the dumbest thing she could have done. You don't kill a man a week before you've paid someone to kill him. What the fuck?

So now I need to manage the potential fall out here. No one

can suspect Chloe today. If they do, then they would go looking for evidence of her desire to 'unalive' – such a fabulous word – her husband. And that could lead back to my company. And we can't possibly have that, now, can we?

'Give me your phones,' I demand of the two women, holding my hand out.

'Our phones?'

'Yes, Tori.' I lace the words with a derision I've hidden up to now. Treating someone with any level of deference feels a little unnecessary when you're about to hide a crime scene for them, if I'm honest.

She blanches slightly at my tone and then seems to debate for a few moments. But eventually she pulls out her fancy new iPhone with its custom case and puts it in my palm.

'Unlock it first,' I tell her. She takes it back and holds it in front of her face, before replacing it in my hand.

I'm checking she isn't recording. That this isn't some kind of set-up designed to have me help them hide the murder and then turn round and finger me for it. It pays to never be too careful in this line of work.

I hand the phone back to her and then angle myself toward Chloe. 'You too,' I demand. Well, I have to keep up the appearance that I'm just a random concierge who's been dragged into this. Tori cannot know that Chloe and I have been plotting together for months.

Chloe takes three attempts to get the facial recognition to work. I wonder if the smears of blood across her skin are stopping the software from working properly. Who would have thought it?

I take a cursory glance at the phone, just so it looks convincing. 'Right then,' I start as I hand it back. 'How about you both tell me the whole story, right from the very beginning. And then we'll figure out where we go from here.'

Chloe swallows and her eyes dart to her husband's body. She seems genuinely shaken up. Perhaps there is more to this story than I'd thought: perhaps she *didn't* kill him, despite her plans for next week.

There's a mini fridge in the room, one I've already stocked with bottles of water and mini champagnes. I open it and hand a water to Chloe, who accepts it gratefully. I offer one to Tori, but she just shakes her head and reaches past me to get one of the champagnes. It's a little early for alcohol in my humble opinion, but whatever helps you cope, I guess. I take a water for myself and straighten up.

'So. Chloe, how about you start?'

She looks nervous, like a child called in front of the head-teacher but who hasn't quite got her story straight yet. 'He was dead when I woke up.'

'So, someone came into the room in the middle of the night and slit his throat next to you, without waking you up?' It sounds ridiculous. It *is* ridiculous.

'I... we went out last night. Me and Tori and Farah. I remember being at the club, having a few drinks, and then... well there's this hole in my memory.'

'A blackout?'

She nods and wraps her arms around her despite the rising heat in the room. She looks vulnerable. Scared. This is not the same woman who booked a service to kill her husband. This is a woman trapped in a nightmare she has no idea how to escape.

'So, you went out last night. Got drunk. Woke up in bed with your dead husband?'

'I wasn't drunk. Not *that* drunk.'

The brain has a curious way of overwriting our memories to stop us remembering the most horrific trauma. I wonder how much trauma it would cause if you slit your husband's throat in the middle of the night; enough to forget?

'What about you?' I ask Tori.

'Me? I just knocked on the door this morning to find Chloe and ended up dragged into all *this*.' She motions around the room.

There is definitely something Tori isn't telling me. Something they both aren't telling me. But I guess it doesn't really matter.

After all, I've got a body to remove and a room to clean.

27

'Right then,' I tell them, slipping into efficiency mode. 'Here's what we're going to do. You,' I point at Tori, 'are going to head out to the terrace and get some breakfast. Complain of a steaming hangover and make a big thing about how late a night you had.'

Tori nods and looks slightly relieved. As well she might, for now at least. She's still helping with clean up later though.

'You,' I point to Chloe, 'need to get in the shower.' I reach out and take one of her hands, inspecting her nails carefully. 'You need to trim these down and then use a brush to clean underneath them. Not a single trace of dried blood left behind. You understand?' I drop her hand and it falls limply to her side.

'Yes,' she says quietly.

'I need to go and make a phone call. Make sure you lock the door behind me, and the patio one. And don't, under any circumstance, let anyone other than me or Tori in. You understand?' My tone is harsh. The last thing we need is even more people sticking their noses in here.

Chloe nods.

'And neither of you says anything, to anyone. OK?'

'We're not stupid,' Tori says.

I want to laugh. I mean, is she freaking serious? I just stare at her until she averts her gaze. Fucking amateur.

I wait in the hallway until I hear that Chloe has locked the door. And then follow Tori down towards the terrace area. I want to make sure that's the only place she goes and check she's playing a convincing hangover for the rest of the family.

'Good night, sweetheart?' Mrs Cooper asks her.

'Hhhmm,' Tori mumbles, hand reaching up to rub her temple. It's a farcical act, full of cliché. But I guess all the Coopers are.

'Little too much to drink?'

'Yeah. I need coffee.'

'How's Chloe feeling?'

I stiffen at the question and wait for Tori to say something dumb. 'Probably worse than me,' she replies and the lie sounds almost smooth.

Satisfied, I leave Tori to her breakfast to call someone about a body.

The company I work for – my real career, not working in this villa – offer a very exclusive and extremely expensive service. This is far more than getting rid of an unwanted spouse or taking out a business rival, or any of the other myriad reasons people want someone else dead. This is about getting away with it clean.

We won't tell you how we'll do it – the murder I mean – that's left up to one of our operatives in the field. And we won't tell you exactly when, merely a window of about a week in which it will take place. We do that on purpose. Too accurate and you'll be waiting for it; your reaction won't be genuine and you might do something to inadvertently fuck the whole thing up. In which case, our operative might have to take you down too and that kind of defeats the whole object really, doesn't it? Too vague on the timeline though and you run the risk that you'll be out of town, or having elective surgery, or be doing something incriminating, perhaps in the middle of an illicit tryst, for example.

So, we give you the window. And we help you to prepare. We'll even suggest ways of shoring up your alibi. Things like going on a big family holiday the week before so everyone thinks you're madly in love with the man you're about to have killed. Every detail is planned; we are meticulous.

There's always a baby-sitter assigned to the person who's taken out the hit. Someone to watch over them in the run-up to make sure everything is ready and in place. It's easy to sneak unseen into the lives of the rich. They always have staff of some description and I'm so good at playing concierge or assistant or even fitness instructor on occasion that the relatives and friends of the client have no idea who I really work for.

It's a perfect system. Or at least it is normally. *Normally* the client doesn't shit the bed in such epic proportions.

* * *

Gary, my boss on the job, answers the phone on the second ring. 'What's happened?' he asks. He knows immediately something is wrong, otherwise I wouldn't have called him. Ours is a strictly 'no news is good news' relationship and we haven't made contact in weeks. Although I do know he's spending this week at a hotel down the road, 'taking some time to observe the family from a distance'. AKA 'checking up on me'.

'We have a problem.'

'No shit.'

'I have a package you need to collect.'

I hear him swear on the other end of the line. I won't repeat the word he uses.

'It was expected, but it's a week early,' I add.

'Do you know who sent it?'

'No.' I say the word carefully, it hasn't escaped my attention that I could end up taking the blame for this. Especially if it does end up being Chloe who killed her husband: my job is to keep an eye on her after all. At least the company doesn't offer a refund scheme and all the payments have already been settled.

'Shitting Christ.' Gary adds a further stream of swears.

'My mate Yannis has a van you can borrow.' I give him the address.

'Fuck's sake. I'll be there ASAP.'

He must have broken a few speed limits because less than fifteen minutes later he pulls up outside the staff quarters. He's in a white van devoid of any livery. He could be anyone: delivery driver, handyman, even just a mate popping round for a cuppa.

He follows me inside the small staff flat adjacent to the villa. 'It's boiling in here,' he says, pulling his polo shirt away from his neck.

'No air-con,' I tell him with a twist of the mouth. It pisses me off that a villa costing tens of thousands of euros a week can't even spring for a little air-con unit for the staff. Talk about cheap.

'Where is he?'

'In one of the side bedrooms.' There's a map of the villa on the wall and I tap the location for him. 'There's a terrace here, only accessed from that room and the one next door.'

'Who's staying in that one?'

'Chloe's parents.'

'Mr Luke Wilson?' Even Gary sounds a little in awe of the great Wilson name.

'Yep.' I'm not in awe. I've seen enough men like him over the years to no longer be impressed by his particular brand of lunatic, even if I fake a level of deference to his face.

'Can we use this side passage?' he asks, tracing a finger over the map.

'It's sealed up,' I tell him. 'No access from the terrace.'

'Shame.' He turns away from the map, a serious expression taking over his features. 'Tell me exactly what happened,' he demands.

'Chloe went out last night, blacked out, woke up in bed with Scott. His throat was cut, looks like it happened in his sleep.'

'So, she killed him?' He gets straight to the point.

'Honestly? I have no idea. I wouldn't think she'd be that stupid, but who else could have done it?'

'What about the cameras?' he asks with a condescending head tilt. What does he think I spent the time waiting for him doing?

'Nothing.'

'Nothing?'

'No one except the guests left or entered the villa last night.'

'And you combed through every second of the footage?'

I really wish he wouldn't take that tone with me: for his own sake really, one day I'm going to make him pay for it. 'There's no need to watch every second. The system only records when it detects motion. Cuts down on expensive data storage.'

'Hmm.' He doesn't sound fully convinced, but I know the villa's owner loves all the mod-cons like the fancy security system but absolutely doesn't want to have to pay for it.

'Who else knows? About the murder?'

'Chloe and the sister-in-law, Tori.'

He raises an eyebrow at me. It says *and why the fuck does* she *know?*

'Chloe told her.' I spread my hands to the side. 'I have no idea why.'

'Do we need to...?' This time he raises both eyebrows.

'If you try to get rid of both Chloe and Tori, with Scott already out of play, there'll be chaos.'

He nods, almost sagely. He would do it. Hit the nuclear destruct button and get as far away from here as possible. There's a motto, in the company: organisation over job over self. I'm not sure I wholly agree, but the men – it's ninety-five percent men – love a bit of declaration of sacrifice. Personally, I think I'll throw everyone else under a bus if – when – the time comes.

'Right,' he says. 'This is the play. I'll deal with the body.'

'Store it,' I interject quickly.

'Why?'

'Scott's the son of a powerful man, the son-in-law of an even more powerful one. When he vanishes, they'll search. I suggest that we keep the body on ice in case we need proof of death later.'

'Fine. I'll move the body, and then you clean house. Literally this time.' He laughs as if that was actually funny.

I smile at him, as if I also thought that lame excuse for a joke was funny. Sometimes I hate that I have to defer to shitty little men like this. One day I'll take his job, and then his boss's job. But this isn't the kind of industry in which you can get an MBA and then leapfrog a few levels in a single promotion. Here you have to earn it with hard work and years of your life. I wouldn't do anything else though. Just imagine having a 9–5 office job filling in spreadsheets with meaningless data so you can create some pointless little charts that no one gives a shit about.

He stops laughing and his face turns to stone, the atmosphere suddenly serious. 'And get those bitches under control. Otherwise I *will* get rid of them.'

Inwardly I sigh.

I need Chloe and Tori alive, there's far more of this story to come.

28

I head back toward the main house, taking the route directly across the dining terrace. In my chino shorts and crisp white t-shirt, I basically blend into the background and so people barely notice me.

'I've had an alert on the smart system about an air-con issue in the master bedroom,' I tell the few people sitting around the table picking at the fresh fruit and last remaining pastries. I really hope they don't finish them all, I'm starving and a left-over custard bougatsa might be my only chance at food this morning.

No one even looks up as I pass.

Inside the welcome cool of the villa, I use the master key to access the utility room. I put a lock on it after the first guests of the summer decided it would be funny to take a shit in the cleaning trolley. Disgusting man boys on a stag party. I wanted to make them eat it, but settled for using their toothbrushes to scrub the toilets a few times. The villa has a full cleaning service between guests, and once a day, normally after lunch, a contractor comes in to give the whole place a spruce up, but I still need to do inter-mittent bits and bobs. Luckily the contractor leaves the trolley stocked and I find everything I'm going to need to bleach the bedroom and remove all traces of murder from the site.

One wheel squeaks as I push it down the corridor towards the room and I add it to the mental to do list, which is threat-ening to overtake my entire life. There is always so much to get done in this job: cleaning and cooking and laundry and shop-ping and errands to the pharmacy and dry cleaner and ferrying people to and from the airport. And that's before you add wiping down a murder scene. I'm already exhausted and a huge yawn threatens to overwhelm me. I leave the trolley and nip back into the kitchen. Inside the fridge is a selection of energy drinks and so I grab three. I'm not meant to drink the stuff bought for guests – we bill it all to them, after all – but at this moment I don't really give a crap.

I knock on the door to the room Chloe and Scott have been sharing.

'Who is it?' Chloe asks, panic in her voice.

'Just me, Grace,' I reply.

She unlocks the door and I push it open, wondering what kind of state I'm going to find her in.

Her hair is still wet from the shower, hanging around her face in thick ropes. She's wearing a simple dress in a pretty abstract pattern of reds and browns and greens. It's a good choice. If there are any stray pinpricks of blood on it, no one would ever notice. I glance at her hands. She's done as instructed and trimmed her nails right down, her hands pink from where she's been scrubbing them.

'The actual fuck, Chloe?' I say as I close the door behind me.

'I didn't kill him, I swear. I woke up and he was like this. I don't know what happened.'

I have no idea if she's telling me the truth, but I guess at this point it's far more important that no one finds out what's happened here. I snap back into professional mode.

'You'll need to go to a nail salon today,' I tell her. Women like her don't have nails like this. I look at my own: I'm hoping my next assignment will have a tiny bit more glamour than chinos, Skechers and clear polish to stop my nails splitting as I scrub all manner of disgusting things. I push aside the thought, one job at a time is the only way to do this and I drag my attention to the problem at hand. 'Actually, that's a good idea. Let's get you out of the house for a few hours, shall we?'

She nods.

I make two phone calls. The first to secure her an appointment with Ariana, one of the best nail technicians on the island. The second to arrange a car to pick Chloe up from here in fifteen minutes.

Done, I turn back to her. 'Put some shoes on and then pop out to the terrace. Tell whoever is out there that you broke a nail and need an emergency manicure. I'll follow you out and say the driver is here so you don't need to make small talk. OK?'

She nods again.

'Use the time in the salon to get your head together.' My lecturing tone seems to catch her off guard and her eyes snap to mine. These rich women are all the same: they need someone to tell them what to do or they'd never actually achieve anything, but they still want to feel superior to the mere minions who serve them. It's exhausting to be around and I really don't have the head space to pander to her this morning. 'Seriously.' I double down. 'You look like a zombie.'

She opens her mouth to speak but then closes it again, her

shoulders rounding as her posture collapses. She simply motions at the body on the bed. He's really starting to stink now, the stench of death assaulting my nostrils.

Maybe tough love isn't going to help here. 'I know it's all a shock,' I say gently. 'It's hardly like I do this all the time either.' I laugh softly. 'But this is serious. If this is discovered, if the police find out, do you know what will happen?'

She nods.

'Say it,' I tell her.

'They'll think I killed him.'

'Exactly. And you don't want that.'

'Of course not.'

'I'm going to help you.' I keep my voice calm and level. 'Because it's my job. But you have to understand that you've now made me an accessory in a very messy murder.'

'I didn't want to. It was Tori who—'

I interrupt her. 'You brought Tori into it too, remember? The three of us are involved now, no matter who did what. If you fuck this up, the rest of us are in serious trouble as well. You understand?'

'Yeah.' She shakes her fingers and jogs on the spot a few times as if trying to psych herself up.

'What's done is done,' I tell her. 'All that matters now is what might happen next. You need to act like there's nothing wrong. Like you broke a nail and need to get it fixed.'

'Where do I say *he* is?'

'I can't help you with that. You need to think of something. And think of it quick.'

'I'll just say he's having a lie in. That he's feeling a bit sick.'

'No. The air-con in here is broken and needs to be fixed. There's a technician coming in twenty minutes.'

She looks puzzled. 'The air-con's fine.'

Jesus, she can be a bit thick. 'It's a cover to move the body.'

'Oh. Right. That makes more sense.' She flashes me a self-deprecating smile. 'I'll say he went out, left before I woke up. Probably gone to look at this diving club course he was banging on about yesterday.'

'That's good. I'll confirm. Say I ordered him a car.'

She doesn't ask what I'm going to do with the body. I'm intrigued as to what she thinks though.

We head out to the terrace. Chloe plays her part beautifully as she excuses herself for the next couple of hours. She also grabs a plate of fruit and bougatsas and carries it into the kitchen. I follow behind her.

'Your car will be here in three minutes,' I tell her, looking at the plate she doesn't have time to eat.

'Oh, I got this for you. I doubt you've had time to eat with all this going on.' She hands me the plate. Hmm, I wasn't expecting that, to be honest.

'Thank you,' I say, now desperate for her to leave so I can cram a bougatsa into my mouth. These little bites of custard and filo pastry are freaking divine.

She shrugs. 'It's nothing. And I should be the one thanking you. You're a literal life saver.' Her words sound genuine. She's full of surprises this morning.

Ten minutes after Chloe's car has driven off, Gary pulls up in front of the villa as if he's just arrived and hasn't been sitting in the van on the patch of drive outside my tiny apartment. I go to let him in.

'Who's that?' a voice asks from behind me in the corridor. I spin round to find Rob, Chloe's brother, who has acted like a total dick this whole trip. He has that swagger of the son of a rich man, you know the type. Guys who have been told they're owed the world because Daddy has money, who no one has said 'no' to, who are so ignorant of their own mediocrity.

'Air-con tech,' I tell him, trying to sound efficient and professional.

'The air-con's fine.' He says it like I might be a little on the simple side. Dick.

'In your sister's room.'

He looks like he's going to ask more questions and I will him to leave me alone. The seconds stretch. Gary will be waiting in the heat and is probably starting to get pissy.

'Do we have a problem?' Rob asks eventually.

'It's probably just a sensor in the room that needs replacing,' I reply.

'Not with the air-con. With *us*.' There's something gross in the way he says 'us'.

'There is no us.' Not that he hasn't tried it on constantly since he got here.

'There could be though...' he twerks an eyebrow and takes a few steps closer.

I tense. It's constant, incessant. Guys like Rob like to hit on the staff. But they do not like to be rebuffed. 'There couldn't.' I've learnt the best way to shut them down is just to be firm. Polite but firm. Not that I won't kick him in the balls the second he crosses a line.

'No need to be a bitch.'

I groan inwardly. 'Please. I have a lot to get done today.'

'Do me instead.'

For fuck's sake. What is it with this guy? 'Rob. Just go back outside. To your wife.'

'She doesn't mind.'

Jesus. 'I mind.'

'Oh, come on. Just a bit of fun. You'd enjoy it. I promise.'

I take a deep breath. 'I have a job to do. Now leave me alone.'

'Yeah, whatever, frigid bitch. You're not even that pretty, you know.'

I sigh. I feel like I've had this conversation twenty times already this summer. I don't reply, just wait for him to leave.

'Prick-teasing whore.' That's his parting line before he turns and heads back through the kitchen.

I shake my head and wait for a moment while my heart rate slows to a more normal level. Then I walk to the front door and open it for Gary.

'Fuck's sake. It's boiling out there and you just left me on the step?'

I'm so done with today and there's still the messy bit to sort out.

Fuck my life.

29

So, here's a conundrum. How do you move a body from a bedroom to a van and then to a chest freezer somewhere? Without anyone seeing you, of course.

How would you do it?

My first thought was to use the laundry trolley, the one we fill with sheets and towels to take to the industrial launderette. You have no idea how many towels a seven-bed luxury villa with a pool goes through. It's like every guest has to use a clean one each time they shower, or go for a swim, and then they use yet more for the beach and for the gym. It's ridiculous, the sheer flagrancy of it all. And there I am, drinking my cocktails through a paper straw to save the planet. But the trolley won't work; the body is covered in blood and the trolley is covered in white fabric. The staining would be catastrophic.

Guess what the brains of my operation – or at least that is what he calls himself – thinks is a good idea?

'You want to just carry him out?' I ask, not even bothering to hide my incredulation.

'We just need to get him in the back of the van.' Gary goes on the defensive.

For God's sake. How am I expected to work like this? Sex pests to the left of me. Morons to the right. This is a fucking joke. 'And what if someone sees?'

'We'll be careful.'

I don't like his use of 'we'. Like I'm going to have anything to do with this charade. This has 'life in prison' written all over it if we get caught. I rub my eyes, I can feel a migraine forming.

'What? Have you got a better idea?' He borders on the aggressive and so I swallow down the retort forming on my lips.

'We need something to move him in. Something to avoid him being seen.'

'Suitcase?'

Has this guy been watching too many dodgy movies? A fucking *suitcase*? Scott is six foot three and weighs well over a hundred kilos. 'Too small.' Then I have a brainwave. Well, actually, the solution is staring me in the face. Quite literally.

You remember the group of disgusting dudes who defecated in the cleaning trolley? Well, they also developed a game they called 'Hide and Sneak'. It involved one of them hiding and then jumping out when no one expected. One of them hid inside the dark wooden ottoman chest running down the bottom of the bed in what is now Scott and Chloe's room. It all ended in disaster when he leapt out and gave his friend the shock of his life, causing him to fall over and smash his head on the tiled floor. He needed five stitches. Guess who had to sit in the hospital with him for four hours while he bitched and moaned?

Anyway, the ottoman is the perfect size and no one will think anything of it if we take it out and pop it into the back of a van. Furniture gets moved around all the time in these posh villas.

As soon as we've loaded the ottoman, complete with grizzly cargo, into the van, Gary drives away and I sigh in relief.

For the final part of the clean up, I need another pair of hands. And, luckily, Tori has already volunteered as tribute. She dragged me into this mess – or at least that's the way it will look to her – and so she's going to help me get out of it.

I find her lounging by the pool as if she doesn't have a care in the world.

'Miss Cooper,' I whisper, conscious that there are other people around and so careful to seem suitably deferent. 'Could I borrow you for a moment?'

'Is everything alright?' she asks, raising her sunglasses to look at me.

'Oh, everything's fine. We've been repairing the air-con in a couple of rooms and I would just like you to check yours.'

'Can't you do that on the smart system thingy?' She flaps a hand.

'No, I need you to come in person.' I say the words through gritted teeth.

'Can't it wait?' She says it like she's busy, like she has something better to do.

'Not really.' I want to slap her.

'Fine.' She huffs loudly and makes a meal out of getting up from the lounger.

Inside the villa, I turn on her. 'I'm cleaning up your fucking mess here.'

She steps back. 'Yeah, I get it. But gotta keep up appearances, you know.' She grins at me. 'Was I convincing?'

Is she actually asking me to judge her acting right now?

Seriously, what did I do in a past life to deserve this?

We make a detour to the cleaning cupboard where I unearth two of the sets of painter's overalls I have stored in there, in case there's a need for any last-minute touches up between groups of guests. Like the time a couple had a huge row and she threw an entire tray of soutzoukakia – meatballs in a tomato sauce, delicious but also bright freaking red – at the wall of the dining room. The overalls are made of a thick waxy type of paper and are hardly the most flattering things in the world. But they do the job.

Back inside the murder room – I feel like that should be a proper noun: the Murder Room – I hand a set to Tori.

'What is this?' she asks, even though it's pretty freaking obvious.

'I'd suggest you strip down to your underwear, or bikini I guess, and then pop those overalls on. They'll protect your clothes from the worst of it.'

She stares at me as though I'm speaking a foreign language.

'So you don't get covered in blood.'

Her brow furrows slightly.

Surely it isn't possible for someone to be this dumb. 'We need to clean up all this blood.'

'You want *me* to...' she trails off and takes a slow spin on the spot as she looks at the carnage around us.

I bite back the laugh that threatens to erupt. Did she really think I was going to do this on my own? The audacity of her. 'Just put them on.'

She does as instructed, although, if I had a pound for every little huff she made, I'd be able to retire tomorrow. I follow suit, folding my chino shorts and white polo carefully and then placing them inside the plastic bag my overalls came in.

Damn. We look ridiculous. The paper overalls rustle slightly with every move and are just see-through enough that I can see the outline of Tori's bikini. I'm glad I wore something presentable in that department. We look like we're doing some kind of shit cosplay of the characters from *Breaking Bad*.

'I'll be Walt and you can be Jesse.' I strike a pose.

Tori looks at me like I've grown another head.

'*Breaking Bad*?' I debate whether to explain, but if you have to spell something out, the other person never finds it funny.

I hand her some gloves and some disposable overshoes and slip on my own, making sure the cuffs of the overalls are tucked inside to keep my skin protected.

Now that we're appropriately dressed, we can get to work. The first problem to solve is the mattress. A human body contains over eight pints of blood and there is a huge amount of it seeped into the memory foam.

I strip off the mattress protector, it's an industrial grade one, used by hotels and villas because people are disgusting and mattresses are expensive. But even the protector didn't stand up to that much blood and there's a circular red stain about the size of a dinner plate on the mattress below. It's ruined.

Tori looks like she's going to be sick. It's the only thing that's making this whole situation bearable, even though I know it's not nice to revel in another's misery.

I make a call to the emergency furniture replacement company I keep on speed dial. They have a massive warehouse up by the port and keep stocks of mattresses and glass coffee tables and sun loungers and all the other stuff that gets constantly broken by overly exuberant or careless guests. They promise to deliver me a new mattress in two hours. They'll also take the stained one that I 'forgot to put the protector on and a guest spilt red wine all over'. They'll know the red wine is hiding something unsavoury but they are the epitome of discretion.

The sheets and the mattress protector will need to be incinerated; there isn't enough Persil in the world to get those stains out. 'Ball them up and put them into a heavy-duty bin bag,' I instruct Tori. I'll deal with them another time.

She does as I ask, but I can see she's holding her breath to avoid the stench of blood. It's a funny smell. Metallic. Thick. Like it's coating the hairs inside your nostrils. It's a smell you think you'll never forget.

'Great. Now for the main event,' I tell her.

'Are you enjoying this?' she asks with a curl in her lip.

'Of course not,' I reply as I motion for her to help me push the furniture to the sides of the room so we can mop.

So much blood.

And it's started to dry, forming hard brown smears across the marble flooring. Thank God it's marble and not carpet though. That would have been game over before we'd even begun.

Tori works hard for about five minutes and then she starts to complain about the overalls.

'They're so hot.'

'I'm sweating.'

'I can't stand it.'

I tune her out. Or at least I try to but it's impossible. She's incessant.

'Just take them off then,' I snap at her.

'My bikini is Zimmermann.'

'So? Either wear the overalls and shut up, or take them off and kiss goodbye to the pretty crochet detailing on your bikini when you can't get the blood out.'

She huffs a few times and then strips off the overalls. She keeps the gloves on but also takes off the overshoe things.

'Just make sure you scrub yourself in the shower afterwards.'

She throws me a look that could curdle milk and gets back to work.

I move on to the bathroom, spraying bleach around like it's going out of fashion. Tori begins to cough and splutter.

'Need... air... burning...' she lurches towards the patio doors and wrenches them open, falling outside and taking huge gulps of air.

'Are you alright, Tori dear?' comes a voice from the patio.

'Oh hi, Mrs Wilson,' Tori replies.

30

Shit. Mrs Wilson is on the patio. I turn to take in the room; the worst of the blood has gone but it's still a mess: the furniture pushed against the walls, a pile of towels in the middle of the space, stained mattress standing upright in front of the door.

If she comes inside, it'll all be over. It's far too much of a risk to bring anyone else into this situation. Plus, I've seen the way she defers to her husband, how he makes every tiny decision for the both of them. She may as well not have an opinion. Or a personality. She's an extension of Mr Wilson; she'll go to him immediately and then there will be pandemonium.

I'm suddenly hit by an image of Peter Cooper. If he realises his eldest son is dead – and that Chloe probably killed him – then he is going to lose his shit. And not in a 'he might get a bit angry' way, but in a 'literal fire will rain down on everyone in his path' way.

'Oh, just borrowing Scott and Chloe's room,' I hear Tori say. 'I need to dye my hair and the light is so much better in their bathroom than in mine. Hence the whole bikini and gloves combo.' She laughs this tinkling laugh, like an innocent child. OK, I'll admit she can be good at this: at the pretence and the lying on her feet at least. Dyeing her hair is a pretty good cover for her unusual get up. I wonder if she'd like a job at my firm?

'You're not going to a salon?' I hear Mrs Wilson ask with a tone of abject horror.

'It's just a temporary hair mask,' Tori replies smoothly. 'My colourist back home would throw a fit if I let someone else go anywhere near his work.' Now I'm even more impressed.

'I wanted to borrow this book Chloe mentioned last night.' Mrs Wilson says.

'She's out at the nail salon,' Tori tells her.

'Of course. Silly me. I'll just...'

She doesn't finish the sentence, but I know she means she will just come in and get it.

I throw the towels into the laundry trolley, thankful I lined it with bin bags earlier just in case. In a panic I strip off my overalls and ball them up, stuffing them in with the towels. I pull my chino shorts from the plastic bag I put them in earlier and pull them on. I'm just about to pull out the polo shirt when I sense someone is watching me.

'Oh. Hi there Grace.'

Fuck. I'm standing in my bra and shorts in the middle of a room with the furniture pushed to the edges and I have literally no explanation for this situation.

I turn slowly, bracing myself for a series of questions I won't be able to answer. My mind is blank, all logic destroyed by blind panic.

'Hi Mrs Wilson,' I say and then fall silent, my eyes darting towards Tori who is standing behind her.

'Grace was just cleaning the room,' Tori says. 'We were chatting about tattoos and Grace was showing me the one she has on her torso.'

My hand moves instinctively to the vine of roses that wraps around the right side of my body.

'I've been debating getting one myself and Grace's is so pretty,' Tori adds. 'I just adore a floral tattoo.'

I want to say it's not just a flower, that it has meaning and importance, but I bite my tongue.

'Oh, that's nice dear,' Mrs Wilson says. There's a tiny undercurrent to her voice. 'I wanted to borrow Chloe's copy of *Sweetpea*. I don't suppose you've come across it while you've been cleaning?' Her eyes roam the room. 'Oh, there it is,' she exclaims and plucks the bright pink paperback from the sideboard near the patio door. She waves it towards me and Tori. 'I'd best let you ladies get on with it.' She raises an eyebrow and gives us both a small smile. She definitely thinks we're up to something, but something far more fun than murder. As if Tori would be interested in me like that.

After Mrs Wilson leaves, I get a call from the furniture company. They're ten minutes away. 'I need you to go and grab a bottle of red wine,' I tell Tori.

She looks at her watch and raises an eyebrow.

'Not to drink. For the mattress.'

She raises the other eyebrow.

'I'm going to pour it over the bloodstain so it looks like a wine related incident.'

She shrugs. 'Seems like a waste of wine, but whatever.'

'Just pick something cheap.'

She takes a step backward as if I've physically assaulted her. 'We don't drink cheap wine.'

I roll my eyes. I'm so not in the mood. 'Just go and get one. Please.'

She stomps out of the room and I lock the door behind her. This whole extended family are the nosiest people I've ever met and I cannot possibly deal with yet another Cooper or Wilson barging into this room.

It takes Tori five minutes to make it back. She's carrying two bottles. 'Cabernet or merlot?' she asks, holding them out to me.

'I don't give a shit. Just tell me you brought a bottle opener with you.'

'No need to be grumpy.' She deliberates for a few moments before handing me the cabernet and then pulling a waiter's friend from inside the cup of her bikini top with a flourish.

I try to ignore the way the metal of the tool has been warmed against her skin as I open the bottle and then slosh the wine all over the bloodstain on the mattress. The rich aroma of blackberry, a hint of tobacco and a deep almost woody scent fills the air.

'Such a waste,' Tori laments.

I decide to address the elephant in the room. Why isn't she more upset over the death of her oldest brother? 'The wine or your brother?'

'Ha! If you knew him, you wouldn't be asking that.'

'You didn't get on?'

'That's the understatement of the century. I don't think anyone got on with Scott.'

'Enough to want him dead?'

A shadow crosses her face. Oh, now that is interesting. She definitely wanted him dead. This isn't ambivalence at his passing, this is joy. Tempered maybe, but only as far as she can act for decorum's sake.

'Is there something you're not telling me?' I ask her.

'No.' The reply is quick. Too quick? Did *she* kill him? Was she the one holding the knife? But how could she have killed him without Chloe waking up?

They could have been in on it together. They could have planned this between themselves. Except that doesn't solve the issue that Chloe already had the hit booked and this would be just a stupid risk.

I keep wondering about self-defence. But self-defence against a sleeping man?

Tori reaches out and takes the waiter's friend back from me. She opens the bottle of merlot and then takes a huge swig, wiping her mouth with the back of her hand.

I look at my watch.

She shrugs. 'Gotta make the story a little more compelling,' she says with an air of the enigmatic.

'Story?'

'Pisshead who can't be trusted with red wine.' She takes another swig and then spills a couple of drops down her bikini top. It soaks into the white crotchet trim. I'm assuming she knows how to get a red wine stain out.

I think it's just an excuse – and a pretty thin one, let's be honest – to get shitfaced in the middle of the day. Although, if I'd killed my brother, I think it'd probably be my plan too.

The furniture guys arrive and a switch flicks in Tori. She slurs slightly and rubs up against one of the men, stumbling a little as she does so.

'I'm so sorry,' she says. 'Such a klutz. I can't believe I ruined the mattress. You must bill me.' That last bit is directed at me.

The taller furniture guy, Leo, makes brief eye contact with me. *Jeez, what a mess.* I return the look. *Tell me about it.*

Tori twirls slowly in a disjointed pirouette. She looks hammered. Exactly the kind of messy rich girl who would stain a mattress in her holiday villa. It's totally convincing and Leo and his colleague will return to their depot, incinerate the ruined mattress and tell stories about the hot but drunk girl who came on to them. They'll dine out on the anecdote for a few days and feel like kings. They will never connect the wine girl with a potential murder.

There's a chance Tori's a genius.

As much as that pains me to say.

31

I look around the room feeling really rather pleased with myself. Now, I'm not one hundred percent sure that a proper CSI crew coming in with their blue lights and their little spray bottles of chemicals wouldn't find anything. But, to the naked eye, it looks perfectly undisturbed, as if nothing has happened.

I'm good at my job. Really good. And I know it. Not in like a braggy way, more in the way that comes from a deep knowledge that I've found my groove, even if my path to get here was hardly smooth. It wasn't my lifelong dream to work for a killing agency; I was pulled into it by a series of stupid choices and a ridiculous belief in my own immortality. At first it was fun to push the boundaries, to see what else I could get away with – I'm sure some psychoanalyst would have a field day with my abandonment issues and attention seeking following my sister's death and the way my parents just kind of stopped caring. And, yes, one day I pushed the boundaries too far and pissed off the wrong people. They gave me a 'choice' – ha! Like I was going to choose the alternative option – and that's how I ended up joining the agency. But I genuinely enjoy my work. You might think this job operates at the fringes of society, it is all a bit hush hush to work for a company that kills for money, I guess. But it allows me to travel, to meet new people, to create new versions of myself frequently and to right wrongs. That moral aspect of it is important to me, the sense that we are – in a tiny way at least – rebalancing the scales. Taking out the men who think nothing of taking us out if it serves them.

Chloe comes back from the salon, her trimmed-to-the-quick nails rescued with acrylics and sporting a rather lovely coral orange gel polish. I'm jealous. I think I might ask for my next posting to be something less menial, perhaps a PA in an office so I can clack around in Louboutins and a well-cut shift dress. Perhaps even dye my hair icy blonde and cut it into a bob like that woman from Serendipity Cosmetics I keep seeing on the news. But, sorry, I digress.

'It looks...' Chloe begins and then trails off as she looks around the room.

'Like none of it happened.' Tori finishes the sentence for her.

A shiver passes visibly across Chloe's shoulders.

'Nothing did happen,' I say, using my firm almost teacherly voice. 'Scott has gone to check out a diving club. You had your nails done. Tori used your bathroom to dye her hair and asked me to help because I was in there cleaning already.'

'And Grace showed me her tattoo of a twisted vine of roses.'

Chloe cocks her head at this last bit.

'Your mum came in and found us. We hadn't quite finished,' Tori explains.

'Why were you dyeing your hair?'

'I wasn't. But I was in my underwear and wearing latex gloves.'

'Right...' Chloe elongates the word.

Tori shrugs. 'There's a chance your mum thinks Grace and I were doing something kinky though.' The words drip from her tongue like they're nothing.

I remember, years ago in another life, a girl whispering in my ear that people might think *we were doing something kinky* and a frisson goes up my spine. It was so long ago and I doubt the other girl has any idea of the effect of those little words on me.

I leave Chloe and Tori in the bedroom and head back to the kitchen. However pleased I am with myself for everything I achieved scrubbing out all signs of the murder, I still need to do my actual job here at the villa and I'm extremely late in starting my to do list.

The first thing is to put in an order for a food delivery and so I sort through the fridge and cupboards looking at what the guests have eaten and drunk over the last twenty-four hours. The food consumption seems to be split between fruit and salad and yoghurt, and full fat crisps and bags of nuts and platefuls of little feta-stuffed pastries called tiropitakia. All pretty standard for a group like this where the women are expected to eat like rabbits to maintain a certain look and the men are allowed to sport a gut and still be drooled over.

The drinking though. These Coopers and Wilsons *really* know how to drink. Vodka, gin, rum, tequila, whisky. Bottles and bottles of wine and champagne. Crates of beer. It's enough to bring down an army.

Food order in, I start on the other random chores that have come my way. First up is checking the security company are actually planning on arriving today to sort out the sodding alarm; the woman I speak to promises me the technician will definitely be there this afternoon. My next task is driving all the way to Nammos to pick up something Jack ordered online and can't be bothered to go and collect himself. I guess that would cut into the time he has to sun himself to an early dose of skin cancer.

* * *

I get back to find Rob Wilson standing in front of the now restocked fridge. Evidently the groceries were delivered while I was out and I'm thankful it's a premium service who actually put everything away instead of leaving it on the doorstep to fester in the heat.

'Where's the oat milk?' Rob asks, without even removing his head from the fridge.

'There was a carton there earlier,' I reply.

'I drank it.'

Well, I guess that explains exactly where it went. But I bite my tongue. How has this manchild drunk two litres of oat milk in an hour and a half? And why does he need more of the stuff?

He extracts himself from the fridge and turns to face me, an expectant look on his face.

Like I don't have enough to do today.

'I can pop out and get you some more,' I say smoothly even though, after his behaviour earlier, I would be entirely within my rights not to help at all.

'Good. Come and find me when you get back.' He walks away.

No please. No thank you. No nothing. Although he does turn round to give me a quick leer.

I wonder if I can persuade Farah that she needs to get rid of her dickhead of a husband? I'd quite enjoy taking his murder on as a new commission.

The Flora supermarket is rammed and it takes me well over

an hour to get the oat milk and return to the villa. It doesn't do much for my mood or the fact that I want Rob to suffer for being such a little prick. Just as I'm about to put it away in the fridge – where I'm sure it won't actually now get touched; a single person cannot possibly get through that much of the stuff and it's gone five so he'll be on the booze now anyway – Farah comes up to me.

'The alarm technician came,' she tells me. 'He was only here five minutes and said it's all fine and he'll email you.'

'Thank you,' I reply, feeling a tad guilty that a guest is passing messages to me about villa admin, but I guess I have had rather a lot to juggle today. I turn round to put the oat milk away.

'Umm... Grace?' she starts. She sounds nervous.

'Yes?' I reply, backing out of the fridge. I've just noticed there isn't much of the smooth orange juice but I'm just going to cross my fingers and hope no one notices as I simply can't stand the thought of going back to Flora.

'I don't suppose you've seen my tennis bracelet somewhere in the villa?'

'You've lost it?' It's a dumb question, but I'm knackered so you'll have to cut me a bit of slack.

'I think so. Though, we went to a club last night – Elysium – and... well...'

'You think you might have left it there?'

She nods.

There's a pause. I know she's waiting for me to offer to go to the club and look for it. If she were her husband, she'd just demand it. But maybe living with someone like Rob has made her at least a little conscious of making demands of others? Or maybe he's just sapped the fire from her? Whichever way it is, she's now nibbling on her bottom lip and she's still waiting for me to offer.

'I'll go to the club and look.' The words are out of my mouth before I can stop them. I've always been far too willing to help people, even if I do bitch about it afterwards.

'Can I come with you?'

That's a surprise. 'Of course.'

'Thanks.' She blushes slightly. Is there something more here?

32

The issue with Farah becomes clear in the car.

'I don't remember coming home last night,' she says quietly about five minutes into the drive. It feels like a confessional. But isn't it always easier to tell your secrets when the other person is facing away and occupied by something else? Like trying not to knock dumb tourists off their scooters?

'Heavy night?' I ask.

'I don't think so. It's like, one moment Chloe and I were having fun and then it all went black.'

I wait for a few moments. That tracks with what Chloe told me. Perhaps Farah knows something more about what happened last night? Or someone at the club might? This might not be such a wasted hour of my time after all. 'Do you think your drink could have been spiked?'

There's a pause, as if she's mulling it over, but she must have already had this thought. 'I don't know.' There's something so vulnerable in her voice that I can't help but feel sorry for her. She might have shit taste in men, but she actually seems pretty normal. Especially in comparison to the rest of the extended family she married into.

She remains silent as we continue to drive towards Elysium. I fiddle with the air-con, blasting it higher as we turn into the late afternoon sun, the road along the clifftop devoid of any shelter and shimmering in the heat. Farah doesn't look up from the blank screen of her phone in her lap, doesn't see the azure sea and the glorious sandy beach spreading out beneath us.

A few minutes later, we pull up in front of the club. It's decidedly less salubrious in the daylight, the painted façade peeling, litter strewn around the entrance, a whiff of something that is probably vomit in the air. I've already messaged Liam, the owner, so I know he's in the vicinity, but we need to wait for him to let us in.

'I wanted to come with you to see if it would jog my memory,' Farah says. 'But it looks so different in the daylight.'

'Yeah, it's amazing the cracks the dark can cover,' I reply. 'Especially when you throw up some fairy lights.' That seems like an analogy for life, but I don't sense that Farah's in the mood for my philosophical musings.

'I remember everything, up until just after Tori left.'

'Tori left early?' This tallies with what I saw on the perimeter cameras, but I want to know why. Her alibi – that she was with Chloe and Farah all night – has been blown wide open. She had an opportunity. If I dig deep enough, am I going to find motive? Motive to kill her brother? Motive to frame Chloe? Trust my luck to have two potential killers in the same villa.

'Yeah. She and Chloe had an argument while I was in the loo and then she stormed out.'

'What were they arguing about?'

'I'm not quite sure. I only caught the tail end and it didn't make sense, to be honest. It sounded like Tori wanted to do something, but Chloe was telling her it had to wait. I don't know what though.'

'So, Tori went back to the villa?'

'With Mikey,' she confirms.

'You were with other friends at the club?'

She shakes her head. 'Just me and Chloe. Mikey said he would come back to pick us up.'

Interesting. Mikey was employed to protect *all* of the women and he left two of them alone so he could take Tori home. Now I know she's the kind of woman men fall over themselves to help, like she's a broken doll they must take care of, but that seems unprofessional at best. Mikey left Chloe and Farah in the club on their own. Anything could have happened to them. Maybe something did happen to them. That bastard put this whole job at risk. I'm not going to lie; I'm seriously pissed off at him.

'Are you alright?' Farah asks.

I instantly slam the professional shutters down on my anger and return to my usual resting bitch face. 'I'm fine.' Luckily that's the moment Liam arrives.

'Hey Gracey,' he says, pulling me into a hug and kissing both of my cheeks in a rather familiar way. We've met about three times but he's one of those people who thinks that makes you best friends. Personally, I find him a little cheesy.

But at least he might be amenable to doing me a favour...

'You want to look at the CCTV from last night?' He sounds dubious.

'My client here and her friend blacked out. I want to see if someone put something in their drinks. And I want to see who they left with.'

'That kind of thing doesn't happen at Elysium.' He's

instantly on the defensive, the hard edge of his Liverpudlian accent rising to the surface. No one on this island is actually local, and there are a surprising number of people from the north of England – I guess all trying to escape the dreary weather and shit towns they grew up in.

I narrow my eyes at him. 'Really?' We all know the rumours. I know he's trying to crack down on it, but he's fighting a losing battle.

He sighs and wipes his hand across his face. His skin is grey, almost ashen. He looks knackered.

'When did you last have a day off?' I ask him, tilting my head a little to ensure he takes it as the question of concern I mean it to be.

He looks surprised. 'What's one of those?' It's a quip, but it belies something more serious.

'Is the club in trouble?'

He raises an eyebrow. I'll take that as a yes and hence the fact he's working all hours to try to make it work.

I groan inwardly: I don't want to be a bitch, but I also know I can leverage this to my advantage. 'Look. I don't want to cause trouble. You know that, right?'

He nods, but his eyes look sceptical.

'So,' I continue. 'Just let me look at the CCTV and then we'll know what happened and we can deal with it. *We*,' I motion between the two of us, 'can deal with it.' I hate the underlying threat, the one that tells him if he doesn't cooperate I'll get the police involved, but otherwise perhaps we don't need to bring anyone else into this.

He stares at me for a moment and I start to wonder if I've played this all wrong. 'Fuck you, Grace,' he says but his tone is friendly. And tinged with relief. 'Follow me to the office and I'll set it up for you.'

There's a camera almost directly focussed on the table in the VIP area where Chloe, Tori and Farah were seated last night. I turn to Liam and roll my eyes. Because of course the club has a 'hot girls' table they can watch from the office with impunity.

Liam shrugs.

We watch the recording from the time they arrive at the club. The three girls look like they're having fun. 'What were you drinking?' I ask, turning to Farah.

'Pornstar Martinis. It was Tori's choice. Oh, and something called a Purple Haze.'

There's a period where they disappear, the table left empty. It's efficiently cleared by a guy in a ridiculously tight t-shirt. The girls return, skin flushed pink, they must have been dancing. They have more drinks.

'Is there sound?' I ask Liam. I want to know exactly what they're saying to each other.

'Of course not.' He sounds horrified. 'We don't eavesdrop on our customers.'

I feel his moral high ground is a little slippery given just how good the camera is that's trained on the table. Like high-definition video is fine but a microphone is crossing a line.

I replay the fight between Chloe and Tori, trying to read their lips but I'm no good at it. I could send the tape off for someone to decipher. *Jeez*, I laugh at myself: I've started to imagine myself as James freaking Bond. My company isn't keeping banks of analysts on staff for this kind of thing, although maybe there's an AI that can do it. Is that a thing?

'I want a copy of the video,' I tell Liam. I wait for him to disagree but he's surprisingly amenable.

On screen, Tori flounces off towards the exit, leaving Chloe and Farah on their own. Mikey, who's been standing with his hands clasped in front of him the whole time looking menacing, follows her.

It takes less than five minutes – well, about twenty seconds, because I speed up the video – before two guys swoop in. I hit pause. 'Who are they?' I direct the question to Liam.

But it's Farah who answers. 'They seemed nice. Offered us a drink and came to sit with us.'

'And could they have slipped something in your glass?'

'It's all waiter service,' Liam jumps in. Hackles up once more. 'Look, I'm doing what I can to stop that shit and especially in the VIP area.'

I won't tell you how I feel about the idea that VIPs deserve more protection from predators than everyone else. I think you can imagine it doesn't exactly fill me with the warm and fuzzies.

I watch carefully as the drinks arrive. There doesn't appear to be any interference from the two guys. But perhaps... I lean forward, nose an inch from the screen as I replay a ten-second section a few times. Did one of them slip something into the drinks there? I can't tell, even with the high resolution of the camera.

'And you definitely don't recognise them?' I ask Liam.

'I've seen one of them around. Him,' he points at the taller of the two. 'I guess he must be working over here.'

'Doing what?'

Liam shrugs. 'No idea, but I'll ask around, see if anyone on the staff knows him.'

'Thanks.'

On screen, Mikey returns and basically shoos the guys away like they are flies on his dessert. As he does so, he turns to face the camera, so close to the lens he's captured perfectly. Now I can see details I couldn't pick up from the villa's perimeter system. He's wearing a different t-shirt to before. That one was dark grey with a white logo on the chest, the new one is dark blue and totally plain. *Is that...?* I hit pause.

There's a streak of something on his neck.

Something brown.

It looks like dried blood.

He slides to sit next to Chloe and pulls out a bottle of water from the cross-body bag he's carrying. He hands it to her and waits as she takes a large drink. He takes out another and hands it to Farah, motioning for her to drink it all. Is he being caring, making sure they hydrate before they head home? Or is there something in the water?

33

Farah and I head back to the villa. It turned out the lost tennis bracelet was just a ruse to go back to the club to try to fill in the blanks in her memory. She seems relieved. I guess she saw something different to me on the CCTV: some guys chatting her up and then leaving, replaced with Mikey, who she trusts, taking her home. Even if she was drugged – and to have two women with gaping holes in their memories looks more than a little suspicious – nothing worse happened to her.

But my thoughts are of Mikey. I would have put him down as a sweet guy – he's huge, obviously, he is a security guard, but a softy at heart – except that something isn't sitting right. He'd changed his t-shirt, had what looked very much like dried blood on him, gave the two women something to drink. It could all be innocent. It's certainly circumstantial at best. Tori could have thrown up on him on the way home so he had to change, he could have cut himself shaving, it could genuinely have been water.

It might be nothing. But it's enough to make me want to keep a more careful eye on him.

Back at the villa, I start to get everything ready for the evening. I've organised for the best pizza chef on the island to cook dinner in the brick oven on the terrace.

'Is pizza Greek?' Rob asks as I lay the table.

Is he really that stupid? 'Pizza's Italian.'

'So why are we having pizza?'

'Because your sister requested it. I believe it's your father's favourite.'

He nods. 'And mine.'

I'd asked Chloe if Rob needed a lactose-free cheese for tonight, given his obsession with oat milk. She'd shaken her head. 'He doesn't realise mozzarella is a dairy product,' she told me, with a look that suggested she was trying not to laugh.

I head back inside to get a tray of glasses and some jugs of water. God I'm tired. I wait for a moment to allow my vision to clear before I pick up the tray. The last thing I need right now is to send everything flying and then have to spend the next hour picking up minuscule shards of glass before one of these fools ends up cutting themselves and needing to go to the hospital.

The pizza chef arrives. Giuseppe – not his real name, he's actually Barry from Broadstairs and yet another British implant here in Mykonos – wraps me into a bear hug as he shouts random Italian words like *bellissima* and *favolosa* and *gustosa*. We head out to the terrace so he can set up the oven. Rob, Farah, Chloe and Mrs Cooper are already outside, sipping cocktails as the sun begins to set over the sea.

'Giuseppe is here to solve your pizza cravings,' Barry tells them, really laying the fake accent on thick. I hide my smirk behind my hand. I love Barry, he always lifts the mood and he cleans up after himself. I've tried to get him in at least once a week this summer; and to be honest it isn't hard to convince a guest they want pizza.

The evening starts well. Barry's on form and the younger Coopers and Wilsons seem to be in fairly good spirits. Chloe and Tori are wearing their masks well, no slips yet and I'm watching them closely. I do wonder what shit they've seen in their lives to be so unphased by spending the morning covering up the murder of a close relative – a murder that one of them may have committed. They should be locked in the bathroom crying, or staring into space, or... well, whatever it is a normal person would do in that scenario. But, instead, they're drinking and joking and planning what toppings they are going to have on their pizzas.

'Goat's cheese, red onion and olives for me,' Chloe says.

'Simple margherita for me,' Tori says. 'Ooh, shall we have champagne? Does that go with pizza?' She directs the last bit towards Barry.

'Does champagne go with pizza? *Mamma mia!* Of course it does!'

Mr Cooper comes onto the terrace just as the cork is popped and he visibly starts, almost as if he heard a gun go off. He looks jumpy. 'What are we celebrating?' he asks, but his tone is wary.

'Pizza,' Tori says and sashays towards her father as she pours a flute. She hands it to him and then kisses his cheek. He laughs and takes a sip, but then puts it down.

Fifteen minutes later and Barry declares the oven has reached the required temperature. '*Perfetto*,' he adds. Everyone takes a seat around the table.

'Where's Scott?' Mrs Cooper asks.

'He texted,' Mr Cooper answers. 'He bumped into someone at that diving club and he's having dinner with them.'

He *what*? I watch Chloe intently. She seems entirely unfazed that her actual freaking *dead* husband is apparently sending texts from beyond the grave. Or did she send the message from his phone? That would make sense. Yes, that must be it. Clever girl: maybe there's a chance she can pull this off after all.

'Oh, did he not want you to join him?' Mrs Cooper asks Chloe.

'Oh, no. Boys' time, you know,' Chloe replies. She pitches it perfectly; a tinge of regret she isn't with her husband while also understanding he needs time with his friends.

'Well, you did have girls' night last night,' Mr Cooper chimes in. It's clear from the way he says 'girls' night' that he doesn't really approve. Although I don't think he approves of much. There's a weird power dynamic in his own marriage. Mrs Cooper is very much the brains of their operation, that much is clear as day, but yet he seems to be the face of it. And who said the patriarchy was dead?

My industry is also run by men. But one day I'm going to set up on my own: an organisation run by women. Brilliant women with vision who will find the sisters who need escape routes and are able to pay handsomely for the privilege, especially once their inheritance or life insurance is paid out. It's very easy to unalive wealthy men – they are so prone to an early death: heart attacks for the CEOs; car wrecks for the mid-life crisis-ers with their brand new Maseratis; a plethora of accidents in boats, falling from high balconies and hunting mishaps for the generationally wealthy; drug overdoses for those in medicine or law. And that's before we've touched on the men who run organisations like the Coopers' and the Wilsons'. Those careers are even more rife with danger; it lurks round every corner.

The rest of the evening goes off without a hitch. Or at least that's the way it looks on the surface. Underneath the pizza and the champagne and the family anecdotes being repeated around the table for probably the hundredth time, there's an undercurrent.

Chloe is distracted, her hand shaking a little as she reaches for another portion of salad.

Tori is faking it, acting like she's getting tipsy when I've seen her dump every other drink into the flower pot behind her.

Mikey is hanging around in the background stealing glances at Tori, Chloe and Farah. I can't read his expression.

Mr Cooper keeps looking at the empty seat in which Scott should be sitting.

A frisson is in the air like a storm is about to break. And something is telling me that more than one of us will end up drowned before the sun chases the clouds away.

34

Everyone slopes off to their own rooms by about ten o'clock. It's certainly the most lowkey evening they've all had so far, but to be fair it has been a pretty busy day for some of them.

I take the opportunity to actually take half an hour to myself. I have a proper shower and pop a deep conditioning mask on my hair. The sun and sweat and everything else has made it dry as straw and I'm hoping the mask really is the miracle it claims to be.

Then I sit on the tiny little terrace that leads from the equally tiny little living space in the staff flat. I found a bottle of alcohol-free beer in my fridge and it's ice cold and delicious. I can't drink when we have guests in the villa – I'm technically on call twenty-four hours a day to respond to their every whim – but at least alcohol-free beer is finally drinkable and it'll do the job to make me feel like I'm unwinding at the end of an exceptionally long day.

* * *

A call comes in the middle of the night, waking me up from what was a rather fun dream about Jodie Comer – as Villanelle, obviously. I knock the phone off my bedside table as I grope to answer it.

'Hello?' My voice is thick with sleep.

'I need you to do a pick up from the airport.'

For a second I struggle to place the voice, my mind immediately thinking it's Scott. But, of course, it's Mr Cooper Senior, they just have the same accent. I pull the phone from my ear to glance at the time. Four thirty in the morning. *For fuck's sake.*

'What flight?' I ask.

'They're arriving from Athens. 05:25.'

He doesn't say *please* or *thank you* or *sorry for waking you up* or even *good morning.* I debate telling him to go to hell and tell his chums to get a taxi, but even I'm not that brave. He is still Peter Cooper.

I stand at the Mykonos airport arrivals with my iPad, the names of the men I'm picking up flashing on the screen.

Aubrey Abbott and George Thorne. I have no idea who they are, but they must be important if they're gatecrashing the Cooper-Wilson family holiday slash dick swinging contest. Oh great, more dicks to add to the mix.

I am, however, proved slightly wrong. Aubrey Abbott most definitely will not be whacking a dick out. I always assumed it was a guy's name but *she's* beautiful: tall and glamorous and wearing the most amazingly starched trouser suit in a white pinstripe, a simple black vest top underneath. I'd say she's probably late forties, but she obviously takes incredibly good care of herself, with glossy chestnut shoulder length hair and the most piercing pair of green eyes I've ever seen.

'Aubrey,' she says, reaching out a hand towards me, her eyes on my iPad.

For a moment I'm frozen in place, a little voice in my head telling me to kiss her hand like a gentleman in an old movie. I shake my head. *Get yourself together,* and reach to shake her hand instead like I'm a vaguely functioning human being. 'Grace.'

'I assume my sister sent you?' She doesn't add a 'hmmm?' to the end of the question, but it wouldn't have been out of place if she had.

'Mr Cooper?' I stumble slightly, the words sounding almost garbled in my ears. What is it about this woman?

She looks flatly back at me as if I'm all kinds of stupid. 'Peter is my brother-in-law.'

'Great,' I reply with more enthusiasm than is strictly necessary.

'And I'm George,' the perma-tanned man with the salt and pepper hair who has been hovering in the background says as he steps forwards to kiss me on the cheek. There's an awkward moment when he goes for the second and then a third kiss. Where are we, Paris?

Where Aubrey is tall and slender, George is short and with the kind of shape you can only achieve through a life lived well. Where Aubrey is haughty and slightly terrifying – who am I kidding, not slightly, completely – George has the kind of smile that lights up a room. They are total opposites. Even down to George's black pinstripe suit and white shirt that perfectly reverses Aubrey's ensemble.

I lead them out to the car and load their cases into the boot. Aubrey is silent on the drive to the villa, whereas George chats away about nothing much at all; the meal they had on the flight, how quiet Athens airport was at three o'clock this morning, that I was kind to come and pick them up. He talks the entire trip, not letting me get a word in edgeways, but I realise as I pull up outside the villa that, really, he's said nothing at all. I have no idea why they are here, or why it was obviously such an impromptu trip. It isn't like anyone would actively plan to leave Heathrow in the evening, overnight in Athens airport, and then arrive before the sun has even risen on Mykonos.

It's six thirty when I push open the door to the villa. I try to slip out to head back to my room for a shower and a gallon of caffeine to try to stay awake this morning, but Mr Cooper's presence in the hallway stops me.

He looks tired, his skin grey, the bags under his eyes pronounced. And he's jumpy, nervous energy emanating from him as he stands in front of me. Very unlike the man who was lounging by the pool yesterday morning as if he didn't have a care in the world.

Does he know? Surely not. I mean, how could he possibly know?

'Find Scott,' he demands. 'We have family business to sort out.' OK, so he definitely doesn't know and I allow myself to relax for a moment.

'Of course,' I tell Mr Cooper and manage to extract myself from the situation. God, I need a coffee.

I use the electric briki I treated myself to at the beginning of the season to make a traditional Greek coffee and take it outside onto my terrace. I like my coffee thick and strong and bitter and the briki even adds that almost burnt edge to the flavour. Sinking into the chair, I feel the last of the tension leave my muscles. What a day yesterday was. And a new one is already beginning, I'm going to be a literal zombie by this afternoon.

I'm just sitting there, minding my own business, when I remember I still have one final thing to do.

For fuck's sake. I stomp inside to grab my laptop and take it back to the terrace. At least I can do this out here, the staff flat is still stuffy as hell.

We're currently living in a world where Scott Cooper is dead but no one knows about it. But they *are* going to find out. I mean, it isn't like the sons of notorious families just disappear, right? Well, actually, they might 'disappear' in euphemistic terms fairly often – it's hardly a stable career path – but, what I mean is, people miss them. People realise they've gone and then all hell breaks loose.

Mr Cooper is already asking questions. How long before the family figure out Scott's not just hanging out with his diving buddy?

How long before they suspect something very bad has happened to him?

How long before they start digging for answers?

The plan before – when my life was nice and simple – was a nasty fall down the marble staircase of Chloe and Scott's home. Chloe had mentioned to me that Scott had terrible taste in home decor and he'd insisted their house had this ostentatious hallway with these uncarpeted stairs curving up to the upper floor. She called it a death-trap and it was. It would have been taken as an accident, no need to look for a culprit. But not now. Now they will look and look and will not finish until they find something.

The digital trail between Chloe and my company has been scrubbed clean, leaving behind only the communications between CC1996@hotmail.com and Grace@premiumvillas.com, which is a really rather dull trail of questions about the number of bedrooms and how many people can dine comfortably on the outside terrace and wouldn't it be fun to have a tomahawk steak on the first night. If anyone goes looking for anything untoward, they will not find a link back to a shadowy company who kills for money.

No, they won't find my company.

But that isn't to say they wouldn't find anything at all.

Chloe thinks I'm helping her to get away with murder. It's almost cute, that blind faith she has placed in me. She was so quick to trust me that she never asked herself the important questions. Like, who was I really and what might be in this for me. Girls like Chloe never think anyone could possibly hate them.

DAY FIVE

CHLOE

35

I've obviously not slept in the bedroom. I know Grace and Tori did a pretty impressive job of cleaning everything and the bedsheets were burnt and a new mattress delivered, but even so. Could you sleep in the room where someone died? I know I hated my husband and wanted him dead. Actively *planned* for him to end up dead. But, actually seeing him like that, the finality of it... well, it was a shock. That image will haunt my dreams for the rest of my life. And there's a tiny part of me that keeps expecting him to walk through the door, blood crusting down the front of his t-shirt, the gaping wound at his neck flapping slightly as he takes stilted steps towards me.

So, instead, I'm curled into an uncomfortable ball on one of the recliner chairs on the patio. The air is gently perfumed with the scent of rosemary and it's a damn sight better than the lingering aroma of death inside my room. *Our* room. I need to keep thinking Scott is alive or I run a serious risk of outing the situation through a grammatical slip of the tongue.

I hear a snatch of conversation from by the front door of the villa. Is that...? No, it can't be.

'Darling Peter,' I hear a voice exclaim, the words dripping with disdain.

It is! Aubrey's here. She's Libby's sister and the main brains of the Cooper operation, even though my father-in-law would never admit it. Part of me loves Aubrey: she's the definition of a boss-bitch and it's hard not to be impressed by the way she gives zero fucks about making waves in what has traditionally been a man's world. Part of me is terrified of her: she's ruthless, holds a grudge like you wouldn't believe and ardently insists on doing her own dirty work. There is also a – massive, if I'm honest – part of me that is horrified by her. She's worse than all the men in the Cooper family. And, remember, they're so bad I organised to have one of them killed for what he did.

Hang on. *Why* is Aubrey here? Scott and I invited her on the holiday – obviously, you don't shun Aubrey Abbott – but she was needed back in the UK to keep an eye on things with the Coopers here on holiday. Like a deputy manager covering for her boss. Actually, scratch that, because she *is* the boss. We all know it, even if everyone pretends my father-in-law runs the show. There's a joke I remember from the summer internship where I discovered corporate finance was the career I wanted: behind every successful man is a successful woman doing all the work for no credit. Never has that applied more fully than with the Coopers.

I go into the bedroom and slip on a lightweight robe over my cami and shorts combo and check my reflection in the mirror. I look like shit, like I haven't slept for days and have had too much sun and too much booze. Leaning closer to the glass, I search for signs that I'm a killer, or at least an accessory to murder, my eyes roaming my own face. Do I look like a widow? If I go out there right now, will they all turn on me like a pack of hyenas sensing weakness and tear me to shreds?

No. No. I'm just being overly dramatic.

I take a deep breath and open the door to find out exactly why Aubrey has turned up at the villa before the sun is even fully risen.

Uncle George is here too. He's an old friend of the family and Tori's godfather. He and Aubrey look like they're performing an amateur version of *Bugsy Malone* in their pinstripe suits, not that I would ever say that to their faces, of course.

'There she is,' George exclaims as he spots me. 'There's the beautiful girl my favourite boy married.' He pulls me into a hug and kisses my cheeks three times.

'Hi Uncle George,' I say quietly. He's always been 'Uncle', since the very first time I met him. Not in any kind of creepy way, more of a testament to his ability to instantly turn a stranger into family. Aubrey on the other hand – who *is* technically one of my relatives as she's Scott's aunt – has never been 'Aunt Aubrey'. Or, heaven forbid, '*Auntie* Aubrey'. I think she'd kill anyone who dared to have the audacity to call her that.

'And where is my favourite boy?' George asks, looking behind me as if all six foot three of my husband could be hiding in my shadow.

'Out,' I reply, trying to keep my tone nonchalant.

'Out?' Aubrey takes a few steps towards me. She looks like she's swallowed a bee. For a moment I feel sorry for the bee, even if it is entirely imaginary.

'He met a friend at some diving club. Had dinner and then too many drinks, so stayed overnight.' I roll my eyes. *You know what he's like.*

'That doesn't sound like Scott.' Aubrey narrows her eyes.

I guess the eyeroll wasn't convincing enough. But she isn't wrong. Scott does tend towards the boring and serious and very rarely lets his hair down. You cannot believe how difficult it was to even get him to agree to this holiday in the first place. And, so, I do something I'm not sure I'm one hundred percent proud of. But needs must and sullying my husband's memory is hardly important, especially after everything he did when he was alive.

'I think...' I allow myself to trail off and shift uncomfortably from foot to foot. 'I don't want to... you know...' I look away, as if this is the most painful thing I've ever had to admit.

'He's with someone?' Aubrey asks.

I nod.

'Well, I guess the apple doesn't fall far from the tree.' She looks Mr Cooper directly in the eye as she says it. My father-in-law's infidelity is hardly a secret.

'I'll talk to him,' Uncle George declares as if that would make everything better. He even goes so far as to pat me on the arm. 'Now then. How about we make some coffee, eh?'

'We have work to do, George.' Aubrey has always been the one who cracks the whip.

'Yes. But I am fifty-seven years old and only slept for two hours. And that was in an airport lounge.' He leans closer to me to whisper in my ear. 'And the lounge was very much not up to par.' Uncle George has always liked the finer things in life. Nice clothes and rich food and fancy wine and surrounding himself with gorgeous people. He orchestrated Tori's modelling career, but I don't think his motives were altruistic, I think he just wanted to be surrounded with youth and beauty and all the best couture.

Aubrey doesn't conceal her scowl as we head towards the kitchen to make coffee. Uncle George turns to me and winks then mimics her stride, nose up in the air in a parody of his business partner. The pair of them are like an old married couple who can't help but take – mostly but not exclusively gentle – digs at each other constantly.

I remember asking him once if there was a history between them. It had taken him a moment to realise what it was I was implying and then he burst into a fit of laughter.

'With that old hag?' His tone had been soft, almost playful, just enough that he could always claim it was a joke.

We're sitting at the breakfast bar, drinking that thick dark sludge the locals call coffee when Tori comes padding into the kitchen.

'Uncle George,' she says, mouth hanging open in surprise. 'What are you doing here?'

'Is that any way to greet your favourite godfather?' He says, jumping off his stool to wrap her into a bear hug.

'Sorry... I'm just kind of surprised to see you. Why are you here?'

'Business,' Aubrey replies.

Concern flashes across Tori's face and her gaze flicks to me. I will her to put on a poker face, now is certainly not the time or place for suspicion around my darling dead husband.

'Oh,' she says, regaining her composure. 'Cool.' She reaches for a cup and presses the buttons on the coffee machine to make a latte.

Aubrey and Uncle George exchange a look.

It is obviously not cool.

Something has happened.

They can't be here about Scott. But it is blindingly obvious they're here for something serious. And serious is always bad.

36

The whole atmosphere shifts as my father-in-law appears at the kitchen door. Business talk is about to begin and so I prepare to make myself scarce.

'Where are you going?' Mr Cooper demands.

I turn slowly, not sure who he's talking to. But his eyes are trained on me.

'Umm... I was going to...' I point in the general direction of my room.

'Sit.'

I comply immediately.

'Tori, make fresh coffee.' He accompanies the command with a flick of the wrist. I can't see her face but I know this will have Tori fuming. She hates it when he treats her like a member of his staff.

'Yes, Daddy.' She sounds like a sullen teenager and I watch as the muscle at the corner of his eye twitches.

He's about to start talking when the door opens and in walks Grace laden with boxes from the local bakery. 'Breakfast,' she announces with a sing-song voice. She places them on the sideboard and then starts to clatter around the space tidying up cups and wiping coffee granules from the work surface.

Mr Cooper stares at her but she doesn't notice.

'Fuck's sake,' I hear him whisper under his breath. 'Let's go out to the terrace.'

We all file out and take up seats around the large table. Although we had established preferred seats earlier this week, the whole seating plan is changed by the arrival of Aubrey and Uncle George: it now becomes a strict hierarchy of who sits where depending on their importance to the Cooper operation. Or at least Mr Cooper's perceived importance; he still thinks he's the lynchpin even though all the evidence points to the contrary.

Tori brings out the boxes of bougatsas and puts them down in front of her father. He looks at them and then up at his daughter, an expectant look on his face.

'Bougatsa, Daddy. Those custard pastries you like.'

His expression doesn't change and he pauses for a moment. 'Coffee, Tori,' he says and actually snaps his fingers at her.

'Be a good girl, Tori,' Uncle George adds. 'You know I can't function without a caffeine hit.'

No one says anything more until we have coffees in front of us and fingers coated in pastry crumbs. Then Mr Cooper taps his cup with his spoon, like the father of the bride at a wedding preparing to make a speech.

Slight aside, he did actually give a speech at my wedding, standing up before the last table had finished eating to get in before my dad. Just in case you'd forgotten about how much of a dick my father-in-law can actually be. Dad was fucking livid, I could see the whites of his knuckles as he clenched the napkin beside him, but managed to keep a lid on his anger. He did smatter his own toast – once Mr Cooper finally relinquished the spotlight – with some passive-aggressive digs. He literally opened with, 'It is such an honour to be the first to raise a toast to the beautiful bride, a gift bestowed on me as her father, as tradition would dictate. And we all understand the importance of tradition when it comes to marriage.'

Anyway, back to the here and now. 'We have a problem,' Mr Cooper says, voice almost gruff with the gravity he's trying to inject into the sentence. He's always had a bit of a flair for the dramatic, but he does sometimes go a little too far with the theatrics. He makes eye contact with each of us around the table in turn. 'A *family* problem.'

His gaze comes to rest on me and I squirm under the intensity of the look. *He knows about Scott.* Somehow he knows what happened and that I've hidden the body to avoid becoming the main suspect even though I genuinely don't think I was the one who killed my husband. Why else would Mr Cooper be staring at me like that?

'You'll notice someone is missing from the table this morning.' He looks pointedly at the empty chair next to me.

I try to paint innocence onto my face but then catch sight of myself in the mirror behind the table. I look constipated. And guilty. It is not an attractive mix.

'That's why I wanted you to stay, Chloe,' he continues. 'Scott has decided that meeting a "friend" is more important than family.' He actually does the air quotes around the word. I can only assume George has told him about my suspicion he's with another woman. My cheeks flame red as if in shame, a gnawing sensation in the pit of my stomach. I know Scott's dead and not cheating, but the fact that his family are so quick to believe the lie makes me oddly angry. Like they're just accepting this fake version of my husband without even batting an eyelid. Was he cheating on me? Cheating on me and everyone else already knew so none of them are surprised now? Bastard.

Mr Cooper continues to talk. 'But with Scott AWOL, you're the representative of his part of the family business.' He smiles at me and I'm surprised at the genuine warmth I see there.

'Daddy, just tell us what's happening,' Tori pipes up.

'Aubrey and George flew out overnight to bring news from home. Yesterday morning, they awoke to discover there'd been a coordinated attack on our operation.' He says each word slowly, carefully. 'A little after midnight, a number of things occurred simultaneously. Two of our most profitable stash houses were raided, the farm on Cumbers Lane was set on fire and one of our distributors was shot.'

'Who?' I ask.

'We don't know who's behind it.'

'No, I mean which distributor.'

'Charlie.'

'Shit,' I whisper. He was a good guy. Or, well, as good as a dealer can be. I think his girlfriend had just had a baby. 'Will we make sure his family is—'

'He wasn't badly hurt,' Aubrey interrupts my question. 'Anyway, the attack was coordinated and well planned. It's obvious whoever is behind it is making a play against us.'

My phone vibrates in my pocket and I pull it out to look at the message.

'Is that my errant son?' Mr Cooper asks.

'Er, no,' I reply. It's Tori sending me a message that is nothing more than a string of question marks. I tuck the phone under the table without replying.

Aubrey stands up and clears her throat. 'There's a lot to discuss. Plans to be made. But, first, I think we need something stronger than coffee.' She stares at Tori.

'Oh right. Yes, of course,' Tori mumbles as she rises from her seat. 'Whisky?'

Aubrey nods.

'Chloe, come help me,' Tori says as she starts to walk towards the villa.

I catch up with her in the kitchen.

'Jesus. Fuck. Do you think...?' her words are so fast they run together, before the sentence peters out to nothing.

'Think what?' Judging by the way her eyes are flashing and a sheen of sweat is creeping across her forehead, her manic brain could be coming up with all manner of random scenarios.

'Scott?' She says it like I'm thick.

'What about him?' I hiss back, taking her arm to pull her further into the house in case our voices manage somehow to carry out onto the terrace.

'You say you didn't kill him,' she says.

'Of course I didn't fucking kill him.'

'And neither did I.' She stares at me. 'Seriously? Nothing?'

'I have no idea what you're talking about.' But I am starting to get annoyed by her obliqueness.

'If you didn't kill him. And I didn't kill him. And, back at home, on the same night, there are raids and fires and that dude was shot...'

'Charlie,' I remind her.

'Whatever.' She flaps her hand in a way that is overly dismissive for the attempted murder of a young man she has definitely met more than once. 'Back home all this shit is going down, like someone is trying to take out the whole operation.

And then here we find the fucking heir to the throne with his throat cu—'

'Jesus! Tori. Keep your voice down.'

'Sorry,' she whispers this time. 'But what if the murder was part of the attack?'

Oh fuck.

37

I think I might have really fucked up this time. Like extremely badly fucked up. Irrevocably fucked up.

What if I covered up my husband getting murdered in his bed by a rival on a mission to destroy the entire Cooper empire?

I just need a moment to think, to play this scenario through.

At some point there is going to come more news from England, some set of demands from whoever is behind these attacks. And, when it comes, they're going to reference the loss of the Cooper heir. Of course they are.

And then what will happen? Will the Coopers just think it's a lie: a way of the attacker making their threats sound even more serious? Or will they start to wonder why there isn't a body?

And then? If they find out I've covered it all up, I know exactly what they are going to think. They will think it was me. Not just that I killed Scott, but that I was part of the attack.

Shit, shit, shit. This just got a hundred times more complicated.

What do you think the Coopers would do to a traitor in their midst?

'Earth to Chloe?' Tori says, still hovering in front of me.

I snap my attention back to her and try to damp down the panic at the thought of Cooper retribution. 'Sorry, I must have zoned out for a moment,' I reply. 'You don't really think...?' I grimace. I need to know if she thinks this is actually what might have happened, to assess the magnitude of the potential risk.

'It's kind of the only logical explanation.'

But there's something off in her tone. Yes, it might be a logical explanation, but could it also be a coincidence? A very convenient coincidence and a way of shifting the blame from where it truly lies?

A picture pops into my head. Mikey: a man who has worked with my husband for years. Mikey: who was out with us the night before last. Mikey: who took Tori back to the villa and then – accordingly to Grace at least – returned to the club with blood on his shirt.

'We need to keep very quiet,' I tell her. 'No one can know what happened.'

'Durrr,' she replies.

'I'm being serious.'

'So am I. What? You really think I'm going to go and tell Daddy that I helped clean up his darling son's murder scene?'

'Seriously, Tori. For fuck's sake. You have to keep your voice down.' I don't even try to hide how frustrated she's making me with her inability to use her inside voice.

'We're on the same team here, Chloe.'

'I know.' And, right now, I really, really wish we weren't. I wish she was absolutely nothing to do with this. Can I trust her? Or will she blabber everything to her father and Uncle George?

'I thought you were getting whisky?' Speak of the devil: Uncle George is standing at the door to the kitchen.

'We're on it,' Tori replies, taking a few steps to the drinks cupboard and pulling out a bottle of Lagavulin.

I busy myself by filling up a tray with crystal tumblers.

'Allow me,' Uncle George says, taking the laden tray from my hands.

I follow him silently out towards the terrace. I feel like I'm walking to the gallows.

Measures of Lagavulin poured, Mr Cooper stands to raise a toast. 'To family,' he says soberly. I feel like we're toasting a lost comrade and my heart hammers in my chest. He reaches his glass towards me, eyes locking onto mine. 'Cheers.'

He knows. Somehow I manage to hold on to the contents of my stomach, gently touching my tumbler to his. 'Cheers.' My voice is high and thin in my ears.

The moment with Mr Cooper is broken by the appearance of my parents, ready for breakfast. 'Bit early for hard liquor, isn't it?' Dad says.

'We're having a family meeting,' Mr Cooper replies, a harsh edge to his tone that says *this is a private matter*.

'Aren't we family?' Dad says with a grin.

Mr Cooper wants nothing more than to be considered family by my father. But I know he will also do anything to keep what is happening back home from Luke Wilson. Nothing says weakness like losing control of your organisation while you're on holiday.

'Of course we are,' Mr Cooper replies. 'Tori, go and get Luke and Erin glasses so they can join us in our toast.'

'And Aubrey and George are here, what a delight,' Dad says, beaming at them both. 'I thought you weren't able to join us?' There's a layered question there. Dad clearly knows something is going on and he's fishing for information.

'Well, everyone needs a holiday,' Mr Cooper says, flapping a hand as if to say it's all nothing.

'Of course they do.' Dad is magnanimous. 'You must have a lot of trust in your teams to take that holiday together though.'

'Do you not?' Mr Cooper replies.

My father doesn't answer, too busy taking a glass from Tori, who has returned from her errand. He pours himself a large measure and then raises the glass to his lips as he studies Mr Cooper. 'Personally, I'd only expect my deputies to join me on holiday if something had gone badly wrong at home.' He sips his whisky, head tilted slightly. I know this look well from my own teenage years: he's waiting to be told what is really going on and he won't give up until he has all the facts.

Mr Cooper laughs, but there's no humour there. 'Everything is fine at home,' he says. 'What a strange thing for you to say.' He smiles at my father.

'So, Aubrey and George are simply here for some sun? How wonderful.'

Mr Cooper tenses, I think he's starting to realise my father is not going to let the lies slide. 'Well... I suppose we are family.' He looks at me for a second and then directs his attention back to my father. 'There has been a small incident back home.'

'What kind of incident?' my father asks carefully.

'A raid and an attempt to hurt one of my men.'

My father nods slowly as if he's mulling this over. 'Who?'

'Now that's the interesting part. No one has stepped forward to claim responsibility.' Mr Cooper takes a step towards my father. 'I don't suppose you know anything about this?'

Mum makes an odd noise, which she covers with a cough. Melodramatic as always.

'Are you implying I have something to do with this?' Dad asks.

'Well, do you?'

'How dare you?' Dad says, voice an octave lower than normal, the words spat in a pure rage at the inference.

Silence descends over the table, cloaking us with the residual awkwardness of the scene.

Eventually Uncle George breaks the atmosphere. 'Right then.' He stands up. 'Chloe and I are going to the diving club.'

What? No we are not. 'Err...' is all that comes out of my mouth.

'Come on. We need to find that husband of yours and bring him back.'

'Bu—'

'No buts.' George cuts me off. 'He's had his fun and now the holiday is over.'

'Bu—'

'What did I say about no buts? You know this friend he met and so I need you to help track him down.'

38

I message Grace to see if she can organise a car for us.

She doesn't reply immediately, but I see her striding across the terrace towards me. 'You need a ride?'

'To the diving club,' I tell her, cutting in quickly before anyone else can say anything. I need to make sure she doesn't let anything slip. 'Scott stayed over in their hotel last night but we need to bring him home.'

'Shall I order a taxi for him instead?'

'We can't get hold of him, he's not answering his phone.'

'Oh. Well, that's difficult. Let me get a car to come here for you.'

The diving club is nestled in a gorgeous cove on the west side of the island. There's an almost colonial style boutique hotel attached to it for the use of the extremely wealthy clientele who dive there.

The sun beats down on the landscape as the car whizzes down the winding road along the coast, but the interior is cool, almost cold, and I find myself wishing I'd bought a sweater with me.

'Are you OK?' Uncle George asks softly.

I nod as I wrap my arms more tightly around myself. 'Just a bit chilly.'

He narrows his eyes at me. 'Is that all? Or is there something more? You know I'm always here if you need someone to talk to.'

Over the years, Uncle George has proven to be a fantastic shoulder to cry on. He's one of the best listeners I've ever met. Unfortunately, he's also a massive gossip who cannot keep a secret and so it isn't like I can share anything serious with him. Like how I wanted my husband dead and now he is but no one knows and perhaps I did kill him or perhaps I covered up someone else's murder scene and it is all a total mess.

'I'm fine. I just...' I shrug. The best thing I can do is make him think I'm upset that Scott may well be cheating on me. 'What if we find him... with *her*?'

'Oh sweetheart.' The pity in his tone makes tears spring to my eyes, even though I know that this is definitely not a scenario we're going to find. Uncle George offers nothing more, no practical advice, no promise that we'll kick Scott in the balls and then find me a really good divorce lawyer. The inference is clear as day: if we find him with another woman, I will have to accept it and move on. That is the Cooper way after all: my mother-in-law has turned a blind eye too many times to count.

The driver parks alongside a plethora of fancy sports cars and we head towards the reception area of the hotel. There's a concierge desk inside.

'We're looking for a friend,' Uncle George says as we approach.

'Are they a guest?'

'Yes. Scott Cooper. Which room is he in please?'

'Oh. Sorry sir. But we can't give out that kind of information.'

'But you can call his room and tell him he has a visitor.' He doesn't ask it like a question, more like an entirely reasonable demand. Uncle George has always been very good at getting people to do what he wants them to.

The concierge nods and turns to their screen. 'Scott Cooper?' They flick their eyes back to Uncle George for confirmation.

He nods.

'Right. Well...' Their brow furrows and they stick out a tiny tip of tongue as they search the screen. 'Unfortunately, we don't have a guest by that name.'

'Check again.'

The concierge takes an almost imperceptible step backwards at his tone. Uncle George is a pussy cat until he's pissed and then he turns into a tiger who will rip your throat right out. There's silence except for the clacking of acrylic nails on the keyboard. 'I'm sorry, sir. No one by that name has checked into the Paradise Cove.'

Uncle George turns to look at me as if he expects me to have a bright idea. 'He told me he met an old friend, perhaps he's staying in their room,' I say.

'Do you know the name of the friend?' the concierge asks me.

'No. Sorry.'

'We think it might have been a woman,' Uncle George adds, raising his eyebrows.

'Right?' The concierge looks confused, evidently not following his line of thinking.

'So perhaps you could look for single women?' Uncle George says it like he thinks it's an entirely reasonable request.

'Sorry, sir. Did you want me to look up all the single women staying at the hotel and ask them if they're entertaining your friend?'

'There can't be that many single women booked into this small resort.'

'Unfortunately, I can't do that, sir.'

'Well, what do you suggest then?' Uncle George fires back. I put my hand on his arm. He needs to stay calm. The poor concierge is only trying to help, but they can hardly just call a load of guests like a lottery system. He softens under my touch. 'Sorry, forgive me. It's just we really need to find him.'

'Is it an emergency?'

'Yes.'

'Right. Well, how about we find you a table in the restaurant and then we'll see if we can locate Mr Cooper.'

'Perfect. Thank you.' He offers them a beaming smile. It is returned with something a little more akin to a grimace.

It's busy, but the concierge finds us a table on the other side of the room to the patio windows with their billowing voile curtains. George's nose curls a little when he realises how close we've been seated to the toilets. He isn't used to being treated as anything other than royalty, but here his reputation doesn't proceed him, and Mykonos is already so full of new money his fancy Rolex and Cartier man bag slung across his chest don't make him look extraordinarily wealthy like they do in Bromley.

At least the table gives us a wide view of the other patrons and we both silently scan the space for Scott. Well, Uncle George scans the space for Scott. I just pretend, while I feel the noose tightening around my neck. This whole situation is such a mess and something is going to go horribly wrong.

'He isn't here,' George says. He turns his attention to the menu in front of him.

'No,' I reply and pick mine up too, although I don't think I can eat.

'Well, not right at this moment anyway.' George smiles at one of the waiting staff in their starched black and white uniform and they hurry over.

'Can I help you, sir?'

'We're looking for someone. He was staying here last night.'

The waiter looks around. 'Ummm...'

'He's not here now. But I wanted to confirm he did stay here.'

'The front desk can help you.' The waiter turns to leave.

'He would have been drinking in the bar. You'd remember him.'

The waiter turns back round. 'What does he look like?' He sounds resigned, like this is definitely happening and he's powerless to stop it.

Uncle George looks at me to do the honours. I hate describing people, I'd be absolutely useless in a police line-up situation. 'Umm...' I stammer slightly. 'He's six foot three, well built, dark brown hair, attractive. Early thirties.'

The waiter looks unimpressed. 'Anything a little more specific?' He motions to a couple of the other tables around us, where men of very similar descriptions are sitting.

'He has a tattoo on his upper arm. A Celtic band.'

There isn't an eye roll from the waiter at the cliched choice my husband made, but I think that's only because he's a professional. 'Anything else?'

Uncle George cuts in. 'He would have been drinking an Old Fashioned with a dash of lemonade instead of soda.'

'Oh. You should have led with that. I'll ask the bartenders.'

He comes back a few minutes later. 'Sorry, but no one has served an Old Fashioned with lemonade in the last few days.'

George looks at me and his gaze burns straight through me. He turns his attention back to the waiter. 'Well, thank you anyway.'

'You're welcome. Are you ready to order?' He motions at the menus. I'm still holding mine like it's a talisman keeping me safe.

'Oh. Not yet. Give us five?'

I watch the waiter leave but I can tell that George is staring at me again.

'Where is he really, sweetheart?' he asks me, his voice soft like I'm a scared child who he's trying not to spook.

'He told me he was here.' I try to sound upset, close to tears. And not at all like I'm lying through my teeth.

'Let's have a drink and then we can talk some more, OK?'

I don't think I have a choice here.

39

Ten minutes later and I've already necked an entire large glass of crisp sauvignon blanc, the wine warming my limbs against the fierce air conditioning – or perhaps it's the chill of terror pressing cold fingers against my skin – when the concierge approaches the table.

'Sir,' they address Uncle George.

'Have you found something?'

'I can't tell you the guest's name. You know, because of confidentiality. But I had a chat with one of the housekeepers and we do have a single female guest whose room looked like she may have been entertaining a friend yesterday.' They pause.

'Go on,' Uncle George coaxes.

'They'd ordered room service, so I checked with the team and they definitely delivered enough food and drinks for two people to the suite. Now, I don't know for sure that it was Mr Cooper, but the waiter did think he overheard her talking to a man. And that she called him after a character from *Star Trek*. The waiter's a big fan apparently.' They add the last bit quickly.

'*Star Trek*?'

'Beam me up, Scotty.'

'Oh. Right.' Uncle George nods a few times. 'Do you know what they ordered for room service?'

'Was it a club sandwich?' I ask quickly.

The concierge looks at me for a moment. 'Yes.'

'Without tomato?'

'Yes.'

'And fries with a load of mayonnaise on the side?'

'Yes.'

I turn to Uncle George. 'That has to be Scott. It doesn't matter where we are in the world; that's all he ever has if he's ordering hotel room service.'

'He always was a basic bitch,' George mutters. 'Well, I guess that solves it.' His demeanour changes and suddenly he's bright and almost chirpy. 'Can you please pass on a message to him?' he asks the concierge.

'It would be my pleasure, sir.'

'Tell him that he's a dickhead, and if he doesn't get his arse to the villa ASAP, I will come back and personally drag him home by his balls.'

The concierge physically blanches.

'Got it?' He shifts back to friendly Uncle George.

'Got it,' they repeat and half scurry away to get back to the safety of the concierge desk.

What the hell just happened?

'Right then, sweetheart,' Uncle George says to me. 'Let's have one more swift drink with our lunch platter to see if Scott makes a quick appearance and then we'll head back to the villa and wait for him there.'

I nod dumbly, my mind too full of questions to string a coherent sentence together.

Why is the concierge lying?

Who are they lying for?

After lunch, Uncle George goes outside to wait for the driver to bring the car round and have a cigarette. He's been trying to give up recently, but can't help himself from having one after meals.

'I'll come find you in a moment. Just popping to the ladies,' I tell him.

But, as soon as he's out of the door I approach the concierge desk instead.

The concierge smiles at me, seeming entirely professional. 'Can I help you with anything else, Madam?'

'Umm...' I have no idea how to ask them why they lied. Or who asked them to.

They lean forward slightly and lower their voice. 'You're staying at Villa Bougainvillea, right?'

I nod.

'Grace is a friend of mine.'

'Oh. Cool.' Well, I guess that answers the question. Well done, Grace. She really does seem to know everyone here on the island. It must be nice to be able to call in that many favours. For a second, I'm jealous that she has so many people to fall back on, but then I remember we're both on the same team. Her resources are my resources and I'm going to need all of them if I'm going to make it out of this mess.

Back at the villa, I make the excuse of a headache and head towards my room. It's not exactly a lie, my head is pounding; a mix of stress, heat and two large glasses of wine.

I need a nap, but I'm still not happy to be inside the room where it all happened. Despite the fierce temperature, I head out onto the terrace. I'm surprised to find it almost cool, the foliage providing plenty of protection from the sun and a handful of hidden mist machines sending occasional bursts of refreshing water into the air.

I sink into one of the recliners, sitting forward, face in my hands. I'm exhausted, like I've run a marathon and then stayed out clubbing all night afterwards. Keeping up the façade of normality is taking its toll on me.

'Are you alright, baby?' Mum is sitting outside the patio door to her and Dad's room.

I didn't even notice her there and I sit up straight, cheeks flushing that she saw me like that. 'I'm fine,' I say quickly.

'Did you find Scott?'

'No. Yes. Well, kind of.' It isn't technically a lie.

'And?'

'He's staying at the diving club's hotel with a woman.' This, however, *is* a lie. 'But we only found out via the concierge, we didn't actually see him.'

She pauses for a few moments. 'I'm really sorry,' she says eventually, choosing her words carefully. I wish I could throw myself into her arms and sob uncontrollably, have her stroke my hair and tell me everything is going to be alright. But we haven't had that kind of relationship for years.

'Have you heard from him directly?' she asks.

'No.'

'He hasn't messaged?'

'No.'

'Is that unusual?' she asks. 'To go so long without hearing from him, I mean?'

'Kind of. He's always been rubbish at keeping in touch, but normally he'd message at some point.'

'But you've messaged him?' She looks at me pointedly.

'Ummm...' I haven't messaged him. Should I have done? Does it look weird that I haven't?

'Maybe you should.'

'Yeah.' She's right. I should. If only for appearances' sake. I take out my phone and fire off a message.

> Scott, just call me, please. I'm getting worried.
> Love you xx

Then I lean back and allow my eyes to close. I try to ignore the sound of Mum rustling around in the bag beside her lounger, no doubt trying to find a tissue amongst the detritus she always insists on carrying around with her. Eventually sleep takes me.

I'm woken by the ping of my phone as I receive a Whats-App. What the fuck?

It's from Scott. Instantly I whip my head to look around me, searching for the threat. But there's no one here but Mum, and she's absorbed in a magazine about posh country houses. I open the message.

> Don't worry I'm fine Love you to S x

'Everything OK?' Mum calls over to me.

I force myself to smile. 'All good, just a message from Scott.' I wave my phone in her direction.

'And?'

'He says not to worry about him.'

Mum makes a harrumphing noise and then returns to her magazine. Learning how to create a chateau style drawing room must be riveting.

I stare at the message. Who sent it? It *sounds* like Scott, the way there's no punctuation and he doesn't know it should be 'too' at the end not 'to'. Actually, he does know, he just doesn't care that he's wrong. But he never signs off as 'S', he's weirdly superstitious about using his own name or initial and will just sign off with a double kiss.

My memory snags on something. Another message sent this week. One that confused me at first because I didn't recognise their new number and they'd just signed off as 'M'. Mikey. I scroll until I find the message. I'd received it the night before we came to Mykonos.

> Just checking timings for tomorrow morning
> don't want to get to the airport to early. M

Questions crowd my mind as I close my eyes and try to fall back to sleep. Did Mikey send the message? Did he kill Scott? Or is he covering for Tori? Why does none of this make any sense?

* * *

I don't want to but I force myself to join the others on the terrace for dinner. No one mentions the empty chair next to me and, in fact, when I excuse myself to go to the bathroom I return to find someone has moved it to one side.

I find myself starting to relax. There is so much tension in the air but none of it is being directed towards me and I allow myself to imagine my secrets really are safe. At least for now. I sip another glass of wine and allow my mind to wander.

But my gaze snags on Mikey standing vigil at the edge of the terrace. Did he send me the message from Scott's phone? Could he really have something to do with all of this? He doesn't look guilty, but then again what exactly does guilty look like?

Grace gives me a wink as she serves baklava cheesecake for dessert. I must remember to go and thank her later for what she did at the diving club. Silence falls as everyone devours the layers of crispy filo pastry, vanilla cheesecake filling and nuts all doused in honey. I'm about to excuse myself and head to bed when Mr Cooper puts down his glass and looks around the table, puzzlement colouring his features.

'One question,' he says, raising his voice to command the attention of the entire table. 'Where the pissing hell is Jack?'

I glance towards Tori. My father-in-law has just raised an excellent question. Because I don't remember seeing Jack since he convinced me to take Tori clubbing.

Jack who was never exactly coy about his disdain for the Coopers, despite the fact they fund a great deal of his extravagant lifestyle via Tori. He wasn't that successful as a model, but Mr Cooper and Uncle George wanted someone to keep an eye on their daughter and he was sufficiently easy to bribe.

Did someone else get to him? Convince him there was something in it for him if he filled in some information about the Coopers and then help him run before he could get caught?

I can believe Jack was a spy and a dirty little snitch. But could he be a murderer too?

DAY SIX

TORI

40

First off, let me be absolutely clear when I say that I did not kill my brother. I had nothing to do with however he ended up dead in that room. Besides, isn't it obvious? It was Chloe. Little miss high and mighty with all her plans and tricks, but then, when it came to it, she just couldn't help herself. I will cover for her, though, I don't exactly have much of a choice. For now, at least.

Now, onto the whole Jack thing. So, full disclosure. Jack and I might have had a teensy little argument that night I went clubbing with Chloe and Farah. It was stupid, a misunderstanding that got way out of control because Jack is a fucking drama queen who thrives on making himself a victim in any situation.

I've had enough of his bullshit if we're being really honest. Always talking shit about everyone we meet, even those people he claims to actually like. I know a lot of people think I'm a bitch, but he is really something else. The little digs and snide comments and constant back-handed compliments.

Look, we work in an industry that's absolutely obsessed

with looks and I know it can seriously mess with your head. I mean, it isn't like I'm exactly normal, is it? But his insecurities bring out the very worst in him.

And the jealousy.

Jesus Christ, the jealousy.

Always so paranoid that I'll cheat on him with someone better, someone hotter, someone with a lower body fat percentage. It's exhausting.

It was only a drunken little kiss with Mikey that night we went to Elysium and he drove me home early. It almost didn't even classify as making out. I was drunk and angry – at Scott mainly, but that anger bubbled over to men in general – and there was Mikey looking all strong and capable and, you know, sometimes a distraction is exactly what you need.

But, of course, Jack came in to the bedroom and found us. He got very upset about it. Started ranting and raving about how I'd never loved him and I'd been leading him on all this time. Well, yes, I didn't think he was 'the one', it wasn't like we were going to get married and buy a house in the suburbs and raise some kids. Even though our kids would be stunning. I knew he was more into the idea of 'us' than I was. But aren't all relationships out of balance? There's always one person who is more into the other and that's OK. That's normal.

Jack got a bit threatening and it was kind of hot – I'm not going to lie – but then he overstepped a little and Mikey put him in his place. Just a tap to the face with his fist – I can't even call it a punch. But Jack decided to go all in and grabbed my dinky knife from on top of the chest of drawers and started waving it about. He had no idea how to use the knife but it's sharp and eventually it found its mark, nicking through Mikey's t-shirt to the skin underneath.

Mikey took the knife off him after that, with a karate chop

to the wrist. And then Mikey picked him up in what looked kind of like a fireman's lift and carried him out of the house. 'Grab his stuff. Just the important things though,' Mikey growled at me as he passed.

I was kind of into this version of Mikey, all husky and brave and a little bit bloodied in the defence of my honour. It was a bit like all my teenage fantasies coming to life in front of me. So, I threw Jack's wallet, passport, tech case and some clothes into a bag and followed Mikey out of the villa.

'I suggest you fuck off for a bit and think about the scene you just caused in there,' Mikey was saying as I caught up with them.

I handed Jack the bag. 'I need to think about things. Don't come back to the villa. I'll call you when I'm back in the UK.'

He cried. Right there in the street with his bag in one hand. Huge fat ugly tears. But I wasn't going to be swayed. I've had enough.

No one noticed Jack was gone. Or at least no one noticed until last night. Which... I don't know. Felt a bit harsh. I knew my family weren't exactly in love with him, but he has been part of our lives for a while now. I'm almost offended on his behalf.

But now my father has noticed and he is acting super weird about it. Take what happened last night. It's almost as if Daddy suspects Jack had something to do with this whole attack thing. Which is just ridiculous, he's totally delusional if he thinks Jack would be capable of something that sophisticated. It isn't like I was dating him for his brain, was it?

Anyway, enough about Jack. He's gone and I think it's properly over between us. It's probably the right thing, we weren't really good for each other. But it does mean that I'm going to be single again, so I'd best make sure I'm in fighting shape to hit the dating market when we get home. Which is why it's only six in the morning but I'm already up and about to head to the gym.

I push open the door and find Aubrey has beaten me to it. She's doing some kind of high intensity kettlebell workout, grunting and sweating in the corner. Props to her though, she is in amazing shape for someone in their late forties. Actually, she might be even older than that, I probably should know how old my aunt is, but she's hardly forthcoming with that kind of intel.

She doesn't even look up as I enter, so she must have headphones in. I decide to leave her to it and instead set myself up in the opposite corner, unrolling my Lululemon yoga mat and then sitting down to slip on my grippy socks. I know they're dumb and no one else bothers with them, but I nearly broke my neck last week transitioning from a wheel into a bridge and so I'm not taking any risks today.

Five minutes later and I'm in a deep stretch, loving the sensation of my muscles lengthening, when Aubrey comes over and stands directly in front of me.

'Where is your brother?' There is no good morning or anything, just straight down to business.

'Umm... At that fancy dive club with some random girl?'

'Hmm.' She purses her lips. 'You don't sound sure.'

'Well...' I struggle to think back to exactly what Chloe said yesterday. I need to keep the story straight and not think about the fact that he's dead.

'And your boyfriend?'

'Ex-boyfriend,' I say. 'I think it's over between us.' I say the last bit quietly, wondering if she'll offer me anything in the way of sympathy.

'Hmmm. And where is he now?'

Well, I guess I'm not getting that sympathy. Not that I

should have expected it. 'I don't know. I don't actually think I care.'

'I care,' Aubrey says. There's an edge there, she isn't implying she cares in any positive way.

'Why?'

Aubrey shrugs, but it looks orchestrated, like she's playing a part and I don't quite understand the script we're performing.

'I don't think I get it,' I say, if only to fill the silence.

'Look, Tori. There's a lot going on at the moment, lots of conjecture about who is really pulling the strings behind the scenes. Who might have coordinated the attacks back home. So, I need you to be really honest with me. OK? Can you do that?'

She's looking at me so intently I can't drag my gaze away. I nod like a zombie.

'Great. I know a lot of people don't give you much credit, but I think there's more to you than just that pretty face.'

She's playing me. Even I'm not stupid enough to think otherwise.

'So, Tori,' she continues. 'I'm going to ask you a question and I need you to tell me the truth.'

I nod again. It's like I can't stop myself, like she's pulling me under her spell.

'Where is Jack? Really?'

41

But, before I can say any more, 'Uncle' George appears at the door to the gym. 'I thought you'd be in here, Aubs,' he says.

'Well, some of us prefer to keep in shape,' she replies, a pointed look at his ever-expanding waistline. My godfather has always been on the larger side, preferring to drink and eat than work out. Although he's made criticising others an Olympic sport.

George doesn't reply.

'What, no pithy comeback?' Aubrey asks. Normally he'd say something about how round is a shape, but not today.

'You need to come to the terrace,' George tells her, then looks at me. 'You too, pumpkin.' He's always loved to call me nicknames, like pumpkin and princess and sweetheart. I hate it. But I smile back at him anyway.

'Has something happen—' Aubrey starts, but he cuts her off.

'Not here.'

This sounds serious.

I trot behind them on our way to the terrace, trying to pick up snatches of their whispered conversation as they walk side-by-side in front of me. George looks over his shoulder a few times, as if he's trying to gauge how far away I am. I pull out my phone and pretend to be engrossed by Instagram.

'Are we sure it's real?' I hear Aubrey say.

'It's real,' George confirms, turning once more to look at me. Evidently, he believes I'm not listening as he continues at a louder level. 'There is no way someone could've staged it and made it look that good.'

'Shit.'

'Yep.'

'This will break Peter.'

'I'm fully aware of that.'

What are they talking about?

Mummy and Daddy are already on the terrace. There's something in the air, something dark and dank hiding beneath the surface. It's already baking hot out here but I shiver despite the heat.

George takes control of the situation, directing us all to take the same seats we sat in yesterday. But this time no one insists I go to get them coffee or whisky or pastries. In fact, no one is expecting me to do anything at all.

Once we're all settled, George stands up at the head of the table and clears his throat. 'There's no easy way to say this,' he starts, his gaze flitting between Mummy and Daddy. 'But we've had a message.'

'About the attacks?' Daddy asks.

'Kind of,' George says. 'Look, it's...' he trails off and looks at Aubrey in desperation.

'Just spit it out,' Daddy demands. 'We're meant to be on holiday and all this shit is not helping my heart condition.'

'It's Scott,' Aubrey says quickly.

Not *about* Scott. Just Scott.

'I'm so, so sorry,' Aubrey continues. 'But we think something has happened to him.'

'What kind of something?' Mummy asks.

No one says anything, but George pulls out his phone and places it in front of my parents.

My mother's scream curdles my blood. It is pure anguish and pain.

'No no no no.' My father is shaking his head, repeating the same word over and over.

Deep down I know what's on that phone. I know it's a picture of my brother. My *dead* brother. But, of course, I'm not meant to know that. And I'm also not meant to care so little either. I take a slow breath, counting to ten as I inhale, the same way I prepare to don the mantle of any other character I play. This one, distraught sister, is going to be the trickiest I've ever attempted.

'Aubrey?' I allow my voice to shake as I say her name. 'What's going on?' I blink a couple of times, feeling the tears already primed to fall. Crying on demand was one of the very first skills I learned to master, it's amazing how often it's useful.

'Don't show her,' my mother says in this hideously broken high pitched way. 'I don't want you to remember him like that,' she adds to me.

Aubrey comes and crouches in front of me. 'It's your brother. He's... well, he's dead.'

'Dead?' I whisper the word as if saying it too loudly might just make it true.

'Murdered.'

'But... he can't be.'

'I'm sorry.' But even as she's telling me this terrible news she still sounds like a robot. Wow, to have that much self-control.

'But...' I start but I'm unable to continue as the tears begin to roll down my face. I lean forward, forehead onto my arms onto the table, shoulders hitching as I sob more and more violently. I open my mouth and allow a tiny sound to escape. A quiet keening, like an injured animal. I found a fox once who had been run over by a car and I channel his spirit, as I build to a crescendo.

God, I'm good at this acting thing.

Five minutes later and my throat feels shredded, my lungs almost itchy from the constant sobbing. Tentatively I dial down my reaction and eventually lift my head from my hands. Mummy is frozen in exactly the same position she was in before. Daddy is shaking his head, fingers drumming the table top as he thrums with anger.

I try to catch my breath. Now what happens?

Actually, that isn't the question.

The question is who sent George a picture of my dead brother? Because there are only three of us who knew he was dead.

'Where's Chloe?' I ask, when I realise she isn't here with us. No one answers, but a look passes between George and Aubrey. Did they forget about Chloe? I know the truth about my brother and sister-in-law's relationship, but the rest of the family thought their marriage was all sunshine and rainbows. She should be at this table wailing with the rest of us.

'I'll get her,' says Aubrey, but I put my hand on her arm to stop her walking away.

'I'll go. We're almost like sisters. She should hear this from me.'

Aubrey nods. 'Bring her out here, though, yeah? We need to have a family meeting.'

Chloe doesn't answer when I knock on the door to her

room. She must be on that little patio she shares with her parents. I let myself in and head out to find her.

'What the hell did you do?' I ask the moment I see she's outside and alone.

'Do? What are you talking about?' she replies. Then she narrows her eyes and looks at me more intently. 'What happened to you? You look like shit.' There's a hint of relish in her words.

'Scott's dead.'

'Well, yeah. We kind of knew that.'

'No. He's dead.' I put a heavy emphasis on the 'dead'. 'As in, everyone knows he's dead and so now we have to pretend to give a shit.'

'What do you mean, everyone knows?'

'Someone,' I jab my finger towards her. 'Someone sent a picture of his body to George.'

'What? And you think it was me?'

'Who else could it be? What the hell were you thinking?'

'I didn't do anything. I'm not an idiot. Why would I do that?'

I pause and watch her for a moment. She makes a good point. 'But if you didn't send the picture then it must have been...'

'The real killer,' she finishes my sentence. Or at least kind of. That isn't what I was going to say; I was going to say it must have been Grace, but I hold my tongue as Chloe's suggestion is much more sensible.

Chloe slumps in her seat. She suddenly looks younger, vulnerable. I don't normally see her like this, I'm far more used to her being calm and in control, every inch the gangster's wife she's been playing for the last decade. I want to look away but I can't help myself. It's like watching a car crash, fascinating and horrifying in equal measure. I can see the young woman my brother manipulated for so long, shaping her and moulding her until there was nothing of the original Chloe left.

'Did you see it?' she asks softly.

'The picture? No, Mummy said I shouldn't remember him like that.' I laugh, a short sharp bark of a laugh that almost takes me by surprise.

Chloe nods. 'What happens now?'

'Well, I guess now we see how good an actress you are. It's time to join the rest of the family and play the grieving widow. I assume you've been practising, this is a role you always knew you were going to have to play.'

'You can be a heartless bitch sometimes, you know that, Tori?'

'It's not mean if it's true,' I reply. It's something Jack used to say, a justification for taking the piss out of someone.

She stands up and rolls her shoulders a few times as if she's just arrived in Pilates class. 'Let's do this then.'

42

Now, I will give credit where it's due, and my sister-in-law is alarmingly convincing as the grieving widow. I'd be impressed if it didn't also make me nervous as hell that she is such a good liar. What bullshit has she told me over the years that I've just taken at face value?

Back with the rest of the Coopers, George tells us to sit down again. But my own period of mourning must already be coming to an end as Daddy sends me back into the villa to get the whisky after all. Charming.

This time I return with the Macallan Daddy bought in the duty free at Gatwick. Daddy pours six measures and then raises the bottle high above his head. 'And this one is for you, Son,' he says to the sky, before sloshing some whisky on the floor by his feet. I think he might have been watching a few too many war movies.

'To Scott,' George says and raises his own glass to the heavens. He too sloshes a little on the floor. I can't believe we're wasting good whisky in commemorating my monster of a brother. We should be celebrating that he's dead and can no longer hurt anyone.

'But now we must get down to business,' Aubrey says. Suddenly the dynamic between her and George makes sense: he's the party guy, the one everyone wants to hang with when times are good; she's the serious one, the one who takes control of the toughest situations even when no one else will step up.

'Someone killed our boy,' Aubrey continues. 'And I think we know who it was.'

Fuck. What did she just say? I can't help myself, my eyes have darted to Chloe before I could stop them. She looks as terrified as I feel.

'Scott's killer was known to us,' George continues. 'He might be someone pretending to be a friend or an employee...' he trails off and looks around the table. I breathe a sigh of relief, he doesn't mean he can name the killer, just that this wasn't a random attack.

'Or someone even closer.' Aubrey directs this comment at me.

I freeze. 'What do you mean?' My voice is squeaky.

'Jack. Do you think he could be part of this?'

Now look, I know I shouldn't, I know it isn't really fair and what Jack did to me – all the cheating and sneaking around – wasn't exactly the end of the world. But he did hurt me and I am in a very difficult situation. So, don't judge. 'Yes.' I make sure I whisper it, but still the word hangs heavy in the air.

Chloe catches my eye, but I avert my gaze quickly. She can keep her opinions to herself. She's the one who got us into this mess in the first place. 'Have you checked his social media?' she asks.

George pulls out his phone, manicured nails tapping the screen as if he's stabbing someone. 'What's his handle?'

'@JackOutTheBox,' I tell him.

'Of course,' he mutters under his breath. 'Hmmm...' He scrolls through Jack's profile. 'So, according to Instagram, Jack is at the NOMAD hotel.'

'Is that a nice place?' Aubrey asks.

I nod. Of course Jack went to the NOMAD. He's probably used my credit card to pay for it too.

'He has captioned this picture,' George turns his phone so we can see Jack in a hammock, swinging above the perfect blue water of the hotel pool. He turns the phone back so he can read the text out to us. 'Waiting for the love of my life to forgive me. I know I messed up baby, but I love you.' George makes a face. 'He tagged you, Tori.'

He puts the phone down on the table. 'Look, I'm not an expert, but I know Jack and he doesn't strike me as a criminal mastermind intent on taking down the family. Frankly, he's such an idiot I'm surprised he manages to function in the real world at all.'

He does have a point.

'Jack isn't our killer.' Aubrey sounds certain – disappointed but resolute – and the rest of the group nods.

We sit around that awful table for another hour and a half. No one has any real ideas, no leads, no action they can take. Every started conversation takes a quick U-turn and heads back to my dead brother and what a tragic waste his death is. I want to scream at them all. In the end, though, I'm able to excuse myself, claiming a headache and a desire to lie down for a while.

I find Grace waiting for me in my room. 'Err. What are you doing here?'

'Waiting for you.'

No shit. 'Why?'

'We have a problem.'

'You think?' What is wrong with her?

'I need you to be honest with me, OK. Did you kill him?'

'No.'

'Did Chloe?'

'I thought she did. But then how did a photo of the body end up with my family? She wouldn't have sent it, she has far too much to lose.'

'So, there was another killer. Someone else was here that night.'

I take a few steps towards the mini fridge. The whisky is pulsing at the back of my brain and I can feel a headache developing. There's only one cure for a midday hangover: hair of the dog. But the fridge is empty. 'Seriously?' I whisper under my breath.

'Apologies,' Grace says. 'You just can't get the staff these days. Or maybe I've just been a little preoccupied with all the murder.'

I shrug off her excuse and open the wardrobe instead, pulling out the bottle of Mermaid Pink gin I picked up as we went through duty free. The bottle is gorgeous and to be fair that's the only reason I bought it; I'm not a huge lover of gin. But needs must and I pull the cap off, the aroma of strawberries hitting me. I take a gulp and it burns the back of my throat, but in a good way. In the absence of champagne, it'll do.

'We need to figure out who really killed him,' I tell Grace. 'That's the key to this all.' Then I have a brainwave. 'What about the cameras?'

Grace huffs. 'You think I haven't... For fuck's sake. There's nothing. No one except the guests came in or out of the villa that night.'

'Daddy will want to check.'

'He already messaged me. I'm going to see him in a minute.' Her nerves are getting the better of her, I can hear it in her voice. She runs her hand across her face. 'But there's still the practical matter that we tried to cover this up. We were the ones who cleaned up and got rid of the body.'

'What did you do with it? The body, I mean?' I feel foolish that I never even thought to ask before.

'I have contacts who can make this kind of thing disappear.'

That doesn't feel like a wholly satisfactory answer.

'The best thing we can do,' Grace continues, 'is to buy some time. Buy ourselves a day or so until we can figure out who the real killer is.'

'And how do you propose we buy time?' I ask, flopping down on the bed. I spill a little of the gin, but who really cares at this point?

Grace clears her throat. 'Has Rob ever tried to make a pass at you?' she asks quietly.

'Rob? As in Chloe's brother, that Rob?'

'Yeah.'

'Well, of course. He can't help but try it on with anyone who moves.' *Oooh.* 'So you think we should make a subtle suggestion that Rob had something to do with all this?'

'He has access to the villa. The ability to come and go as he pleases without anyone batting an eyelid.'

'Motive?' I ask.

'He owed Scott a ton of money from poker.'

Very *very* interesting.

43

You probably think I'm a terrible person. And that's OK. I am a terrible person with a dodgy moral compass and a stubborn streak of self-preservation that trumps any other consideration. I'm not apologising here, I'm just making sure we're all on the same page.

I'm standing outside my parents' room, hand poised to knock on the door and tell Daddy my 'suspicions', when Farah comes down the corridor.

'How are you doing?' she asks, her voice full of sympathy.

'Fine,' I say quickly. Absolutely not about to falsely accuse your husband of murder. Nope. Absolutely not.

'Fine?' She cocks her head slightly and looks at me.

Shit. I'm meant to be playing the grieving sister. 'Sorry. Force of habit to pretend everything's OK,' I tell her, dropping my eyes to the floor and waiting for them to fill with crocodile tears. 'It's just such a shock.'

'Yeah, I can't believe it.' Farah looks genuinely sad. She's so nice and I feel a little more guilty for what I'm about to do to her husband. 'Well, look, I'm here if you need someone to talk to. Any time, even if it's the middle of the night.' Then she squeezes my shoulder and walks away. The knife in my heart twists slightly.

'Hey Mummy,' I say as she opens the door to her and Daddy's room.

'Darling.' She pulls me into a hug and for a moment I allow myself to relax into her arms, my body heavy. She smells of cigarette smoke and vodka and Chanel No. 5.

'I need to talk to Daddy.' I pull back to look her in the face.

'He's on the terrace,' she tells me, pointing towards the figure of my father standing frozen in place just staring out across the sea.

'Daddy,' I whisper softly as I approach. I don't want to scare him.

He brushes the tears from his face before he turns round. I've never seen him cry, barely seen him express any kind of deep emotion. He thinks it would be a sign of weakness and that 'real men' don't cry. I wonder how much of Scott's inability to play nicely with others was because Daddy forced him to repress his feelings when he was little, trying to make him into the perfect little mini-me and creating a monster in the process.

'Daddy,' I repeat, making sure I actually do have his attention.

'Yes, sweetheart.'

I've debated how to tell him about my 'suspicions' but, in the end, I think it's better just to come right out with it. Blurting something out always looks more genuine than trying to preamble up to it. 'I know who it was.'

I hold my breath as I wait for his response. 'Who?' he asks eventually.

'Rob Wilson.'

'Why?'

'He has a hideous temper and he owed Scott a boatload of cash.'

'No. Why do you think it was Rob?'

Oh. I should probably have thought this through a bit more, got my story fully straight before running in here with my baseless thoughts. 'He—'

'Did he do something to you?' Daddy interrupts to ask.

'What? No.' I scrunch my face up at the mere thought. Rob would've felt the edge of my knife if he'd even tried to go there.

'So?'

'I heard him on the phone. Earlier today. He was bragging to whoever was on the other end that his debt had been wiped clean.'

'And he was specifically talking about the money he owed Scott?' Daddy sounds sceptical.

'He said he'd taken matters into his own hands and he'd be royally fucked if anyone found out what he did.' I'm panicking a little, trying to make it sound convincing.

'Hmmm.'

He definitely doesn't believe me. I need to double down. 'He was talking on a burner phone, but not the one I've seen him use a few times while we've been here.'

'A third phone?' This gets Daddy's attention. Practically everyone I know has two phones: the legit one and the anonymous one that gets changed regularly. But it is suspicious as hell to have a third.

I nod.

'Interesting,' says Daddy. 'Let me do some digging. See what I can find. Now, why don't you go and get your mother and me a proper drink from the kitchen?'

'Of course. Shall I do you a whisky sour?'

'Do me an Old Fashioned with lemonade, not soda.'

George finds me in the kitchen a few minutes later. I'd just poured Mummy's triple vodka but I down it myself before I turn back to face him.

'Well, well, well,' he says. 'Aren't you the little detective?' There's an ugly snarl to his tone, but it's one I've grown very used to over the years.

'Daddy told you what I heard?'

'He told me what you told him, yes.' There's a glint in his eye, like he's already caught me in a lie and he's just waiting for me to slip up. He likes to play these kinds of games.

'I heard what I heard,' I tell him.

'Yes. Apparently, you did. But Rob didn't actually say he'd killed Scott, did he?'

'Well, not in so many words, no.'

'And you know how you often exaggerate and catastrophise, and see things that aren't really true?'

It's rare that I overreact, but that isn't the persona I play with George. 'Well, yes, but—'

'It isn't nice to point the finger, Tori. You know that.' His voice is dripping with sweetness, like he's saying this for my own good. For ten years – ever since he realised that my fledgling modelling career could be useful to him – I've put up with this bullshit, having this man manipulate and gaslight me into doing everything he tells me to, making me weak and reliant on him. But I've seen the light and there is no going back to how things were before; no more 'Uncle' George.

'Now you see, here's the problem.' He takes a few steps towards me, so close now I can smell the garlic on his breath. 'Rob can't possibly have killed your brother.'

'Why not?'

'Because he has an alibi.'

'Farah's lying. She was with me and Chloe that night.'

'It isn't Farah.'

'And you trust this alibi?' I raise an eyebrow at him.

'Don't sass me.'

I return my expression to neutral, an instinctive reaction I hate myself for. 'Who is it?'

'Your aunt.' He offers me a slow smile.

'Aubrey? But that doesn't make any sen—'

'Are you going to make me explain?' he asks.

'I... I... But Aubrey wasn't here. You were both back in the UK.' *Weren't they?* Yes, they definitely were. George and Aubrey only arrived yesterday.

He shakes his head slowly as if I'm an annoying little kid who asks too many questions and the adults are all a little tired of it. 'Rob owed your mother a lot of money from their poker games. She suggested that perhaps he might do a little favour for the family. You know, to clear some of the debt. Aubrey had a personal matter on the island he was able to assist her with.'

'Oh.' I don't really know what else to say. Except... 'But why didn't Daddy just tell me that?'

'Your father didn't know; you know how he feels about people who don't pay what they owe.'

Well, I guess that makes sense.

'So, it begs the question. Why are you trying to blame Rob? Who are you really trying to protect?'

DAY SEVEN

CHLOE

44

I took the easy way out yesterday and excused myself from the others in the late afternoon claiming I just needed some time alone. It wasn't like anyone could say anything, I had apparently just found out my husband was dead. Mum bought me some dinner of a simple chicken salad and a whole bottle of Sancerre to wash it down with.

'I'm here, you know,' she told me. 'If you need anything at all.'

I could tell she wanted a big emotional heart to heart, but that's really not my style. Plus, Mum does have a bit of a tendency to hijack other people's misery and make it about herself, and I am definitely not in the mood to deal with that.

I spent most of the evening sitting on the patio, a book balanced in my lap. But I wasn't reading, I couldn't make it through a single paragraph without my brain wandering off the page and back to the shit storm my life has become.

I'm seriously concerned about Tori. I was watching her yesterday, whispering in the kitchen with Uncle George, heads together like they're the best of friends. What was she telling him? Who else is she going to throw to the wolves?

That moment when she suggested the traitor could be Jack shocked me to the core. That she'd so casually just point the finger at him like that. I know their relationship wasn't perfect, that it wasn't exactly a great love story but more of a situationship. But still. She cared about him – at least in some small way – but she hung him out to dry in an instant like he meant nothing to her. Luckily for him, he had a vaguely convincing counter story with that NOMAD post. Well, it isn't like he'd have advertised his location if he actually had anything to do with the whole situation, would he?

But I do not have an alibi. And my story that we were madly in love? Is that actually going to be convincing enough when it's put under scrutiny? Plus, of course, there is always the whole 'crime of passion' angle that someone could spin if they felt so inclined. It would be so easy to say I loved my husband too much, that I discovered he was cheating and slit his throat in some kind of 'if I can't have him then nobody can' moment of madness. His family didn't exactly take much convincing that he was seeing someone else on the side.

I must have fallen asleep at some point, because I wake up with a start as dawn begins to creep across the horizon, painting the sky pink. My neck aches and my book lies crumpled on the floor, pages bent where it must have slid off my lap. I smooth the pages as if the state of a novel I picked up as a holiday read still matters.

Half an hour later and I've had a long hot shower, working out the kinks in my neck and shoulders under the pressure of the water. I feel almost human for a few moments, until my memories catch up with me and I'm back to worrying. Worrying about how I can be the convincing grieving widow.

Worrying how to stop the finger of suspicion turning towards me. Worrying if Grace will somehow let the truth of how we know each other slip. Worrying about Tori. I'm knackered from it all.

I dress in a plain white t-shirt and navy linen wide leg trousers. I don't have anything black – well except the outfit I wore to the club the other night and that is hardly appropriate – so this ensemble will have to do. My hair is still wet, so I scrape it back into a ponytail, squeezing the water from the ends with my towel so it doesn't make my t-shirt see-through.

Do I look the part? I can't even judge any more. But it's going to have to do, I can hear that other people in the villa are starting to stir and it's time for me to face them. Nerves gnaw deep in my belly but I tamp them down. A few deep breaths and I'm ready as I'll ever be.

Out on the terrace I find breakfast pastries and a French press of coffee already prepared. But no one else has made it outside yet. I stuff three pastries into my mouth in quick succession, I'm assuming grieving widows don't smash down breakfast so I need to eat while I'm alone. Then I pour a large coffee and sit down to wait for someone else to arrive.

I don't need to wait for long, but I'm surprised the first up is Tori. She looks her usual gorgeous self from a distance. But, as she approaches, I can see that her eyes are rimmed in red like she's been crying all night, and there's some smudging to her mascara, as if she was applying her makeup through a veil of tears. It's an act but no one else would ever suspect. How is she so good at this?

'How are you doing this morning?' she asks softly as she takes a seat, her hand reaching for the coffee. 'Did you manage to get any sleep?'

I glance around me to check we're alone. 'You don't have to put on the act with me, Tori.'

'What act?' She widens her eyes.

'Don't play the innocent.'

She flashes me a wicked grin. 'Just keeping in character.'

'Tori, this is serious.'

'For fuck's sake, Chloe. I do understand that. You don't always have to treat me like an idiot, you know.'

'Sorry.' But my apology is a reflex. I'm not sorry at all, I'm increasingly concerned my sister-in-law is a bone-fide psychopath who will shove me off a cliff without a single thought.

'Any more ideas on who the actual killer is?' Tori asks but then she gets side-tracked by the box from the bakery. 'Ooh, are there any of the chocolate ones?'

'Umm...' she's thrown me with her ability to switch between subjects.

'Yes.' She punches the air as she opens the box and sees what's inside. 'These are the absolute tits.' She takes a huge bite, smearing chocolate around her mouth.

I look away. The more I see her like this, the more I think she could have killed Scott. I know there's probably a more politically correct term to use, but she's a nut job. It doesn't take too much imagination to believe she could commit murder and then smile and laugh in the next moment.

'I did wonder if it could have been Rob,' she says as she casually licks icing sugar from her fingers.

'Rob? As in my brother?'

'There's only one Rob here, Chloe.'

'Did you...?' but I can't bear to finish the sentence as ice runs down the back of my neck. Surely she wouldn't accuse my brother? He's a dick and everything, but he isn't a killer.

Tori shrugs and then reaches for another pastry, this time pulling out one filled with a bright pink filling. 'Ooh, this looks lush.'

'Tori.' I use my best prefect voice to get her attention. 'Who did you tell that you thought it might have been Rob?'

She puts up a hand to tell me to wait while she finishes her mouthful. 'You really need to try these strawberry ones,' she says eventually.

'Tori. So help me Go—'

'Oh, chill out, Chloe. Jesus. I only mentioned it to George, that's all.'

'That's all?' Uncle George might be soft and fluffy on the outside, but I've seen him break a man's fingers because he didn't like the way the guy was looking at him.

'Chill.' She huffs and leans back in her seat. 'He had an alibi. He was running some kind of personal errand for Aubrey.'

I feel relief wash over me. I don't always see eye to eye with my brother, but I'm glad he's safe. 'Any other ideas?' I ask. 'Preferably ones that aren't members of my immediate family,' I add under my breath, but loud enough for her to hear.

'I do have one other idea.' She leans forward, balancing her face in her hands, elbows on the table.

'Who?'

She smiles. 'You.'

'Ha ha. We know it wasn't me.'

'Do we?' She smiles sweetly.

'Don't fuck about, Tori.'

We're interrupted by the arrival of Uncle George. 'How are you ladies doing?' he asks gently.

Tori drops her gaze to the table and then sniffles. 'Not great,' she answers.

'And how about you, Chloe?'

I try to think sad thoughts and not get distracted by Tori's superior acting skills. 'Not great either.'

'I was thinking I should take you for lunch later,' he tells me. 'Get you away from this place for a little while. Just the two of us. Does that sound OK?'

I nod. 'Thanks Uncle George.'

Tori narrows her eyes and I watch in horror as something flashes across her features. Jealousy. Resentment. Hatred. She stares at me for a moment and then turns to Uncle George.

'Umm...' she starts, snapping into the persona she always uses around her godfather. 'Could we have a little chat, Uncle George? Just the two of us?' She glares at me.

'Of course. Why don't you come with me to the kitchen so you can help me figure out one of those coffee machines.'

They walk away from me and Tori looks back over her shoulder. She winks.

What the hell is that supposed to mean?

45

Uncle George comes to find me just before midday. It's not a moment too soon. I've spent the entire morning stewing about Tori, camped out on the terrace just waiting for a sign that she's done something to incriminate me in all of this. I never should have trusted her. And I never should have thought she would keep quiet in our mutually assured destruction scenario. She doesn't care about me, or seemingly anyone, and I'm going to pay a price for my naivety in thinking she might.

'You alright to head to lunch?' Uncle George asks, his voice gentle.

I nod. I've spent most of the morning staring into space, a look on my face that I'm hoping has been saying 'quiet contemplation on the brevity of life' and not 'guilty as sin and having an internal meltdown'.

'Great, let's get going. Grace has sorted out a hire car for us.'

'You're driving?' I quip – Uncle George is a notoriously bad driver. But then I realise it's probably not the time or the place for such jokes so I crinkle my nose. 'Sorry.'

'I promise to drive like a gentleman,' Uncle George tells me as we walk through the kitchen and head towards the sleek BMW on the driveway.

'How's Tori coping?' I ask him as the car accelerates away from the villa.

'Hmmm.' He says nothing more for a minute or two, almost as if he's debating how to phrase what he wants to say. 'You know Tori,' he says eventually, the words loaded with inference.

'So not well then.' It's a statement more than a question.

'She's spiralling, spinning out of control.' He doesn't sound surprised.

'In what way?'

Uncle George takes a deep breath and then turns off the main road, taking a tiny track down to the rocky beach below us. He pulls into a parking space and switches off the engine. His shoulders slump for a moment before he sits back up straight. 'Let's go for a little walk.'

We don't talk as we pick our way towards the water, careful not to slip and break our necks. There is a smooth flat rock facing the Aegean and we both sit on it, shoulders touching.

'Tori is in a state,' Uncle George says. 'She's grieving and she's angry and she's lashing out at everything and everyone.'

'How do you mean by lashing out?' I ask, dreading the answer.

'She has suggested a number of people who could be involved in Scott's death.'

'Like who?' My voice is small in my ears.

'Well, you were there when she suggested Jack.' He turns to look at me as he says it, waiting for my reaction.

'Poor Jack.'

'Poor Jack indeed. And he's such a nice chap. You know, I was hoping he and Tori would get married one day.' He's wistful, almost melancholic.

I want to laugh at how ridiculous an idea that is; fuck buddies yes, but soulmates they absolutely were not. 'I think she's still hung up on Markus.'

Uncle George shakes his head. 'He was so wrong for Tori.' He leans in closer to me, as if we're teenagers whispering secrets. 'You know he wanted her to give up the modelling? What kind of man makes his woman give up her dreams like that, eh?'

If Tori hadn't told me she wanted to quit, I would have believed the narrative from Uncle George completely. Unless of course, the one spinning a false narrative is Tori herself? Perhaps I can't trust *anything* she says.

'Anyway, that's by the by. She also suggested that perhaps your brother was involved.'

'Rob? Wasn't he running an errand for Aubrey?'

Uncle George narrows his eyes for a moment.

'Well, yes.'

'So, he couldn't have been involved.' I make it sound so simple, but in truth I'm testing the efficacy of Rob's alibi, making doubly sure no one is going to try to come for him.

'No, he could not.' He waits for a few moments before continuing. 'So, you see what I mean about Tori?'

'Yeah. Should we be worried about her?'

'I've asked Aubrey to keep a closer eye on her.'

'Good idea.'

Uncle George stands and extends a hand to help me up. 'Let's go eat, eh?'

Ten minutes later we're pulling up outside the front of the diving club hotel. 'Why are we back here?' I ask.

'I thought it would only be right to come to the last place we know Scott was.'

I stay silent.

'Oh,' Uncle George says as the penny drops. 'I didn't think. This is where he was...' he trails off. He doesn't need to add the part about this being the place my husband was shagging someone else. Or at least in my version of events anyway.

'It's OK,' I say, deliberately removing all emotion from my tone, like I'm some kind of robot or operating on autopilot.

'You're sure? I'm so sorry.' He slams the palm of his hand against the steering wheel. 'We can go somewhere else?' He sounds so annoyed with himself – and I know he's prone to self-flagellation for his mistakes – that I can't bear to make him take me elsewhere. And to be fair; it *isn't* actually where my dead husband was shagging someone else.

'It's fine, honestly. It's just nice to get away from the villa for a while. Thank you for this.'

'Aww, sweetheart. You're more than welcome. I know this must be hideous for you. Now, let's go and get some wine, eh?'

He links his arm through mine and I allow myself to lean against him a little. My eyes search for the concierge from before as we walk through the lobby area, but they're not behind the desk. Must be their day off.

This time we are seated by the French doors with a glorious view out across the patio area and down towards the water. We order salads and wine and then settle back in our seats making idle chit chat. Uncle George is obviously trying to distract me from thoughts of my dead husband and he keeps up a stream of commentary on our fellow diners. It's similar to what Tori does, but Uncle George is far harsher and a hell of a lot funnier in his pithy observations.

'Ooh,' he says staring at a table in the corner. 'That guy behind you just blatantly took a Viagra in front of the whole restaurant.' He sounds scandalised, but in that overly theatrical way that makes you realise it doesn't shock him one little bit.

I make a face. 'Ewww.'

Our food arrives and we fall into a companionable silence as we eat. Once he's finished, Uncle George puts down his knife and fork. 'So, how did you know about Rob's alibi?' he asks.

'Um... He told me.' Of course he didn't tell me, Tori did, but I don't want Uncle George to know I've been chatting to her about these things.

'And did he tell you what he was doing that night?'

'Umm...' I scramble for something that sounds legitimate and convincing. 'Just picking something up.' Yes, that's suitably innocuous.

'He went to collect Aubrey's HRT drugs. There's a very strong black market here in Mykonos.'

'Oh.' Well, that wasn't what I was expecting. Uncle George tilts his head slightly as he looks at me.

'But I guess your brother wouldn't tell you that kind of detail, would he? It would be a little...' He pauses for a moment. 'Indiscreet of him, wouldn't it? Although I'm surprised he mentioned it to you at all. Unless you were discussing things, making sure you both had watertight alibis, seeing if perhaps you'd need to cover for each other?'

'Ha,' I say, trying to cover the panic creeping up on me. But then I remember one of the random Never Have I Ever questions from the other night and something my brother said about 'performance enhancing drugs'. 'Rob told me because he wanted my advice; he wanted to know if he should use this same black market contact to help score some Viagra while he's here.'

'Your brother asked you to help him get Via—?'

I cut him off. 'You've met my brother, you know he has zero shame. He's far worse than that guy behind you taking it at lunch. And you know girls talk to each other, you think Farah hasn't mentioned his troubles too?'

Uncle George stares at me for a second and then laughs. 'You're right.' I feel myself relax again. 'He is definitely an over-sharer.'

I make eye contact with the waiter and then pick up my wine glass so he knows I'd like another. He makes a beeline to the table.

'Another sauvignon blanc?' he asks me. I nod in reply. 'And for you, sir?' he asks Uncle George.

'Just a sparkling water for me. I'm driving.'

I wait until the waiter has left us alone. 'Do you know who was responsible?' I ask.

'We're working on it,' he replies. 'But, don't worry about it, OK? The person responsible for killing Scott is going to pay for what they did. The photo from that morning should give us more clues.'

* * *

It's not until we're in the car heading back to the villa that I realise what Uncle George said about the photo. Scott was killed in the night: I woke up in the morning to find him dead, but we were alone. So how was the photo of the body taken in the daylight?

I glance sideways at Uncle George. He's grinding his teeth, the tension clear in the set of his jaw. He doesn't say anything as he takes the next exit off the main road. It's signposted to a little marina, a handful of small yachts bobbing gently on the water.

'Where are we going?'

'I need your help with something, if you don't mind.'

'Of course.'

'Here we are,' he says, pulling in to a space in front of one of the boats. It's called the *Ianassa* and there's a jet ski next to it, attached by two strong bars.

'You're buying a boat?'

'Something like that,' he replies before getting out of the car and ushering me aboard.

I take a seat on one of the small sofas on the deck, feeling the rise and fall of the Aegean beneath my feet. My stomach churns, but I don't think it's motion sickness.

'I think it's time you were a little more honest with me, don't you?' Uncle George says over the roar of the engine as he switches it on and then unmoors the boat.

'I...' But my words die in my throat as he expertly guides the boat from the dock and out into the open sea.

He cuts the engine a few hundred metres from the shore and allows the *Ianassa* to drift in the deeper water. 'Let's start with you telling me why you killed your husband.'

46

I laugh. It's an instinctive reaction, a short bark of mirth that erupts without me being able to stop it. I clap my hand over my mouth.

'You think I'm joking?' George asks.

'You think I killed Scott?' I counter.

Uncle George tilts his head and looks me directly in the eye. 'Yes, I think you killed him.' He makes it sound so convincing. So obvious. Such a foregone conclusion.

'I didn't.' I'm not lying. I genuinely did not kill him. Yes, I wanted to, plotted to even. And, yes, I persuaded Grace to clean up the murder scene. But I did not kill him.

'You're lying.'

'I'm not.'

Uncle George takes a deep breath. He holds it for a few counts and then exhales slowly. I want to drag my gaze away from him but I can't, it's like I'm locked in place, unable to look away. 'So, you see, Chloe, we have a problem here. I know you killed him. But I need you to tell me exactly what happened, in your own words. Do you think you can do that?'

'I didn't kill him.'

'Chloe, Chloe, Chloe.' He sounds almost patronising, like a father who is bored of his daughter's lies. 'Of course you did.'

He takes a few steps towards me and I shrink away from him. He sounds so sure of my guilt. *Did* I? Have I been chasing a phantom alternative murderer this whole time?

'You need to tell me the truth.'

'I didn't ki—'

'Yes, you did,' he interrupts me, his voice raised. I can see the soft and cuddly Uncle George mask slipping to reveal the savage man beneath. 'This is pointless,' he says, almost under his breath. 'For fuck's sake.' He shakes his head a few times. 'I didn't want to have to do this.'

'Do what?' I ask.

He doesn't answer. Instead, he puts the keys to the boat into his little designer man bag and then stuffs it into another bag, this one with a roll over top. He slings this one across his body and then, without even a second look, he dives overboard. Within a few strokes he's at the jet ski, pulling himself up onto it, flicking water from his hair as he does so. He's not the most athletic man in the world, but he makes it look fairly easy, like a former James Bond gone to seed.

'I suggest you think things through properly,' he calls from the jet ski as he disconnects the arms that attach it to the boat.

'Where are you going? You can't leave me here.' My panic is rising.

'I can.'

'You can't strand me like this. I'll...' but I trail off, I have no idea what will actually happen to me if he leaves.

He reaches into his bag and pulls out what looks like a red TV remote. Behind me there's a whirring noise.

'What's that?' I ask.

'Just the anchor. We can't have you drifting too far, can we?'

Eventually he tucks the remote back into the bag, then switches on the jet ski and throttles the engine a few times, the sound loud in the vast expanse of sea around us. He swings around so he's adjacent to the side of the boat and looks up at me.

'You know, Chloe, I always liked you. I always thought you were one of the good ones. You have no idea how disappointed I am; you've broken my heart into a million pieces. So, you just sit tight and have a good old think. I'll come tomorrow and then we'll talk properly.'

'Tomorrow? What the hell? You can't lea—'

'Yes, Chloe. Yes, I can. No one knows you're here. You don't have your phone.'

My hand goes to my bag. Of course I have my phone...

Oh shit.

Uncle George grins at me. 'I took it from your bag at lunch. You didn't even notice. It's safe in the car so don't worry. There's water in the cooler underneath your seat. And some snacks if you get hungry. I'm not a monster, Chloe.'

'But you can't do this.' Jesus, the panic is really taking hold now.

'Be thankful it's me here and not Aubrey. Do you have any idea what she wanted to do? Let's just say she wouldn't have put down the anchor, or left water and snacks. She would have left you to drift out to sea without any supplies. Either that or you'd already have a bullet in the back of your brain.'

And with that parting shot, he revs the jet ski engine and roars off.

* * *

OK. I'm not going to panic. *Everything is fine. Everything is fine. Nothing to see here. Just a woman in a boat in the middle of the ocean with no phone and no way to get back to shore. Everything is fine.*

I should start with gathering an inventory of what I have on board. Yes, that feels like a sensible and pragmatic thing to do. Starting with the cooler beneath the seat. Inside is a single five hundred millilitre bottle of water and a sad looking cookies-and-cream flavour protein bar.

Uncle George can't honestly be planning on leaving me here until tomorrow with just this? There have to be more supplies.

The boat is small, little more than a few sofas on a deck, a raised seat for whoever is driving, a tiny toilet that smells like chemicals and death – the stench almost burning my nasal hairs the second I open the door and I'm forced to immediately close it again – and a miniature galley area, barely big enough to make a sandwich.

There are no other provisions. No more water. No more food. My tongue feels like it's coated in fur, but it's just my lunchtime wine turning into a mid-afternoon hangover. Soon my head is going to start pounding. I should drink the water.

But what if he doesn't return until later in the day tomorrow? He wasn't exactly specific in terms of details. It could be any time. I should save the water.

* * *

I search the boat again, this time looking for a spare set of keys. Perhaps there's a set hidden somewhere on board? It feels almost reckless to only have one key. What if you dropped it overboard? But I come up empty.

* * *

I try to use the radio to call for help. I'm kind of annoyed at myself for not thinking of this right at the beginning, but better late than never. There is nothing but static.

* * *

Should I pull up the anchor? He took the remote but there must be a switch somewhere too. I look over the side of the boat and into the apparently still water. If there isn't a current, then I'd just gradually drift towards the shore, wouldn't I? Raising my hand to cut out the glare from the sun, I look towards land. It isn't that far – although definitely not close enough to risk swimming – and almost the entire coastline is dotted with villas and hotels. If I washed up on someone's private beach they'd have to help me.

But what if there is a current? Would I just drift out to sea? Drift away with no water and no food and zero survival instincts because I've spent my entire life as a pampered princess who was handed everything on a silver platter.

* * *

The sun begins to set and the temperature starts to drop. I'm only wearing a t-shirt and some lightweight trousers and I shiver in the cooling air. There was a towel in the galley and so I wrap it around my shoulders like some kind of shawl.

On land, the villas transform from white blocks against the pale landscape into fireflies of light blazing in the dark. It's oddly beautiful.

* * *

My stomach growls and I debate eating half the protein bar. But, no, I need to save it. I wonder what they're eating back at the villa. It's day seven of the holiday, what had I planned?

Tonight was meant to be the last night, before everyone knew about Scott and we had to extend the trip. No new guests were coming to the villa so Grace had agreed we could stay a few more nights. But, originally, we were going to go to a traditional taverna for kleftiko and I can almost taste the rich slow cooked lamb and potatoes on my tongue. My stomach growls again, even louder this time.

Where do my family think I am? What has Uncle George told them? Should I even call him Uncle any more? It feels kind of odd to use such a familial title for the man who has marooned me at sea.

Surely Dad knows I'm missing by now? He won't buy whatever bullshit George and Aubrey make up about where I am. He'll know something's wrong. And then he'll come and find me and everything will be OK.

* * *

Dad will be here soon. I know he will.

* * *

Dawn breaks and I break with it, finally opening the water and gulping down half the bottle in seconds. The protein bar tastes like cardboard. It's the most delicious thing I've ever eaten.

* * *

The sun is high in the sky, the heat bouncing off the water. I've been dozing lethargically as I try to ignore my burning thirst.

I hear it in the distance. The sound of the jet ski. He's coming back.

But what am I going to tell him?

Ha! Who am I kidding; I'm going to tell him whatever will get him to take me back to civilisation.

DAY EIGHT

GRACE

47

It's yet another glorious day here in Mykonos, not a cloud in the sky and the morning sun already warm on my skin.

The Coopers and Wilsons think I've gone out to run some errands – yes, including picking up more oat milk for that idiot, Rob. The atmosphere in the villa is hard to describe; shock and grief and anger and a desire for action all melding into a single ball of general discomfort. It's been excruciating to watch and an absolute nightmare to judge what each of them want: I do have to keep up the pretence that I'm just the concierge after all.

Chloe excused herself yesterday and went to stay the night in the Belvedere Hotel. At least she kept up a stream of texts to her mother so she didn't have a meltdown. Chloe had warned me about Erin Wilson's propensity to overreact and so I made sure I kept an eye on her last night. Erin did ask me at around ten if I could organise a taxi to take her to the hotel to speak with her daughter, but I managed to convince her that wasn't the best idea.

'But she's my baby,' Erin had said, fingers twisting in front of her.

'She's almost thirty,' I had replied, placing a hand gently on Erin's arm. 'She's just lost her husband. She needs time to mourn.'

'She needs her mother.'

'My best friend lost her husband last year,' I'd told her. 'She needed some space to come to terms with it. It's normal to want to run away and hide, especially at the beginning.' I was lying through my teeth about this fake friend, but I do coach my clients on how to act when their hit is enacted in order to be convincing, so I know what I'm talking about.

'You're right,' Erin had eventually agreed and dropped the idea of heading to the Belvedere.

Finally done with babysitting Erin, I'd turned my attention to George Thorne. George, with his barely contained glee that he knew who the killer was and all he had to do was wait for them to hand over their confession to him in exchange for a glass of water. He milked it with the others but refused to name the perpetrator. 'Just wait until they tell me everything,' he told the others.

He's waiting until midday to go back to the *Ianassa*, I overheard him and Aubrey – who seems to be the one who is really in charge of the whole Cooper empire – discussing it late last night. Which gives me a window of a few hours to do what I need to do.

I thought he liked Chloe. I mean, she literally called him 'Uncle' George. But it turns out he's a sadistic bastard under all that cuddly demeanour. Luckily for Chloe, I slipped a GPS tracker into her handbag on day one of the trip so I know exactly where she is.

Spray hits me in the face as I zip over the calm sea on the jet ski. It's exhilarating and I'm tempted to increase the speed, really feel the power of this machine. But I've been on the island for long enough to hear a few horror stories about jet ski accidents and I'd really rather not end up the victim of one. Especially as no one knows I'm out here.

The *Ianassa* bobs gently on the horizon line as I head towards it. I wonder what kind of state Chloe will be in? It's only been about eighteen hours, but it's hot out here and she'll be starting to feel the effects of the dehydration. Plus, she's had a lot of time to imagine all the things that could happen to her when George returns.

She's standing on the bow of the boat waiting for me as I pull alongside. The look on her face when she realises it's me and not George is priceless.

'Grace. Oh, thank God,' she exclaims. It's sweet that she thinks I've come to rescue her.

I pull a bottle of water from the bag across my chest and throw it to her. She grabs it from the air, twists off the top and immediately starts to chug it down. But then she stops and spits a mouthful over the side of the boat. 'What the fuck?' she screams at me.

I chuckle. Yes, it was cruel to throw her a bottle of salt water, but she deserves everything she's going to get. 'Oops,' I call up to her.

'What are you doing?' she shouts. Despite the eighteen-hour ordeal she's already experienced, she still hasn't shaken off that aura of entitlement, that belief that everyone else exists to make her life easier. 'Grace, stop messing around.' The prefect voice she puts on has a little less impact with the rasp at the edge from her unquenched dehydration.

I nudge the jet ski a little closer to the boat. I need to be careful that she doesn't try and jump from the deck and try to topple me from it. When she realises which side I'm on, her desperation is going to increase and people often do very stupid and reckless things when they feel backed into a corner with no obvious means of escape.

'Grace, I'm being serious now. I need to get off this boat. I'm thirsty and hungry.'

I appraise her for a moment. Her white t-shirt is grubby, sweat staining the armpits and around the neckline. Her hair, normally so sleek, is a total mess, as if she's been running her hands through it all night. The bridge of her nose is bright pink from the sun; another hour or two and that is going to start to blister and peel. I should pity her.

But I don't. 'I'm not here to rescue you,' I say.

'You what?'

'I am not here to rescue you,' I repeat, making sure to enunciate each word even more clearly this time.

'Of course you are.' She's blind in her conviction.

'I'm really not.' But I'm getting a bit frustrated that her insistence is ruining the gravity of the moment. I had this conversation all planned out and now she's going off script.

She crosses her arms and looks at me. Really looks. I paint on a little smile for her benefit. 'I... I... I... don't understand.' Confusion skitters across her face.

She needn't worry, everything is about to come clear. 'I'm going to tell you a little story, Chloe. It's about a young girl and the big sister she absolutely adored.'

She actually has the audacity to roll her eyes. 'Grace. Can we do this back on dry land, please?' She sounds bored. Like my story will hold no interest for her and so she can't be bothered to listen.

'My big sister was everything to me. Three years older and the best friend I could ever have asked for. A lot of girls ignore their little sisters, treat them like annoying bugs. But not mine. She always tried to include me, even when her friends thought she shouldn't and said I was just a kid. My sister had one friend in particular who thought she was all that and hated me hanging around. We were all at the same boarding school and this friend would try to get me into trouble so I'd be grounded and not allowed out with my sister.'

Chloe tilts her head slightly at this, as though I've sparked a memory.

'You really don't recognise me?' I ask. 'I know I've changed a bit, dyed my hair and lost the puppy fat, but seriously?'

Her brow creases and her head tilts further.

'I didn't even change my first name.' I changed my surname, I didn't want to be *too* obvious, but I've hardly been hiding.

'Grace? But I don't know any Graces...' She trails off. Oh. Is that a spark of recognition behind her eyes? Finally.

'Rosie was my sister.' My left hand strays subconsciously towards my tattoo. I got it two years ago to commemorate the tenth anniversary of her murder. Something about the fact it had been a decade since her death lit a fire in me. And so I set about laying a plan to snare her killer.

A plan that led me all the way here. It was going perfectly until Scott turned up dead a week early, but I can still save the situation.

Chloe deserves everything that's coming for her.

She did help kill my sister after all.

48

'Grace?' Chloe whispers. 'I had no idea it was you.' She sounds relieved. Like she's discovered the tie that binds us and now of course I'll rescue her. 'I loved your sister,' she continues. 'What happened to her broke me. We're on the same side here. Let's just go back to shore.'

'I know the truth, Chloe.'

She starts slightly, as if a ghost has slapped her across the face. 'The truth?'

'About what happened that night.'

'Scott killed her.'

'Scott didn't kill her,' I correct. '*You* killed her.'

She laughs. Actually laughs. 'You're kidding me? You think I killed Rosie? Is that what this is all about? Scott pushed her off that roof.'

'Scott pushed her. I know that. But he did it because of you. You're the reason Rosie is dead.'

'He did it because he's a cunt.' She spits the word and I blanche.

'He did it because you asked him to.'

She physically steps backwards. 'No.' The word is strangled as it leaves her lips. 'No.'

'You had an argument, you and Rosie. She told me everything. You were so jealous of her getting that summer internship instead of you. And then the next morning she was dead and didn't you have a fabulous time milking the whole situation?'

'That's not what happened.'

'Oh, come on Chloe. You've convinced yourself you were the victim. Just like you always do. Nothing is ever your fault, even as you leave a trail of chaos and destruction behind you. And you revel in it. You just love to be the one everyone is lavishing pity on. Do you remember, back then? Everyone swarmed around you, poor Chloe who lost her best friend. More people came to comfort you than me and she was my *sister.*'

'No.' This time she's louder, more forceful. 'That isn't true. Scott killed Rosie.' She sags slightly into the railing around the edge of the boat. 'Perhaps it was my fault, in a way. Or at least because of me. I'd dumped him, but, then, after Rosie's death I went back to him, he offered me support and a shoulder to cry on. Without Rosie, I had no one and he exploited that.'

'Oh, piss off, Chloe. *I* was the one who had no one. *I* was the one left on their own. You were never exploited. You told him you were mad at Rosie because you wanted that internship for yourself and so he killed her for you.'

'No, that isn't—'

'It is,' I scream back at her. 'Chloe Wilson got her own way again. I know you took the summer placement that should have been hers and then leveraged it to get that plummy job the second you graduated from uni. You always got your own way. Don't you see? You think everything is about you.'

'No, I—'

'Well, the joke's on you now. This time it is going to be all about you. Finally Chloe can stop being the innocent victim. In this story, you're the villain. And everyone is going to know about it.'

'What do you mean?' Chloe drops her voice and stares at me.

'Like I said, I'm not here to rescue you. I'm here to tell you exactly the way the rest of the story is going to play out. I've been planning this for so long, moving the pieces into play, waiting for the perfect moment to strike.' I reach into my bag and pull out a bottle of Fanta. Chloe watches me take a long drink from it, she's practically salivating. Or at least she would be if her body had any moisture left to give. I don't really like Fanta, I'd rather have had a bottle of water, but I didn't want to risk mixing up my bottle with the salt water one.

'You nearly messed everything up,' I tell her as I put the rest of the bottle in my bag. Her eyes follow it. 'But I'm quick to react and everything is now ready for the big finale.'

'I don't understand.' She sounds almost broken.

'I have enough to prove you killed Scott and that you'd been planning it for a while. George, or should I call him "Uncle" George, is killing time at the villa before he comes back here. And, before he leaves, I'm going to make sure he has that proof. He'll still want a confession from you, of course, but what do you think he'll do then?'

'My father will rescue me,' she replies. She tilts up her chin like a child trying to be brave.

'Your father thinks you're at the Belvedere Hotel having a little "me time".' I tell her. 'You've been texting your mother every few hours so she knows you're OK. Did you really think George wouldn't have a plan for that?'

She takes a deep breath, as if her predicament is finally starting to become clear. 'So, you killed Scott? To frame me?'

'I didn't need to kill him. *You* killed him, Chloe. But, instead of helping you get away with it, I was lining all the evidence up at your door.'

'The photo. Of course.' She hits the heel of her hand against her temple. 'You were the one who sent it. Stupid, stupid girl.' She repeats the motion, harder this time, and I can hear the thud each time she makes contact.

I wait patiently as she berates herself for her own stupidity. I'm not going to lie and say I'm not enjoying this. Eventually, she speaks again, this time she's quieter than before, her innate confidence starting to erode. 'Grace, do you really think I killed Scott?'

'Of course you killed him. I know you're in denial, but come on. For fuck's sake, do you really think some stranger just walked into the villa and slit your husband's throat while you lay sleeping next to him?'

'He might have already been dead when I got home.'

'So, you think you just got into bed with a fucking corpse?' *Jesus Christ.*

'Maybe...' but even she doesn't sound convinced.

'Let's just say you didn't, OK? So that means you were there when it happened.'

'OK. That's probably right.' But her voice sounds small.

She's actually going to make me break this down for her, isn't she? I glance at my watch. Nine thirty. I need to be back at the villa in two hours – with the damn oat milk and a good excuse for my delay. It goes without saying that no one can know I came here this morning. Chloe will obviously try to convince George I set her up, but she's going to sound like nothing more than a rambling fool who spent the morning hallucinating in the middle of the ocean.

'Chloe,' I say, trying to keep my tone neutral. Jesus this is exhausting. 'Let's just think this through logically, shall we? Why the hell would Scott's murderer have left you alive? You'd be a potential witness. People who kill for money don't leave witnesses.'

'I was passed out. I didn't witness anything.'

She says it like it's a gotcha. 'Yeah, because the killer would risk that. You think a hired killer would hesitate for even a moment? You're a fool.'

'I didn't kill him.' But she sounds less sure than she did before.

'Yes, you did. And the Cooper family are going to make sure you pay for it.'

* * *

I leave her on the boat and head back to shore on the jet ski. But there is one thing that's bothering me. Just a tiny little niggle at the back of my brain. What if there *was* another killer? And what if he knew Chloe couldn't be a witness because she'd been drugged? What if he knew because he was the one who drugged her?

49

I pull up outside the villa just after eleven. I'd swung past the Flora supermarket on my way back from the marina and the boot of the car is full of pre-made lunch platters. They were meant to be leaving today but have extended their stay for a few more days. I didn't have time to organise anything better than some sandwiches and fruit.

A noise behind me causes me to jump and the large carton of oat milk in my hand slips onto the paving slabs. It feels like it's happening in slow motion as white foamy liquid splashes everywhere, including up the leg of my trousers. 'Fuck,' I all but scream.

'Woah, overreaction much?' It's Rob. 'No point crying over spilt milk.'

'It was your oat milk,' I say pointedly.

'Oh.' I can see the conflict in his features as he debates just how much he does actually want to cry. 'No, no,' he says eventually. 'It's fine. I can drink my coffee black. I like it just as much that way.'

Of course he does. But yet he's made me go to the shop at least twice to get him more bloody non-dairy milk. I take a breath to allow my irritation to dissipate. Then I realise something. 'Umm, how did you get out here?' I ask. He didn't use the front door.

'There's a side entrance.' He points behind him as if I'm stupid.

He's right. There is a side entrance. But the gate is permanently locked, secured on the inside by a heavy-duty padlock, the kind of one you cannot cut off no matter how hard you try.

'Do you have the key?'

He shrugs. 'There's no lock.'

I leave him standing there and stride over to the tall, heavy wooden gate. It swings open at the slightest push. There's a narrow passageway between the villa and the outer wall, covered with a canopy of the bright pink bougainvillea the villa is named after. Half way down is a door into a side room off the kitchen. In theory, this entrance could be used to allow the staff to come and go without interrupting the guests, but I've never bothered, it always felt like far too much of a faff. At the end of the floral canopy is another gate, but that one is sealed shut.

'There should be a padlock on here,' I tell Rob.

'Nope.'

'Yes, Rob.'

'Look, I don't know what to tell you, there isn't.' He gives me this look that makes me suddenly aware I'm acting oddly. And round here, especially at the moment, odd is definitely not the way to be acting.

'Sorry. Of course,' I put up my hands in acquiescence. 'I must be mistaken.' I take a few steps down the corridor as I cast around for a glimpse of the metal padlock.

'You know, Grace,' Rob says following me down the corridor. I hear the sound of the gate click shut behind him and swing round to face him. His face is twisted into that same leer he's used a number of times already this week.

'Rob? What are you doing?' I look around, searching for something that I could use to defend myself. I don't like the way he's staring at me. It's like he's hungry.

'This is such a lovely spot, don't you think?' he asks and the leer morphs into something even more threatening.

I step towards him and try to pass by.

He moves to block my way. The passageway is too narrow. 'No, Rob,' I say forcefully.

'Oh, don't be like that. You've been giving me the come on all week.'

'I've turned you down every time,' I tell him.

'But only because you enjoy the thrill of the chase.'

He's close now, really close. I can feel the heat of his body. I take a few steps backwards, then a few more. The door from the little side room is locked; it's on the smart key system and I can see the small red flashing light. The only way to unlock it is by using the keypad on the inside.

'Don't tease me any more, Grace.' He licks his lips and reaches a hand out towards me. I step backwards again, and again, and again, but every time he closes the distance. One more step and my back is against the sealed shut gate at the far end of the passageway.

I open my mouth to scream, hoping if I can make enough noise it'll scare Rob into backing the fuck away from me. But, before I can make a sound, I'm falling backwards as the gate swings open behind me.

Mrs Wilson cries out as I come crashing onto her patio where she was peacefully sitting with a book in her hand.

'Grace?' She says, clutching her hand to her chest. 'Are you alright?'

I struggle back upright and pull my t-shirt back down from where it had ridden up.

'She's fine, Mum,' Rob says, pushing past me.

'What were you two doing out there?'

'Oh, nothing,' he replies but I see the wink he gives her.

I want to punch him in his disgusting face. 'I was just checking something,' I say, but the words come out a little mangled, like I'm making a lame excuse.

'What's that up your trousers?' Mrs Wilson asks me.

'Oh, that. Just milk. I dropped some getting it out of the car. Actually, that reminds me, I need to bring the lunch in.' I scurry back down the passageway and out of the gate at the other end. I'm fuming at Rob. He had absolutely no right to make me feel like that. Or to imply I was with him under my own volition. I fucking hate these rich twats who think none of the rules apply to them.

He follows me out to the car.

'Get away from me,' I tell him, not bothering to hide my anger.

'Oh, come on. I was just playing.' He raises his arms by his side as if to say *no harm, no foul*.

'I wasn't playing, Rob,' I hiss back.

'Oh my God. Did you think I was going to do something to you? Get over yourself, Grace. Like I'd risk getting caught for someone like you. There's a camera in that alleyway.' He shakes his head a few times and makes this 'tssk' noise under his breath. 'Un-fucking-believable,' he says. 'I was going to help you inside with that lot,' he motions to the platters. 'But I don't think I'll bother.' He heads to the front door of the villa.

'What camera?' I call to him.

'The one at the second gate. I could see the light blinking.'

I carry the platters inside, taking three journeys since Rob couldn't bring himself to help. Then I head back outside and grab the hose to rinse away the lake of oat milk. I'm half expecting Rob to reappear, but I don't see him again.

Why did he lie about the camera? Was he just gaslighting me? But what an odd way to do it, why not tell me I was overreacting and had misconstrued the whole situation?

Unless...

There's a six-digit code to open the door from the side room into the passageway with the bougainvillea canopy. The system flashes up an error when I type it in. Fuck's sake. I pull my phone from my pocket and navigate to the app for the security system. Someone has changed the code. How the hell have they done that? And who?

I reset the code on the app and punch the new one into the door's keypad. The lock beeps and the light turns green. I'll have to check the logs to see if I can figure out who was messing with the system. I tap my screen a few times to set this door to remain open, I'm not going to risk Rob finding me here and cornering me again by locking this door.

Now to see if he was lying about the camera.

He wasn't. Although how he managed to spot it is a miracle to me, it's practically embedded in the bougainvillea. The camera is old, slightly yellow with age. How long has it been here? There are cameras all around the perimeter of the villa, but they're much newer looking than this one. Besides, they're all numbered and accounted for. I've never seen a feed from this camera.

It's attached to the wall with a cable, which must be how it's drawing power to blink. But is it recording? And, if it is, where is it sending the video?

Back in the sweltering staff flat, I grab my laptop and head outside. It's possibly one degree cooler on my patio than inside, but that's being generous.

I log in to the CCTV website and bring up the list of cameras. Yep, I was right before, that old camera doesn't exist on the system. Maybe it's just a decoy, but why would someone bother? Hang on. All the cameras are listed in a folder called 2022. I'm sure the villa owner told me the system was installed two years ago, so that makes sense. But there, right at the bottom of the page is another folder. 2018. There are twenty cameras listed in that one.

The first one I click on comes with an error message. *Camera not found.* The same with the next five. The seventh shows me a view of the pool, but it's not one I recognise. The angle looks like it comes from the corner of the pergola, in fact I can see the edge of the dark wood in the corner of the shot. There must be a camera there that I've never noticed before. I right click on the camera icon and it brings up a description. In the notes field is a single word: *hidden*. There's a concealed camera trained on the pool. I wonder what I'll find if I watch back that footage?

I click through the rest of the cameras listed, but get that error message every time. The old system must have been decommissioned, but the concealed one by the pool remained. Perhaps no one even realised it was there. There's one final camera on the list and I hold my breath as I click on the link.

The light is low under the bougainvillea canopy, but it's clear this is the one I've been looking for. I bring up the list of dates but there's only a handful of files. There's one for today but I ignore it. I don't want to re-live those moments in that claustrophobic space with Rob. There's a file from Thursday morning at 02.54. The image is shades of green, captured in night vision. And there he is. A man with a balaclava covering his face, first sneaking onto Scott and Chloe's patio and then less than a minute afterwards coming back. The perfect window of time.

There's a second file, from Wednesday afternoon. This time the film is in broad daylight and I can see his face clearly.

50

There's a knock on the door of the staff flat, a sharp rap of the knuckles and for a moment I'm convinced it's Mr Cooper come to tell me he knows exactly what part I've played in this whole thing. But it isn't Mr Cooper; it's Tori.

'What are you doing here?' I ask.

'Well, that's hardly a greeting,' she replies as she pushes past me into my apartment. 'Jesus, it's hotter than the fucking sun in here. Why haven't you got the air-con on?'

'There isn't any air-con.'

She sniffs the air. 'What's that smell?'

She's right, there is a distinctively iffy smell in here. I look down. Of course. The oat milk has curdled and is now starting to stink. 'I spilt some milk earlier. I'll go change.'

I pull off the offending trousers and grab the Citizens of Humanity shorts from the other day out of the washing basket. Don't judge, it isn't like I've had time for personal laundry, is it? And, besides, Tori was kind of complimentary about these ones. She's on the patio when I head out of the bedroom.

'Where's this?' She asks, pointing at my computer screen

and the still shot of the man under the shadow of the bougainvillea.

'The passageway between the front of the villa and the patio from Chloe's room.'

She whips round to look at me and then raises an eyebrow in question.

'This is the afternoon before Scott...' I trail off. I don't think I need to clarify further. 'The same guy came back in the early hours.'

'Interesting. Very interesting.' She turns back to study the image again. 'Do you know who he is?'

'No,' I reply, turning my attention back to him. 'But he was at the club that night. After you'd left. He bought Chloe and Farah a drink.'

'He was at ELIAS too,' Tori tells me, her voice little more than a whisper. 'He's the man with the pretty blue eyes.'

'I think he's the one who killed your brother.'

She lets out a stream of expletives under her breath. 'But that would mean Chloe didn't kill him.'

'You thought she did?'

'Of course.' She twerks an eyebrow at me. 'Tell me you didn't?'

I don't reply but my expression gives me away. Of course I thought she'd done it.

'I need a drink,' Tori tells me.

'Oh, I don't have anything here.' I motion towards the inside of the flat in case she could be in any doubt what I mean.

'Nothing? Jeez. OK, stay here. I'll be back in five.' And then she's gone, leaving the flat shrouded in silence once more.

So, I know what you're thinking. Chloe's innocent. But is she really? She was always going to kill him, it's just that our mystery man with the blue eyes beat her to it. So, I'm not actually setting her up. I'm just making sure justice is served. This blue-eyed stranger merely complicates things a little.

Tori knocks on the door and I let her back in. She's carrying a bottle of vodka and another of white rum. 'I didn't know what you drank so I hedged my bets,' she says, brandishing both towards me.

'I'm on duty.'

'So?'

'I can't drink when there are guests in the villa.'

'That feels boring.' But she shrugs and puts down the rum. 'I'll just go for vodka then.'

'Do you need a glass?'

She grins and then twists off the cap, taking a swig directly from the bottle. I'll take that as a 'no' then.

She steps around me and out onto the patio. She has no concept of private space, seemingly no sense that this is my home and she's just invited herself in without a second thought. She even picks up a takeaway menu from the side as she walks past and uses it to fan herself. 'I have no idea how you cope without air-con.'

I follow her outside and we squish onto the two tiny patio chairs, our knees practically touching.

'You're sure he was at the club after I'd left?' she asks, once again scrutinising the man's features on the screen.

'One hundred percent.'

She nods. 'OK.' She lifts the bottle of vodka to her lips and takes a large gulp. Then she laughs, but the kind of laugh that's not born of humour, more from disbelief. 'I was so convinced it was Chloe.'

I make a non-committal noise in the back of my throat.

'Can you keep a secret?' she asks.

'I freaking hope so. I did help you get rid of a body.'

'You did,' she exclaims and points the vodka bottle towards me. 'I keep forgetting you're an accessory here. Anyway, Chloe had a plan.' She leans towards me and glances over her shoulder. Given my patio is less than two metres square there isn't exactly anywhere for an eavesdropper to hide. 'She hired a hitman to kill Scott.' She sits back and looks at me like she just imparted the juiciest gossip known to man.

'A hitman?' I raise an eyebrow. *How does Tori know this?* If George wasn't going to do it for me, I'd kill Chloe myself for not keeping her mouth shut.

'Seriously. She was mad as hell with him. She'd been plotting his demise for months.'

'Why was she mad at him?' I ask and then hold my breath to discover whatever bullshit reason Chloe gave her sister-in-law.

'Where do I even begin? He was abusive. Cruel. Cut her off from her friends. Constantly talked her down, you know how men do, like a constant stream of criticisms. Made promises he never kept.'

'Sounds like she should have walked away a long time ago.'

'She should. But, if I'm honest, I don't think she realised how bad he was. I mean, he was a literal walking red flag but she never saw it.'

'What changed her mind?'

'She discovered he killed someone she was close to. A long time ago. At first, she blamed herself; she was convinced that it was her fault he did it.' Tori pauses for a moment to swig more vodka. 'You can't make yourself responsible for someone else's wrongdoings. She wasn't the psychopath. Scott was.'

'Rosie would still be alive if it wasn't for her.' The words are out of my mouth before I realise she didn't actually use my sister's name.

'I knew I recognised you.' Tori grins at me. 'You have a little dimple when you smile.' She reaches out to touch the corner of my mouth and I recoil from her touch. 'Eloise's party. It was fun; it felt like we were doing something kinky.' She laughs softly. 'We were so young.'

'Sixteen.' Rosie had been dead for two years and I was going through what my mother called a 'phase'. Only it wasn't a phase, of course it wasn't, even though Mum's still waiting for me to bring home a boyfriend. She's going to be waiting a long time. 'When did you realise who I was?'

'Not 'til yesterday, that was when I finally figured it all out. I knew something was going on when I saw the tattoo, though; it was obvious it meant more to you than just a pretty flower. I know I come across as an uncaring bitch, but I'm always paying attention.' She shrugs, as if it's just a teeny foible in her personality and not a huge gaping problem in her psyche.

'Why didn't you say something?'

'Like what? Besides, I needed to see what you were up to. Why you're here.'

'Coincidence,' I tell her quickly.

'Yeah, of course.' She smirks. 'There's no such thing as coincidence. Come on.'

'Honestly.'

'Look, Grace. I know you're part of this. You're the pretty face of the operation, the one who sits down with the clients and guides them gently through the process of getting rid of their problems. But then you got someone else to do your dirty work.' She theatrically taps my laptop screen.

'I had nothing to do with it. I don't know this man.' I sigh. Fuck it, I really want a drink. I flap my hand at her until she hands over the vodka. I only take a little sip, just enough to feel the burn of it in the back of my throat. 'I'll tell you the truth.

Yes, I'm part of the team Chloe hired to get rid of Scott. But the plan we put in place was for next week. Back in the UK. Everything that's happened over the last few days is nothing to do with me or my organisation. This man,' I point at the screen. 'He isn't with me.'

'Such a dark horse.' She sounds so pleased with herself, like a child who has finally put two and two together and made six.

'But, tell me this, Tori. Why aren't you more upset that someone killed your brother?'

She throws her head back and cackles, like I've told the dirtiest joke she's ever heard. 'Oh, trust me, I am *thrilled* he's dead. I just wish I could have done it myself. Right then,' she says with a sense of action as she stands up. 'So, this guy can't get traced back to you?'

I shake my head.

'Cool. So, I guess we should show this to George and Aubrey. Prove Chloe wasn't the killer and get her back from that boat.' She grins as confusion flashes across my face. 'You're not the only one with a tracker.'

I know the whole dumb blonde thing is an act, but she's still missing a very important piece of the puzzle here. 'We can't say anything.'

'We have to.' She's matter of fact.

'OK. But only if you can tell me how we explain us moving Scott's body and cleaning the murder scene. That hardly screams innocent, does it?'

51

'Jesus Christ, Grace. Are you always this much of a downer?' she asks. 'There is no problem so great it cannot be solved.' She sounds like she's quoting someone.

'Who said that?'

'No idea.' She shrugs. 'I think I've heard Daddy say it. Anyway, it's true.'

I sit back in my chair and cross my arms over my chest. 'I'm waiting for you to tell me how we explain cleaning the scene.' I imagine I'll be sitting here for a very long time. I may as well have another nip of vodka while I'm waiting.

'Why can't your organisation get involved?' Tori asks eventually. 'They must have the resources to come up with some kind of plan to get Chloe out of this mess. In fact,' she pauses and narrows her eyes at me. 'Aren't they already working on something? Surely you've been in contact with them to get them to help?'

I don't reply.

Tori narrows her eyes further. 'There's something you're not telling me.'

I remain quiet.

'You don't want them to get involved, do you? Because they'll think it was your fault, that you lost control of the situation? No. I don't think that is it.' She continues to stare at me and I can feel her searching my soul.

She sits back and crosses her arms over her chest, exactly mimicking my own position. 'What is it I'm missing?' she asks softly. 'Oh,' she says. 'Oh.' The second 'oh' is far more animated. She picks up the vodka and takes a sip, her eyes still trained on me.

'Chloe killed my sister,' I tell her.

'No. That isn't what happened. Chloe—'

'It is what happened,' I interrupt her. 'And she's going to pay for what she did.'

'Woah, woah,' she puts both hands up, like I'm a wild horse about to bolt. 'OK. Let's say, just for the sake of argument mind, that she did. Is that why you're here?'

I nod in reply.

'And so, just pretending everything had gone to your original plan, you were going to kill Scott next week and then frame Chloe?'

'No, well, not exactly.'

'No, because that would look very bad for your organisation, wouldn't it? Hardly a glowing endorsement of your services if one of your clients gets sent down for the murder. Especially with all those guarantees I assume your bosses like to make.' She pauses for a moment. 'So, what *were* you going to do? An unfortunate accident afterwards?'

'I didn't want her dead. I just wanted her to feel some of the pain I did. It was her fault that my sister was dead. Chloe ruined my life and so I wanted to ruin hers.'

'But how?' she spreads her fingers out on the table. 'I just don't understand the angle you were going for here.'

'I was going to wait until the life insurance paid out,' I say softly.

'Oh. Blackmail. That feels a little...' Tori gropes for the word. 'I dunno. Tacky?'

'I was going to take the money and then use it to set up my own agency, make something good out of my sister's death.'

'I mean, I'm not sure "good" is the word I'd use for a company that kills people, but you do you I guess.'

'I'm going to specialise. A team of women who help other women get rid of the shitty men in their lives.'

'Ooh, taking out the trash. I take back what I said. I love it.' She grins at me. But then her face drops. 'And your current employer would let you just walk away? Walk away and then set up in competition?' She says it like she thinks I'm an idiot, a stupid trusting fool.

I open my mouth to reply but then I shut it again. Hearing her say it makes me realise how naive I was.

Tori sits back in her seat. 'You know why my family was able to grow their business so quickly at the beginning? Before my brother managed to get in with the Wilsons, I mean.' She raises an eyebrow. 'It wasn't by asking nicely, or having a robust business plan, or even being particularly smart – even though Aubrey *is* objectively brilliant. They destroyed the people they took it from. Simple as that.'

'What are you saying?' I ask.

'You have this dream. And I respect that. But if you want to make it a reality...' she trails off and leans forward. 'You have to take it from them,' she whispers.

'How?'

I watch her eyes. I can see that she's thinking, scheming,

running a million different variations on how things could work out in order to select the best one. She really is something else, this brilliant woman who has no idea of the power she could wield if she stopped hiding it.

'Got it,' she says eventually and her face lights up. She stands and reaches a hand out to me. 'Come on then.'

'Come on what?'

'Do you trust me?' she asks.

'No.' *Is she serious?*

'Fair.' She nods a couple of times. 'I probably wouldn't trust me either. But, still, I don't think you have a choice.'

'Just tell me what you're going to do.'

'Where's the fun in that?'

'This isn't a joke, Tori.'

'Eughh. Please don't do that same prefect voice Chloe uses. It drives me insane.' She looks at me for a second and then sits down again, ramming her hands under her thighs to try to stop the energy I can see thrumming through her. 'Alright. So, we need a murderer. And we need alibis for all three of us.'

'Three?'

'You, me, Chloe.'

'I don't care about Chloe.'

'Yeah, and I get that, I really do.' She reaches out and pats my shoulder gently. 'But you're wrong about her and she's kind of my sister and it's non-negotiable. Anyway,' she continues. 'We need alibis. And you need freedom from your employer.'

I nod at that one.

'And we need cash,' she adds. 'This business of ours needs money to get it off the ground.'

Ours? Did she just say *our*—

She interrupts my thoughts. 'Yes, *ours*. I want in, Grace. Come on, you know you need me.' She says it like it's a statement of fact. And I can't deny she would be an asset to have on board. *And a liability if she wasn't,* whispers a voice in the back of my brain.

* * *

In the end, with Tori's help, it didn't take much to build a convincing narrative for the Coopers.

An unknown assailant in the house, getting in and out down the side passageway. Ethan falls on his sword when questioned over why it wasn't secured. Mikey was quick to confirm it was Ethan's responsibility, zero qualms about twisting the knife against his colleague. Mr Cooper has promised Ethan leniency, but I'm not convinced.

A video of two men in the middle of the night dragging a heavy case from the villa and loading it into a van. It was filmed a few weeks ago when some guests hired a DJ for the evening, but Tori was able to doctor the timestamp. It looks convincing enough that it could have been the body being moved. I email it to myself from a dummy account and tell the Coopers the security service was able to recover a file some hacker-for-hire had deleted from that night to cover the killer's tracks. It's the weakest part of the story, but Mr Cooper believes it without question.

A second video, this time showing Gary's face as clear as day. The number plate on the van he's driving proves it's the same one the 'body' was loaded into: this week wasn't the first time I've borrowed Yannis's Transporter. Mikey is dispatched to deal with Gary. He tracks him to a warehouse where he kills him with a single bullet. In a chest freezer, Mikey finds a body. He makes an anonymous tip off to the police and returns to the villa. The police will identify Scott but will never find any evidence of his killer on the body.

Gary's phone – swiped by Mikey from the warehouse – contains only two numbers. The first doesn't ring; it's already sitting at the bottom of the sea, I made damn sure of that. The second will lead the Coopers to an address in London and the head of my organisation. Sure, they'll try to deny any involvement in Scott's death, or the wider attacks on the Cooper business, but whoever is sent to exact revenge won't listen to them anyway.

* * *

Chloe looks shell-shocked as she arrives back at the villa. Tori did an OK job of patching her up; the sunburn across her nose covered with concealer, a fresh pair of clothes, her hair combed out. In truth, you'd just assume she is a poor widow who has been smashed in the face by grief. And that's the story she's going to maintain, the price of her freedom. If she tells the Wilsons what George put her through there will be all out war.

'Oh, my darling,' Erin Wilson says, rushing toward her daughter and enfolding her in a hug. It's still making my blood boil that Chloe isn't going to pay for what she did to Rosie. For all that Tori insists Chloe was another victim, I know it's bullshit.

'I'll still force her to pay reparations,' Tori whispers in my ear as she comes to stand next to me. 'We're going to need seed money after all.'

'Promise?'

'Promise.'

Erin leads Chloe away, leaving Tori and me alone.

I turn to face her. 'There is one final thing. Who did actually kill Scott?'

She smiles at me, a slow languid smile. She knows, it's written plain as day on her features. 'Maybe one day I'll tell you.'

'Tell me now.'

Her smile stretches wider as she pulls out her phone and shows me a photo from the night they went to ELIAS. 'I can never resist a man with pretty blue eyes.'

EPILOGUE

It was meant to look like a break in. Like someone had scaled the walls of the villa and slit his throat in his sleep. There should have been an investigation. All the evidence pointing back to an up-and-coming guy from a rival group operating out of Manchester. Brandon knew Scott from back in the day, but he'd been sent down and never moved back to Bromley on his release. I even planted some of his hair at the scene. A slam dunk case of murder. And then the Coopers would have retaliated, of course they would. It's what we do in this world.

I planned it all so meticulously, every tiny detail perfectly constructed. The stuff back home: tip offs about stash houses and burning down one of the farms was a piece of cake. I sent one of the Wilson men, someone we've trusted for decades, to meet Brandon to pass on the addresses along with the promise that the evening of 10 July would be the best date, what with the Coopers out of the country. Brandon didn't even notice my man plucking a few rogue hairs from the back of his jumper.

Here on Mykonos it was surprisingly easy to tamper with

the smart house system. I don't think it's a good idea to convert everything to being 'smart'; mainly because these things never are that clever. All I needed to do was enough damage to the system to get an engineer out, and then a little spy while he was there and bingo, I had his universal access code to disengage the lock into the side passage and delete the footage from the perimeter cameras. That huge padlock to the front of the villa was a bit more of a problem, but in the end I was able to pick it open. The gate to the patio was apparently sealed shut, at least according to the layouts Chloe sent around, but a gentle shove revealed that to be a lie.

I even made sure there was an actual stranger skulking around, someone to leave footprints in the mud, even though they wouldn't be traceable back to anyone. That was why I'd convinced Chloe to take us all to that awful ELIAS place; I needed to confirm the plan was a go in person – well, you always need an escape route in case you change your mind just before, don't you? And I made sure Chloe couldn't be a suspect by getting the same stranger to slip something into her drink in the nightclub. Enough to knock her out and leave a lasting impression in her system for the police to determine her innocence.

A perfect plan for the perfect murder.

And goodness, the *rush*. The feeling of absolute power as I held the knife in my hand. The pure pleasure of killing that bastard.

But when the villa awoke the morning after there was silence.

No body.

No crime.

I considered all the possible angles, all the myriad things

that could have gone wrong. Perhaps I hadn't killed him and someone had found him? No, that would have resulted in pandemonium, not all of us sleeping soundly through the night. Or perhaps he had somehow managed to get himself to a hospital? But it would have been very difficult for him to make his own way to A&E, what with that six-inch slash across his throat, the flesh separating like a raw steak being sliced for a nice bourguignon.

He couldn't have called for help; I had his phone. I don't even know why I took it at the time, except that it seemed the kind of thing a killer would do. Obviously I switched it off and then hid it, tucking it behind all the foliage growing around the walls of the patio from my room.

And so, in the end, I went to Chloe's room, desperate to ask her what was going on. But all I found was Tori in her underwear and the concierge in the final throws of cleaning up the scene. I decided to wait and see what happened for the rest of the day. When Chloe spun some story about the diving club, I knew she was part of whatever Tori and Grace were up to. I secretly helped her by sending a few texts from his phone to Peter as I waited to figure out what exactly had happened.

I wanted there to be chaos. I wanted there to be a war. And, in the midst of it all, my daughter would walk free. Free from that terrible man and the prison he built for her. I know she's capable of doing so much with her life; I even left her a couple of notes at the start of the holiday, just so she'd remember how fierce she really is.

Chloe should have walked away from her marriage years ago, but she always defended Scott's shitty behaviour, piled the blame for the way he treated her on work stress or even on herself.

I blame myself, I should have modelled better behaviours for my daughter; I should have stood up to her father more, shown her that strength is admirable. I should have told her she could be anything, that she didn't need a man to complete her. I should have shown her the stars and encouraged her to try to reach them instead of shackling herself to such a broken little twat.

So many shoulds. So many regrets.

My daughter and I used to be close, like we were best friends, the two of us against the world. Then Luke sent her off to Chelsham Park. I didn't want her to go to boarding school but he was insistent. 'It'll be the making of her,' he told me. He'd always been so obsessed with the kids getting what he thought was the best education. I worried she'd be lonely – she always struggled a little to make friends. At first, I was proved wrong and she met Rosie. Such a sweet girl and she was always so kind to Chloe. But then Scott came into her life and she changed. That's why we went to Val d'Isère that Christmas, I wanted to get her away from that boy. Gosh, you should have seen my relief when she met Sébastien. But Scott already had his dirty little claws in her, and she couldn't get free.

I should have put my foot down. I should have insisted she stay at home and go to the local school. I should have kept her safe.

But I didn't protect her back then. And so I decided to take matters into my own hands now and get rid of him for her.

Besides, Scott knew the truth. Even Chloe has convinced herself that something else happened that night on the roof of Chelsham Park School. I couldn't risk the real story bubbling to the surface. It would break Chloe's heart if she remembered what she did.

Some secrets are better left buried.

* * *

MORE FROM SARAH BONNER

Another book from Sarah Bonner, *How to Slay at Work*, is available to order now here:

www.mybook.to/HowSlayBackAd

ACKNOWLEDGEMENTS

Firstly, a huge thank you to my brilliant agent, Hannah Sheppard. I am so incredibly lucky to have such a supportive champion in my corner.

To the fabulous Francesca Best for your editorial wizardry and ability to take my rambling muses and whip them into a coherent novel! Your enthusiasm for my work blows me away and I can't thank you enough for everything you do. To Amanda Ridout, Nia Beynon, Wendy Neale, Niamh Wallace, Isabelle Flynn, Leila Mauger, Hayley Russell, Sue Lamprell, Ben Wilson, Paul Martin, Justinia Baird-Murray, Arbaiah Aird and everyone else at Boldwood for all your work in getting my books out into the world.

To my family and friends for everything you do. Special mention to Mum for being an early reader, cheerleader, and finder of typos and grammatical errors – I promise that one day I'll get practice vs practise right! To my lovely husband for keeping me sane and always reminding me that every book has its challenges but there is nothing that work (and chocolate) can't fix. I couldn't do this without you. And of course to Lily for being the best furbaby in the world.

Special shoutout to the Sbooky Bitches. You've welcomed me into the coven and I'm so blessed to have such a wonderful group of other writers to learn from, vent to, and laugh with.

And finally to all the other authors, reviewers, bloggers, and readers. Bookish people really are the best people!

ABOUT THE AUTHOR

Sarah Bonner is the author of bestselling psychological thrillers, including *Her Perfect Twin*. She lives in West Sussex with her husband and very spoiled rescue dog.

Sign up to Sarah Bonner's newsletter for news, competitions and updates on future books.

Follow Sarah on social media here:

X x.com/sarahbonner101

f facebook.com/sarah.bonner.35574

📷 instagram.com/sarahbonner101

♪ tiktok.com/@sarahbonner101

ALSO BY SARAH BONNER

How to Slay at Work

How to Slay on Holiday

THE

Murder

LIST

**THE MURDER LIST IS A NEWSLETTER
DEDICATED TO ALL THINGS CRIME AND
THRILLER FICTION!**

**SIGN UP TO MAKE SURE YOU'RE ON OUR
HIT LIST FOR GRIPPING PAGE-TURNERS
AND HEARTSTOPPING READS.**

SIGN UP TO OUR
NEWSLETTER

BIT.LY/THEMURDERLISTNEWS

Boldwood

Boldwood Books is an award-winning fiction publishing company seeking out the best stories from around the world.

Find out more at www.boldwoodbooks.com

Join our reader community for brilliant books, competitions and offers!

Follow us
@BoldwoodBooks
@TheBoldBookClub

Sign up to our weekly deals newsletter

https://bit.ly/BoldwoodBNewsletter